Vengeance for a Fallen Angel

Vengeance for a Fallen Angel

Published by The Conrad Press Ltd. in the United Kingdom 2024

Tel: +44(0)1227 472 874

www.theconradpress.com

info@theconradpress.com

ISBN 978-1-916966-25-3

Copyright © Christophe Medler, 2024

This is a work of fiction. Names, characters, places, and incidents either are the product of the author's imagination or are used fictitiously.

All rights reserved.

Typesetting and Cover Design by: Charlotte Mouncey, www.bookstyle.co.uk

The Conrad Press logo was designed by Maria Priestley.

Printed and bound in Great Britain by Clays Ltd, Elcograf S.p.A.

Vengeance for a Fallen Angel

Christophe Medler

Dedicated to my children,
Faye Louise and David Elliott

Our greatest goal in life
is not never failing
but rising every time we fall.

Confucius

Acknowledgements

This novel would never have been written without the love, support and dedication of my editor and wife, Lyn.

With thanks also to :

Justin Schamotta of The Madrigal Brewery,

James Essinger, my publisher, and all of the team at The Conrad Press Ltd,

Immortal Technique 'Dance with the Devil'.

1

Sunday 24th September 1967

The sunset's fiery orb was sinking slowly beyond the horizon, the sea glassy and calm reflecting its orange, red and yellow. As the colours started to fade, the foreboding moon started to rise, revealing the dark eyes of the night. That aura of peace, that feel good factor at the end of a summer season, was about to be shattered by one of the most heinous and horrific acts ever committed in such a tranquil North Devon community.

There was a full moon that night, the tide was high, and the waves were crashing against the cliff face of Hillsborough Head, at the top of which was the site of an iron age fort and burial ground. After dark it was a spooky place, damp and salty. As the waves pounded against the rocky shoreline below, the sea spray formed liquid crystals caught by the moonlight and a veil of darkness fell like an enormous blanket over the landscape.

A young girl, who not long before had been dancing in abandon in front of a roaring log fire with LSD coursing through her veins, was now tumbling down that cliff face, her frail body smashing on the rocks below. Atop, a mysterious figure dressed in a hooded black cloak shook his feathered rattle calling unto the sea below, 'Oh, mighty Bondye, accept this sacrifice, the soul of this harlot is now yours.'

Earlier that day on a bright sunny afternoon, Woolacombe Bay with its long sweeping beach had just held its annual

International Surfing Competition, attracting surfers from all over Europe and some as far away as the USA and Australia. The winner of the main event, the Woolacombe Wave Cup and a prize of £250 was none other than the Australian, Nat Young, the 1966 World Surfing Champion, who was in the midst of a world tour attending sponsored international surfing events such as that at Woolacombe.

The surf might be miniscule compared to that of the Big Sur in California or Shipstone Bluff in Australia that Nat was used to, but he entertained and wowed the spectators with his flips and cutbacks. He even managed an Ally Oop on his second run. The shore breeze had got up and Nat found an open facing wave enabling him to accelerate toward it, bottom turn at forty-five degrees and kick his tail out as he flipped the lid of the top of the wave. The shore's inward breeze kept his board stuck to his feet. The crowd roared; they could hardly believe it was possible on the Woolacombe surf that rose no higher than eight feet.

Among the crowd on the beach was a local policeman, Detective Inspector Richard (Rick) McCarthy, accompanied by his partner Kay Stone and a group of surfing friends. Rick was competing in the final event of the weekend, The Novices Cup, open to anyone who had not competed in an international competition. It was regarded as a bit of fun by the locals to see who could embarrass themselves the most. The time flew, and before they knew it the announcer was calling for competitors in The Novices Cup to come down to the shoreline to be briefed by the referee and judge.

Rick looked round at Kay and his friends, giving the thumbs up as if to say, *It's now or never guys.* He proceeded to strip down to his wet suit and picked up his surfboard. Kay watched him get ready then kissed him good luck. *God I love you, Rick McCarthy, you are one in a million, My Adonis,* she thought to herself as he walked away.

In her eyes, Rick was very different from all the others, handsome, not perhaps in the conventional sense, but his appearance made him stand out in the crowd. He had dark hair and naturally lightly tanned skin, with unfathomable dark brown eyes that complemented his toned face. His eyes were deep and expressive, inviting you to get lost in them if you looked into them long enough, but he sometimes had that faraway look, making him appear disinterested. This was due to his enquiring mind which, almost like a chess player, was five moves ahead of his opponent. At other times you could see a hint of sadness in his eyes, which would disappear as suddenly as it emerged. Above all was his frame and his stature. He was not exactly muscular, but he kept himself in good shape and carried himself with a confidence that was incredibly attractive.

He may not have all the girls swooning over him, thought Kay, watching him striding down the beach, his surfboard under his arm, *he's an enigma to many, but he's mine.*

Rick was unusually tense; it was a big crowd. He was riding his Blaker surfboard, his favorite, and had spent hours polishing the underside to glide over the waves and rough sanded the top for better grip on the soles of his feet. On his first run he tried a back flip and ploughed into the wave. This was greeted with hoots of laughter from Kay and those friends not competing.

His second run was much better, and he managed a double cut back before running out of wave and gliding upright to the shoreline. Kay rushed towards him and threw herself at him to give him a salty kiss as they both tumbled into the water. That run moved him up on the leader board and he finished third for a bronze medal, the highest he had achieved in the competition in five years of trying. The competition winner and the winner of The Novices Cup and gold medal was none other than one of Rick's colleagues, Ethan James, head of the SOC team at Barnstable Police HQ.

Many of the spectators stayed behind after the surfing event had finished. The fast food vendors were still doing a roaring trade serving hot and cold drinks, burgers, hot dogs, and fish and chips. Families with young children were having picnics enjoying the last of the late afternoon's sunshine. Some children were building sandcastles with moats, trying to stem the incoming tide from breaching the outer wall, while others flew paper kites of multi colours, swooping up and down as if mimicking the gulls searching for any morsels to be found dropped on the beach. An impromptu game of beach cricket struck up with Nat Young captaining the overseas team v England made up of a sporadic bunch of local and visiting surfers.

Rick and Kay spent the evening with friends around a beach fire, watching the sun go down, with copious amounts of beer from a cooler box. Camping out, up on the hillside overlooking the beach, were a remnant of hippies with their beaten-up VW Surfmobiles. The surfing event had attracted a following of the hippie movement, dressed in their unconventional clothes of vibrant colours, some with psychedelic images, barefoot, and wearing flowers in their hair. Many of them were anti-establishment, suspicious of the government, rejected capitalism and consumerist values, were generally opposed to the Vietnam War and supported the Ban The Bomb movement.

There was a sweet smell of marijuana, a fusion of citrus and rosemary, permeating the air and the magical sound of Procul Harum's *A Whiter Shade of Pale*. The haunting sound of Bach's *Orchestral Suite No 3 in D Major Air on a G String*, featuring as a countermelody to the song, resonated across the campsite and beach. It was a time for peace and love.

'Can you hear it, Kay? That's a Hammond Organ, playing Bach on a psychedelic pop record. I love it, it's so innovative, pure jazz.'

'It's beautiful, Rick. I find it kind of perverse, even incredulous that Engelbert Humperdinck is top of the Hit Parade, with his song *The Last Waltz* at the moment. It's as if the middle classes of England are rebelling against this new phenomenon. They seem to be challenging and dismissing all the great songs such as *If You're Going to San Francisco* and *Flowers in the Rain*. OK, the songs, including *Itchycoo Park*, have drug connections, but they are great music. They'll be classics one day.'

As they sat and watched the sun go down, Rick cuddled Kay and murmured rather poetically, 'The world is changing fast, and the young are the future of our country. Let them have their fun, let them protest peacefully against tyranny and war.' Little did Rick know that his own values, his belief in humanity, were about to be challenged in the most disturbing way that would make many a person's blood run cold. It would take all of his detective skills and the skill of his dedicated team to solve the most abominable crime driven by man, so evil as to be beyond redemption.

2

Seven miles up the coastline at Ilfracombe it was nearly midnight. Ilfracombe, a seaside resort with a working harbour, sat snugly in a recess on the shoreline encircled by massive cliffs. The harbour was protected seaward by Lantern Hill which was capped with the oldest functioning lighthouse in the UK. There is a wild majesty to the place, as the terrain rises suddenly at Lantern Hill and again across the water at Hillsborough Head where, at its highest, the cliff face is four hundred feet high above sea level.

Hillsborough Head had long been designated as a nature reserve and was popular with tourists, ramblers walking the North Devon Coast path, and the local population alike. The Head had been revered over the centuries by various pagan religious factions that practised Wicca, Druidism and more recently, Voodoo. Here, on that balmy late summer's night, the North Devon Voodoo Cauldron had gathered. They practiced their own version of Voodoo worship based on the ancient rituals of Voudun, together with that of Wakan Tanka, the Great Spirit of the Creole nation.

Circled around a makeshift altar, the cauldron celebrants were dressed in white cloaks emblazoned with the golden image of Bondye, the Voodoo God of Creation, on their backs.

The warlock, the elected leader of the cauldron, dressed in a black cloak emblazoned with the same golden Bondye image, shook his rattle adorned with Creole Indian feathers, and pronounced:

'Oh, mighty Bondye and Wakan Tanka, we worship you. Let the evil beast of Wendigo receive our sacrifice tonight.'

With that he threw powders of crushed mugwort, and black powder extracted from fireworks onto the fire creating a massive flash that lit up the clifftop and sent out shafts of flames and white smoke into the night sky. The cauldron reeled back. The explosion and shafts of flames lit up the faces that were painted with designs reminiscent of ancient Creole Indian warpaint to protect their anonymity.

A young girl no more than eighteen years old was dancing in abandon in front of the group with the drug LSD coursing through her veins. She was singing *Eight Miles High* by the American west coast country rock group The Byrds, the recording having the inimitable guitar chords and voice of David Crosby. The LSD had been given to her by one of her past lovers on the climb up to the summit. 'What's this?' she had asked him on the climb up to their secret place where they used to make love under the stars.

'It's LSD, or Acid as it is sometimes called. It blows your mind with all beautiful thoughts and a kaleidoscope of colours. It's way above marijuana, speed or ecstasy. Sometimes you feel an out of body experience. They call it the purple fierce little heart on the streets and in the clubs in Barnstaple, as the pills are heart shaped and coloured purple.'

'OK. I will if you will,' she said as she swallowed hers. He spat his own out without her noticing. The LSD did not take long to take effect, a matter of minutes as it coursed through her veins. She was used to taking ecstasy in the clubs, but this was a whole new experience. She started to lose all sense of time and space as the drug's mind-bending experience took effect. Sounds around her were being projected as colours, patterns and shapes.

Her lover held her close to prevent her stumbling as they continued to climb up the footpath toward the summit. As they neared the clearing, he took hold of her, kissed her passionately, fondled her and whispered in her ear, 'Here Babe, take another, it's groovy.' She was too far gone, tripping out from the effect of the first pill to care, so she swallowed another.

On reaching the clearing she was seeing bright multi-coloured stars like diamonds spinning around in the sky, and white robed monks dancing. Her lover took her by the hand and handed her over to one of warlock's two acolytes.

The acolyte paraded her before the cauldron as if she were a prize-winning contestant in a TV games show. After she had twirled and bowed before them, he proceeded to strip her naked, throwing her clothes onto the log fire crying out, 'Faithfull followers of our almighty God the Creator, Bondye, I give you this harlot who has betrayed the cauldron.'

She made no resistance, the silhouette of her lithe body looked almost transparent as she gyrated against the backcloth of the roaring fire that was lighting up the dark sky. Her image reminded some of the cauldron of the opening scene of 'Tales of The Unexpected' a popular TV dramatization, as they salivated with hardening erections at the thought of what was to come.

The acolyte who had stripped her, took her by the hand and handed her over to the warlock who offered her a ceremonial chalice with a secret potion of drugs and herbal medicines. The young girl drank the potion with gusto and in an almost manic trance started to gyrate again, provocatively running her hands slowly up and down her torso.

She was laid upon the altar and each member of the cauldron took their turn in subjecting her to continuous sexual abuse with no orifice remaining sacred. The cauldron continued to chant in an ever-increasing tempo. Whilst one of them was engaged in rough anal sex and performing sexual asphyxiation on her, the naked girl passed out. She lay motionless spread eagled, face down, like a suckling pig roasting on a spit.

The chanting had reached fever pitch, there was no stopping the cauldron now.

'You've killed her,' cried out the second of the warlock's acolytes, prompting the rest of the chanting of the cauldron to reach an almighty crescendo.

'She's dead, she's dead, the wicked white witch is dead,' they chanted manically in unison as they danced round the altar.

The warlock waved, shook his rattle, danced in circles, and then decreed, 'Toujou' *(still, in the Haitian Creole language)*.

The cauldron's chanting subsided to almost silence as they formed a semi-circle around the altar facing the man in black. He cried out:

'Touye' *(Kill)*.

Go harlot into the eternal flames of Wendigo.

Steal no more secrets, say no more lies.

Seek no more to break the Cauldon Oath.'

The full moon emerged again from behind the clouds. The still night air was suddenly cut by the swishing sound of the falling of a heavy blade crashing down with a thud on the altar, severing the girl's right hand which fell to the earthen floor.

The severing of a hand was an ancient ritual of the Creole as punishment for stealing, breaking an oath or telling a lie. It also had religious connotations as an act of destroying the omnipotence of God by severing 'God's Right Hand.'

A deadly hush fell upon Hillsborough Head. Turning to face the others, the warlock pronounced, 'Let the witch's blood flow into the chasm of Wendigo.' He held up the hand dripping with blood and tossed it onto the fire, a stench of burning flesh permeating the air.

The girl remained motionless on the alter. The warlock shook his rattle again and threw more mugwort onto the fire causing a drift of white smoke to rise as he signalled the close of the ceremony.

'Go brethren, may the mighty Bondye hold and protect your damned souls until we meet again.'

The moon drifted back behind a cloud and darkness fell. As if by magic, members disappeared into the shadows of the night leaving the warlock and his two acolytes to dispose of the girl's body. They picked her up from the altar and carried her to the cliff edge, casting her into the sea below. Her body spun, jerked, and tumbled like a rag doll in the jaws of a puppy dog, smashing against the rocky cliff face on the way down. The tide was high against the base of the cliffs and the current immediately began to carry her body away and round into Hele Bay.

3

Monday 25th

The following morning, not long after dawn, Gram Parsons was walking his springer spaniel, Digby, down on Hele Bay Beach. He was always up at the crack of dawn, a quick cup of tea and then out of his cottage and down to the beach to give Digby his morning exercise and ablutions. That day he was earlier than usual as he planned to go to the Pannier Market at Barnstaple. After walking the dog, he needed to catch the 8.00 a.m. bus at the Hele Bay Hotel at the top of the road. It would take him to Ilfracombe Station to catch the 8.30 a.m. train to Barnstaple. Digby had an inbuilt clock and knew almost to the minute when it was 6.30 a.m. and time to wake his master up. Gram was always amazed how Digby even adjusted to the time change when the clocks either went forward in the spring to announce British Summer Time and back again in the autumn.

There would be no market for Gram that morning. No joy at the sound and sights of belching steam and smoke and slipping loco wheels as the train left Ilfracombe to climb the Torrs embankment on its way to Mortehoe, the steepest climb out of a train terminus in the country. No smell of sizzling fresh west country saddleback pork bacon rashers from Nellies' Hash and Grill making his mouth water as he strolled into the marketplace to enjoy a late breakfast. No pint of Imperial beer in The Panniers pub with the locals over an early ploughmans lunch, catching up on any gossip. Worst of all there would be no stroll round the market, buying his favorite homemade pork pies, sausages, bacon and not forgetting the bones for Digby from the same butcher that supplies Nellies' bacon.

Gram was a retired merchant seaman and lived alone with his dog in Salty Bay Cottage overlooking the beach at the end of Beach Road. He was the son of a methodist preacher and raised in a strict household in North Devon, leaving to go to sea as soon as he could at 14 years of age. Born Graeme, ever since he took to the high seas his fellow crew had called him Gram and the name had stuck with him for the rest of his life.

Behind his cottage to the west was the dramatic steep escarpment of Hillsborough Head.

He missed life at sea. Every summer holiday as a boy he would spend his holidays with his grandparents who lived by the sea, and he fell in love with it. He would watch the merchant ships sail by and wonder what part of the world they were off to, and he dreamed that one day it would be him. Life as a merchant seaman was hard, often having to work a grueling day and sometimes night, but it was the making of Gram. He loved the freedom of being at one with mother nature, and at other times having to battle nature in the form of raging storms, huge swells, and waves as tall as a double decker bus.

It was cool that morning but not cold as he walked down to the beach. The early morning drizzle of rain had stopped. Dawn had broken around 6.30 and the rising sun was wrestling to break through the sea mist glistening on the calm blue sea. The crews of the fishing boats in Ilfracombe Harbour were busy preparing the vessels to sail on the high tide. The trawlers would be heading for the shoals of mackerel, ray, and megrim sole to be found further out into the Atlantic and the much smaller crab and lobster boats, often operated by either one or two people, would be heading out to check their pots in the various bays and coves up and down the coastline.

The tide was now crawling slowly up the beach like a serpent, spewing out occasional flotsam and seaweed. Gram was wearing his well-worn Barbour jacket with the collar turned up against the south westerly breeze, and his trusty Breton fishing hat. Digby was loving it, running back and forth returning the ball that Gram was throwing into the mild surf of the incoming tide. As he strolled up the beach, he lit a Players Navy Cut cigarette, an old seafaring habit, took a satisfying drag, coughed twice, and then threw the ball one more time some fifty yards ahead into the surf. This time Digby did not return.

'Here boy,' Gram called but there was still no response from his dog who was now barking at something half in the water partially covered in seaweed and moving inch by inch up the beach on each incoming wave.

As he approached, Gram thought it was just more flotsam from the yacht Lady Louise that had floundered not two months before on the rocks off Hillsborough Head. She was approaching Ilfracombe Harbour when a sudden squall and change of wind direction drove her onto the rocks. Fortunately, there was no loss of life and the crew of three had been taken off by the Ilfracombe Lifeboat's inshore rib.

'Digby, leave,' called Gram as he got nearer. Digby duly obliged and sat pointing his nose at the object. 'Good boy' said Gram not realizing what he was about to discover.

As he got nearer, Gram was stopped in his tracks and reeled back in horror. He was a seasoned merchant seaman who had served in the Second World War and had seen many war-torn dead bodies, but nothing had prepared him for what he was now witnessing.

There, lying half in, half out of the water, was a nude female body with multiple wounds and her right hand severed at the wrist. It took a moment for Gram to take in what he saw. *Dear God*, he said to himself and then ran back to his cottage with Digby in tow, his ball in his mouth. He no doubt thought it was part of a game they were playing.

Gram dashed in knocking over the boot rack in the porch and immediately grabbed hold of the phone. Shaking, he misdialed the number. *Shit,* he said to himself *pull yourself together man.*

He redialed; a voice answered, 'PC Nigel Worthy.'

'Nige, its Gram. I hope I haven't woken you and Annie.' He didn't know why he had said that given the circumstances.

'What's up Gram, you wouldn't call me at this unearthly hour it wasn't important' replied PC Worthy.

'Nige, you'd better get yourself down to the beach, there's a dead body floating in and out at the water's edge.'

'That's all I need on my day off, another suicide off Hillsborough Head' replied Nigel, still half asleep.

'This isn't suicide Nige, it's a dead girl with a hand missing,' said Gram rather tersely.

'Jesus, I'll be as quick as I can,' he said. 'Gram, can you go back down to the beach and stop any bystanders getting anywhere near the body, although I can't think of anyone being there at this hour other than Jim Derbyshire with his black labrador, Bruno. I'd better phone HQ and let them know before I come down, so hold the fort for me until I get there.'

'No worries, Nige, I'll get back down there straight away.'

Nothing much happened in Hele Bay, a small inlet east of Ilfracombe on the other side of Hillsborough Head. It had become a popular spot for bathers and families seeking a safe cove since Victorian times, as it had a gently sloping sand and shingle beach, and there were rocks and rock pools for children to climb and play in.

The sparse local population grew in the times of quicklime production in the 18th century when lime kilns were prevalent all along the North Devon coast. Hele Bay was ideally situated to bring in coal from Swansea in Wales which is directly opposite across the Bristol Channel. The coal was transported in small shallow draft ships and was used to fire up and feed the kilns of limestone on the beach that had been hewn from the rocks of Hillsborough Head. There are still remnants of the oak stanchions used to tie up the ships, and limestone shale on the beach.

The most excitement Nigel had experienced since becoming the local Bobby was regularly arresting drunken summer seaside revelers or giving a warning to a bunch of hippies gathered around a campfire on the beach knocking back cans of Stellar, a strong lager beer, and smoking spliffs of marijuana.

PC Worthy phoned the North Devon Police Headquarters at Barnstaple, where desk sergeant George Nelson took the call and said that he would let Detective Inspector McCarthy know. It was now 7.15 a.m.

Gram left the cottage to go back down to the beach. 'Digby, stay, be a good boy,' said Gram as he closed the door. Digby just sauntered over to his bed by the Aga and curled up, contented after his run on the beach and his homecoming treats.

PC Worthy lived with his wife Annie in a police house

almost opposite The Hele Bay Hotel on the junction of Beach Road and the main Ilfracombe to Combe Martin Road. He had been the local PC at Hele for going on twenty years and was well known to the locals. He was what was known on the force as an 'old timer' and never had any ambition to gain promotion, for that would take him away from his beloved birthplace. He put down the phone, threw on his underwear and police uniform as quick as lightning, almost falling over trying to get his trousers on.

'What on earth's going on, Nige?' asked Annie, dressed in her pink floral winceyette nightgown.

'A girl's body has been found down on the beach. Washed up by the tide by all accounts. Looks like I shall be busy all day, so don't make me lunch. I'll grab something from the café when I get a moment.'

With that he kissed his wife on the cheek and then left the house. He grabbed his police bicycle stored in the shed, jumped on and pedaled furiously down Beach Road. As Gram stepped back onto the beach, sure enough, coming from the eastern end was Jim with his dog Bruno. Jim Derbyshire was middle aged and the owner and landlord of The Hele Bay Hotel. He was known to be a 'ladies' man with a penchant for young girls, often barmaids or chambermaids at the hotel.

Gram approached him frantically waving his hands in the air. 'Stay back Jim, and can you put Bruno on the leash, there's a dead body in the surf up ahead. Nige is on his way, but I reckon this will be a major crime scene before much longer. God knows how they're going to cope with the incoming tide.'

Jim stopped in his tracks and held Bruno firmly on his lead. He looked at the dead body without flinching, showing no sign of recognition, concern or for that matter, care.

PC Worthy arrived shortly afterwards and immediately took control. 'Right, I've informed HQ and a Detective Inspector McCarthy and a crime scene investigation team from Barnstaple will be taking over as soon as they can get here. In the meantime, Jim, can you take Bruno home and then come back and help Gram to cordon off the beach as best as you can.'

'What about the girl, Nige? It seems indecent just to leave her lying there exposed and as naked as the day she was born,' asked Gram.

'She's best left as you found her; DI McCarthy will be here soon and decide things from then on.'

The sun had now cut through the early morning mist and beams of sunlight shone down on the shoreline like theatre spotlights picking out the dead girl's body. A tattoo of a small slithering snake climbing up on the girl's right buttock was shimmering, almost dancing in tune to the waves lapping up against the body. Her long copper-coloured red hair was swirling in the sea with each ripple of an incoming tide.

Nige looked back up at Hillsborough Head and noticed someone coming down the coastal path. As Sod's Law would have it, a holidaymaker, camera in hand, was making her way down to the beach. She had been up early, camera in hand, to catch the morning dawn. She was a journalist from a national tabloid newspaper.

A journalist's sixth sense kicked in as she got nearer to the beach, and she began to snap away taking pictures of the scene below. Nigel, without realizing the consequence of her taking photos, walked over to meet her and asked her, as a potential witness, to await the arrival of DI McCarthy.

4

The telephone sprang into life on the bedside table in the penthouse apartment at 15 Kipling Terrace, which overlooked Bideford Quay on the Taw Estuary. Its shrill sounded like the squawks of the gulls outside, swooping along the river seeking anything they could find being jettisoned by fishing trawlers returning to harbour on the incoming morning tide.

Rick McCarthy reached out from deep slumber knocking the telephone off the table. He leant over the side of the bed, groaned, and grabbed the phone which was now off its cradle. He looked at the alarm clock, it had just gone 7.00 a.m.

'Rick McCarthy,' he answered in a daze.

'It's George, sir, sorry to disturb you so early but PC Worthy has just phoned in from Hele Bay. There is a dead female body washed in on the tide. It looks like murder, and a bad one at that,' said the desk sergeant at H.Q.

'Now then sergeant, don't let's be too quick to jump to conclusions. Didn't they teach you anything at Middlemore?' said Rick tersely.

'Well sir, PC Worthy said the body washed up has a severed hand, so I think it's a fair bet that she didn't kill herself or maybe she cut it off with a machete and went for a swim. That would be novel, wouldn't it?' the sergeant replied, tongue in cheek.

'Touché, George. Phone Dave and get him to pick me up in twenty.'

Rick sat up, turned round, yawned, and looked across at the other side of the bed where Kay was now wide awake. She was wearing one of Rick's faded old T shirts emblazoned with the poster of the 1960 Newport Rhode Island Jazz Festival featuring many of his jazz idols. The T shirt just about covered up her bum and the most intimate part of her body. They had been together for six months, ever since they had met on Rick's first murder case, the infamous 'North Devon Coastal Path Strangler.'

The strangler turned out to be a schizophrenic psychopath who, when in his delusional psychotic persona, went about strangling holiday makers walking the coastal footpath. He was found to be insane and committed to the St Thomas Lunatic Asylum in Exeter.

Rick had joined the police force as one of the new breeds of graduate entrant detective constables in 1962 and had risen to sergeant and then detective inspector by early 1967. He was not the archetypal policeman. His modern sartorial attire and unconventional ways were tolerated by the hierarchy as he was a brilliant detective who got results when all seemed lost. He often either bent or ignored the established rules of policing to gain advantage and had no time for the 'pen pushers' in senior roles who had not served their time at the 'coal face.' He was a keen advocate of the use of emerging technologies and supported the increasingly important role of the use of forensic pathologists in crime detection.

Rick was an avid jazz fan and loved all the American greats. Whenever he had a weekend off you could often find him rummaging through the imported jazz records at John Surman's record store in Barnstaple. Surman, a prominent west country saxophonist and composer, had recently moved up to London to be part of the burgeoning London jazz scene but kept his record store in Barnstaple going. He was now playing with such English modern jazz and R&B greats as Alexis Horner and Georgie Fame.

He was even known to drag Kay off for a long weekend to London to go to Ronnie Scott's jazz club in Soho when Ronnie was bringing over the likes of Sonny Rollins and Dexter Gordon from New York to play. When Rick was there, taking in the club's dingy intimate atmosphere, he was immersed in listening and swinging to the dulcet tones of jazz and blues. Rick was 'in heaven.' It seemed to him that jazz mirrored human life as it's lived from moment to moment. Reliant on the fleeting glance, and the startled smile between players rather than the written score, jazz can be at its most engaging when you can experience that impromptu process unfolding before your eyes as well as your ears.

Rick lent over and softly said to Kay, 'You always look ravishing first thing in the early morning light Babe, that's the time I love the best,' quoting a line from one of his favorite Donovan songs currently in the hit parade. 'Making love to you, stripped of all your war paint, in fact, when you are stripped of everything!'

Kay had always looked young for her age, fresh-faced with high cheek bones, wearing only minimal make-up. She wore her bouncy blonde hair in loose curls tied up in a top knot. She had perfectly shaped eyebrows surrounding her dewy blue eyes that sparkled like the sunlight on the sea. She was petite, but not short, with legs of a fashion model and she wore her clothes well.

'Away with you, you charmer. If you weren't a copper, you could have been a romantic poet or a jazz crooner. I suppose you're leaving me now. Will I be seeing you later?'

'Maybe sooner than you think, down on Hele Bay Beach if the coroner gives you the case I've just been given.'

'Ooh, that sounds promising. Is it right up my street?'

Kay was the senior forensic pathologist at Barnstable Mortuary and reported to the county coroner. She had first met Rick at Exeter University where Rick took a degree in criminology and where she qualified as a doctor. She had always set her heart on being a forensic pathologist since embarking on her degree. Perceptive, with a sense of drama and the macabre made her ideally suited for the job. She had recently been promoted to the post on the retirement of the incumbent, much to the abhorrence of Nathan Faraday, a colleague who had been a pathologist much longer than her and believed he would get the job, especially as his father was, William Faraday, the Coroner.

Rick filled her in on what he knew so far so that she would be ahead of the game and come prepared if called upon. He then quickly washed and shaved whilst Kay made a pot of filtered Colombian arabica coffee and some slices of toast and marmalade.

He put on a freshly ironed white cotton Van Heusen shirt with an Exeter Rugby Club tie to compliment his navy-blue Canali suit. It had narrow lapels and sloping side pockets making him look as cool as one of his jazz heroes, Miles Davis, or so he thought.

'I've made the coffee strong, darling; I'm thinking you need this given the scene you're going to face down at Hele Beach.'

Rick grabbed the cup of black coffee and woofed down a slice of toast as the entry phone burst into life. It was his sergeant, Dave Elliot.

David Elliot, 'Dave', was a 'salt of the earth' Devonian who had lived in Barnstaple all his life. He came up the hard way after his father died in a tragic accident when he was twelve years old, drowning whilst out fishing on one of the trawlers based in the town. His mother never remarried and brought Dave and his younger sister Jenny up on her own.

He took the death of his father badly and started running wild, getting into all sorts of scrapes at school and on the streets around the Harbourside where they lived, but none that warranted the attention of the law. It was only when an ex-copper encouraged him to join the local boxing club that he began to sort himself out. The ex-copper became a father figure to him, and it was no surprise to his mother that he decided to join the police force as a cadet at the earliest opportunity after he left school.

Once old enough, he became a young PC on the beat and earned his 'spurs' by sorting out a lot of the problems created by teenagers loitering in the town centre and down on the harbourside with little or nothing to do. He related to them and saw himself in their shoes at an earlier age. They came to trust him and would confide in him.

After spending five years on the beat, he was encouraged to sit his sergeant's exam and passed with flying colours. An opportunity came up with CID and Dave jumped at it. He soon became noticed within the squad as a hard-nosed and tenacious sergeant with a feel for what he called 'life on the street.'

As luck would have it, when Rick's sergeant moved on to be a detective inspector in another force, Dave's own governor retired. Rick didn't hesitate in requesting Dave as his new partner. They never looked back, the Yin with the Yang, like Napoleon Solo and Ilya Kuryakin in the popular TV series 'The Man form UNCLE.' They became the most successful duo that Devon and Cornwall CID had ever seen, solving some of the most difficult cases in the history of the force.

Rick answered the entry phone, 'I'll be right down, Dave.'

With that he slipped on a pair of Italian black patent leather pointed toe shoes, kissed Kay goodbye and was out of the apartment in a flash.

I'm glad he's not that quick in coming in bed, she mused to herself.

Dave was waiting outside in Rick's allocated Daimler Dart SP250 police car. It was sleek and fast. It had a boot big enough for all their scene of crime paraphernalia and was packed with new white scene of crime suits, sterile gloves, boots, evidence bags, camera, film etc.

'Where are we off to, Guv?' enquired Dave.

'Hele Bay Beach, a female has been washed up with a hand chopped off. Have you managed to grab any brekkie?'

'No chance!' exclaimed Dave.

'I thought so, you look as if you have just fallen out of bed, what do I keep telling you?'

'Clothes maketh the man,' said Dave with a sigh and a grimace.

'That's right. If you are ever going to set your sights on getting promoted you really must smarten yourself up.'

'I could never carry off that New York jazz look like yourself, it's just not my style.'

'I don't expect or want you to. North Devon only has room for one Rick McCarthy, or should I say Ricardo,' he said with a big grin. 'No, just get yourself down to Burtons and buy yourself a decent suit,' he said, looking up to the heavens and shaking his head.

'OK, pull into Ilfracombe railway station on the way and we will grab a couple of bacon sarnies and black coffees from the café. That'll keep us going,' said Rick not admitting that he had already had a cup of coffee and a slice of toast back at the apartment.

Ilfracombe station was on the north-western outskirts of the town, two hundred and twenty-five feet above sea level. The 1–in–36 gradient between Ilfracombe and Mortehoe, a further four hundred feet climb, was one of the steepest sections of double-track railway line in the country and was most certainly the fiercest climb from any terminus station in the UK. The Devon Belle, a luxury express passenger train carrying hundreds of holiday makers, ran between London Waterloo station and Ilfracombe.

At that time of the morning, it took them just over thirty minutes with their blue lights flashing, and bell ringing all the way from Bideford to Ilfracombe and a further five minutes to Hele Bay. They arrived just after 8.00. Dave screeched to a halt in the car park next to the beach with a sideways skid, throwing up sand blown in off the beach and spilling the remains of Rick's coffee all over his shoes. Rick often wondered why police drivers always did that on arrival at a crime scene as they were perfectly capable of controlling the car. *Must come from watching all those American TV cop programs such as Murder*

Squad and Dragnet he thought to himself.

After getting out of the Dart, Rick swapped his fine shoes for a pair of Timberland boots and proceeded to walk the remaining twenty-five yards down the road to the beach where they were met by PC Worthy.

'Good morning, sir,' he said, whilst also nodding at Dave, who he knew from schooldays. 'The body is about fifty yards up the beach, you can just make it out from here.'

'OK constable, you don't mind if I call you Nigel?'

'It's Nige, sir.'

'Right Nige, fill me in on the basics as we walk to the body.'

As they stepped onto the beach Rick paid particular attention to the café and public toilets to the left, above which was Hillsborough Head. It rose above them, reaching up to the sky, and touched by the morning light. A giant escarpment of limestone rock, carpeted with heathland, and with ferns, juniper and thistles nestling in the cracks of the rock.

The café was closed that time of the morning, more to the pity, thought Dave. It was now late in the summer season with few tourists about, so they only opened from 11.00.a.m till 2.00p.m, finally closing at the end of September and not reopening until the following Easter. On the right-hand side, immediately next to the car park was a reception building being the entrance to a caravan site that ran along the shoreline right round the beach above the sand dunes. The caravan site was still open to tourists, and a few had gathered behind the low open fence above the sand dunes to watch what was going on. By the time they reached the body Nige had told them all he knew so far and ended up by telling Rick about the lady with the camera.

'What do you mean, a lady with a camera? Make sure she doesn't go anywhere, I'll need to question her later, she may be a material witness or at least the pictures in her camera may contain vital information.'

5

The body had moved a further ten yards up the beach on the incoming tide and was now 'beached' as the tide was turning. Rick and Dave looked at the corpse from all angles, being careful not to disturb any traces of evidence.

'What do you make of it so far, Dave?'

'Nothing much more than Nige has told us really, apart from the obvious possible attempt to prevent identification, but why sever a hand, if that was the objective why not sever both? A revenge killing maybe? I would guess that she had been in the water no more than 12 hours and was obviously a pretty little thing, of maybe eighteen to twenty years old before being mutilated and suffering unimaginable injuries.'

'I agree, but let's wait for the forensic pathologist and SOC (scene of crime) boys to arrive.'

'What's this?' asked Dave pointing to a tattoo on the right cheek of her buttock.

'It looks like a tattoo of a snake,' replied Rick leaning over to take a closer look. 'It has a copper-coloured head, similar in colour to the girl's own hair, and reddish-brown scales, so I would guess it's a Copperhead Viper. That's the same snake that Queen Cleopatra of Egypt used to commit suicide in 30 BC. In those days it was called an Asp.'

'You and your passion for history as well as jazz. What has that got to do with the girl's murder?'

'Nothing, as far as I can think of, but history repeats itself and broadens the mind. Somebody is going to recognize it but given where it is on her body, I would imagine only her closest most intimate friends would have seen it. She is also wearing a strange pendant, the image of which is not one that I have ever seen before.'

'Nor me,' replied Dave, 'but it looks almost satanic to me.'

It wasn't long before Kay turned up dressed in a white body suit, wearing a mask, sterile gloves and booties, her hair tied back.

'Hi Kay, I had a feeling that it would be you who would be given the case, given its unusual nature,' greeted Rick trying not to show too much endearment in front of his colleagues, even though they all knew that they were an item. At the same time, SOC arrived headed up by Sergeant Ethan James together with two further constables from Ilfracombe and Combe Martin.

'Right, I need the whole beach cordoned off. Nige, I want you to do that with the other two constables. I then want the SOC team to search the entire beach, paying particular attention to the tide line in case any evidence had also been washed up or signs that she may have been murdered or dumped in the sea here. Sergeant James will assist Ms. Stone in examining the body and the immediate surrounding area.'

Turning to Ethan, he said 'Can we have a verbal report of your observations and the photos as quickly as you can. You can write up your report later. I particularly want to see photos of the tattoo and pendant close up.'

'No problem, sir. Shall we say first thing tomorrow morning?' Rick nodded his agreement.

'Now where is that lady with the camera?'

Turning full circle, he spotted her sitting on a rock and walked over to her.

'Good morning, Madam. You are?'

'Felicity Wainwright, Travel Correspondent at The Daily Chronicle.'

Rick was taken aback but kept his feelings to himself. *That's all we need, pictures of the crime scene splashed on the front page of tomorrow's edition.*

'And what may I ask are you doing down here?'

'A busman's holiday, taking photos of the local landmarks for a piece I intend to write about holidaying in North Devon.'

'What time were you out this morning?'

'Just after six. I wanted to capture the dawn from up on Hillsborough Head looking out over Hele Bay towards Combe Martin.'

'Did you see anyone else out at that time or anything suspicious?'

'No, I came back down from the cliff to be met by PC Worthy,' she said, as she looked across the bay to see him cordoning off the entrance to the beach with blue and white tape.

'Right. I'll have to take that camera if you please,' he said, holding out his hand.

'No, I don't please,' Felicity said sharply in reply. 'As an accredited journalist I don't have to do that without a court order.'

'Well, that can be arranged within a few hours if need be. Let's be sensible shall we?'

After some discussion, Felicity agreed to hand over the camera and film after Rick gave her an assurance that he would give her the scoop on any major developments in the case. Unknown to Rick, Felicity Wainwright also had a small pocket camera on which she had taken photos of the crime scene as she stepped onto the beach after walking down from Hillsborough Head.

Kay finished her work in about an hour and gave Rick her initial findings.

'Do you know what, I think; she may have died from poisoning and not the immediate inclination of drowning, nor through loss of blood from the severing of the hand. There's some bruising round her wrists and neck but a slight tinge of colour on her lips is leading me towards poisoning. Her right hand was severed when she was either unconscious or postmortem. The time of death was certainly within the last twelve hours, most likely between 11.00 p.m. and 2.00 a.m. It looks like she either fell or more likely was thrown over the sea facing clifftop up on the Head. She has severe lacerations, a broken pelvis and broken left leg. I'll carry out the postmortem this afternoon and let you have my preliminary report tonight, but if I am right about poisoning, we'll have to wait until tomorrow for the toxicology report.'

From that Rick assumed that the post mortem report would make interesting after dinner reading and discussions with Kay. *No nookie for him that night* he mused to himself.

Ethan and the SOC boys would be there for the rest of the day. Rick took Dave to one side and walked a few yards away out of earshot of the others.

'There is not much more we can do here Dave. When we get back to HQ, I want you to send Matt and Adam to do house to house calls and can you look up the tide timetables for

Hillsborough Head and Hele Bay. Also get Theo and a search party up on the Head looking for anything unusual, paying particular attention to the north cliff top that drops straight down into the sea.'

Rick looked around the cove. It was now closed off to the public, Kay was bent over the body with Ethan, Nige was standing guard. It was organised and under control. Turning back to Dave, he said, 'Can you also get your thinking cap on as to the significance or otherwise of the tattoo? It's an unusual one and I can't help but think that the tattoo of a snake and a severed hand has something to do with who she is and why she was murdered. When the body is ready to go to the mortuary for the postmortem, bag that pendant in an evidence bag and get an expert to try and identify the image on it.'

It was now past eleven o'clock. The café had opened. 'Right, coffee and a doughnut all round I think,' said Rick loudly. Nige was nearby and took the hint and duly went off to the café.

'Morning Nige, what's going on? I don't know whether this is good or bad for my trade,' said Tracy the café owner.

'I'm afraid a dead girl has been washed up on the beach. The SOC boys will be here all day, but I suspect once the word gets out the morbid gawkers will be down in their droves, cameras in hand. It'd be good for trade for you and the Hotel for the next few days after the Press Release and DI McCarthy's statement on the radio this evening. I would make hay whist you can, Trace.'

'Thanks for the tip off. I'll get more supplies in and also let the bakers know. Now, what can I do for you?' 'Six coffees, three black, one with sugar, three white, two with sugar, and half a dozen doughnuts please. Are the doughnuts fresh?'

'Of course, I picked them up at the bakery on my way in this morning.'

'Thanks Tracy, what do I owe you?'

'On the house Nige, I always like to help the boys in blue. I'll probably clean up with the increased trade. I think I'll put the prices up for all the Grockles, then the locals that I recognize can have a discount.'

Dave couldn't wait for his 'elevensies.' He looked over to the cafe anxiously to see where Nige was and saw him strolling over with the coffees and doughnuts. All were gratefully consumed by the whole team. After drinking his coffee and eating the finger-licking doughnut, Rick looked out to sea and lit up a Camel cigarette. He'd been smoking ever since his university days at Exeter when he thought it was cool to smoke the same brand as one of his Hollywood western movie idols, John Wayne. The habit and the brand stuck.

He decided to drive back to HQ alone and stop off on the way to have lunch at The Crab and Lobster Inn on the harbour quayside at Ilfracombe where his mother was the landlady. He asked Dave to get a lift back to Barnstaple with Kay.

On returning to the car park, Rick changed back into his shiny Italian shoes and climbed into the Dart. As he turned the ignition key, he thought to himself, *I don't like the look of this one, it has shades of the occult to me.* Little did he know that his intuition would be proved right, and that he was about to expose a local devil worship cauldron. They met and practiced their deviant activities at sacred ancient sites across North Devon that were located on the Lundy Island to Glastonbury ley-line. The first one such place was Hillsborough Head.

6

Rick drove into Ilfracombe High Street along the Hillsborough Road and then immediately turned hard right and wound the Dart down Fore Street to the harbour. He parked in the car park at the end of the main quay just past The Crab and Lobster Inn. The car park was only about half full, it being near the end of the tourist season. There were a few people fishing at the end of the quay, casting their lines out into the breakers with either bait or lures in an attempt to catch wild sea bass that came in on the tide.

The weather had brightened up and it had turned out to be another fine late-summer's day. The sun was now high in the sky and beaming down on the harbour, reflecting on the water like spilt diesel oil and creating a kaleidoscope of colour as if it were at the end of a rainbow. As Rick got out of the car the reflections of the white hulls of the yachts moored in the harbour were blinding, causing him to reach in the Dart glove box for his Ray-Ban aviator sunglasses.

A number of late holidaymakers were enjoying strolling round the harbour. They were mainly retired folk as the schools had reopened three weeks earlier. A few had ice creams in their hands, others were happily sitting on a bench watching the world go by, some nodding off with the after-effects of their lunch of fish and chips or a few pints of beer.

Rick had never tired of coming to Ilfracombe. He grew up

in Barnstaple which together with Bideford, is on the Taw and Torridge Estuary, but in his opinion, there was nothing like the views of the cliffs and the bays as you drove or walked along the coastal path from Ilfracombe all the way up the rugged North Devon coastline to Lynmouth. When Rick's parents retired, they bought the rundown Pier Inn, on the quayside at Ilfracombe harbour, renovated it and changed its name to The Crab and Lobster. His mother, Rose, ran it as the landlady and his father, Bob, bought a small crabbing boat, the Marie Rose, which he moored in the inner harbour beyond the middle jetty.

The Inn became renowned for its crab and lobster dishes created from the catch of the day from the Marie Rose, and for its good selection of local ales. Rose was an established cook, having previously worked in the catering trade and she prepared and served everything from plain fresh crab sandwiches to lobster thermidor. In this instance Rick would have one of his mother's house specialties, a crab soup full of a generous helping of cooked crab from his Dad's earlier catch, together with a crusty bread roll from the local bakers.

Rick had been adopted by Margaret (Rose) and Robert (Bob) McCarthy when his birth mother Elizabeth, who was Rose's younger sister, had died giving birth to him. Rick's father, Major Richard (mad Dickie) Devonport, Intelligence Corps, SBS, VC had died at Guernica in active service having volunteered for a covert undercover operation in the Spanish Civil War.

'Hello mother,' he said with much warm affection beaming from ear to ear as he entered the Inn.

'Darling Rick, come here and give your old mum a hug. My you do look smart,' replied Rose as she came round from behind the bar.

'What brings you here on your own on a Friday lunchtime? Is everything OK with you and Kay? Your dad's out on the Marie Rose checking his lobster pots off Lee Bay.'

'Oh, we're both fine. It's just business I'm afraid up at Hele Bay. You'll hear about it soon enough on the local radio and TV tonight, so I might as well tell you what will be in the press statement, but it must obviously remain under your hat. A young girl has been found washed up on Hele Bay beach, murdered.'

'Oh dear, poor soul. Do you know who it is?'

'Not at this stage. That's all I can tell you for now, you know how these things go.'

'Yes dear, you will solve it in due course, that I have no doubt,' his mother said sounding like a cross between motherly love and being patronizing.

'And whilst I am about it, it's about time you married that lovely girl.'

Rick just let his mother's comments go over his head. He loved Kay with all his might, but they had both come to an understanding that for now their careers must come first. Rick was a rising star and the demands of his job meant that he was called out at all hours. In all probability he would be promoted in the not-too-distant future, possibly to a more senior CID role in Exeter. In his eyes, fully supported by Kay, there would be plenty of time to settle down, get married and have kids of their own.

'Now, what can I get you?' asked his mother.

Rick ordered his crab soup and looking up and down the bar, asked what guest beers were on tap.

'Well, we have a new IPA beer called Ogun. It's the latest

one from the Madrigal Renaissance Brewery. A bit scary title if you ask me but it's proving to be popular with the locals, especially the younger set.'

'I'll try a pint of that then,' replied Rick without thinking of its significance. After a splendid lunch and catching up on day-to-day affairs with his mother, he strolled out of the Inn to the quayside. He took out his pack of Camels, flipped one out from its soft pack and lit up. Glancing over to the far side of the harbour. 'Our Olivia Belle,' the largest fishing boat operating out of Ilfracombe had returned on the morning tide and was unloading its catch.

The seagulls were swooping and diving, making their distinctive high shrill piercing cry hoping to scoop up any smaller fish or offal thrown overboard by the crew, or to take advantage of any scraps dropped by late holidaymakers strolling along the quay and eating fish and chips from the 'chippee.' A couple of the sightseeing boat trips were still operating. There were trips to see the splendour of the bays and coves up and down the coastline or to venture a bit further out to Lundy Island to see the flora and fauna, the basking seals and puffins from which Lundy was named in Norske.

The rigging of the sailing boats moored in the inner harbour could be heard chinking against the masts. In another month or so they would be lifted out of the water and parked up on the hard for the winter, protecting them from any storms that breached the harbour defenses. Whilst there, the owners could make any necessary repairs, and their hulls could be cleared of any barnacles below the waterline and anti-fouling painted on.

You could not wish for a more peaceful scene. It was idyllic.

Rick strolled down to the car park at the end of the quay,

flicked his cigarette butt into the glistening water shining in the midday sun and looked out to sea. Taking in a deep breath of intoxicating sea air he looked to his right at the towering sight of Hillsborough Head with its rocky promontory below. *Who are you, my beautiful sea urchin? What secrets are you holding up there?* He wondered. *Someone is missing you today, parents, husband, boyfriend, lover, sister, brother, friend? I will find who did this to you, I will find them, and I will get you justice.*

He got back in the Dart, took one last glance at the Head, and set off for Barnstaple. The car climbed its way out of the town, up past the railway station and further up the Torr embankment to Higher Mullacott. Rick dropped down a gear and floored the accelerator and the Dart surged forward. He smiled at the throaty sound from the exhaust of the V8 engine pushing him back into the leather sports seat. He took the corners with ease, just like Kay's ex-racing car father had taught him. Outside line, accelerating into the bend and out without braking. He was just approaching the outskirts of Braunton, halfway to Barnstaple, when it suddenly came to him. It was his turn to skid to a halt. *Of course, you idiot* he said to himself. *How could I have missed that?*

Turning on the blue flashing lights, much to the annoyance of traffic building up behind him, he did a three-point turn and headed back to Ilfracombe. He could hardly contain himself as he drove back to The Crab and Lobster. He parked outside, leaving his hazard warning lights flashing and ran in.

As he rushed in his mother looked up, 'Back already son, have you left something?'

'Only my brain, mother.'

Rick walked over to the bar and sure enough he found what

he was looking for. There, on the sign of one of the traditional real ale beer pumps and also on the labels of the bottles of beer on the shelves behind the bar was the name and image of Ogun. He grabbed hold of a bottle and looked closely at the label. On the front was the image of Ogun holding a machete and the words 'God of Justice' beneath it. On the back of the bottle label, the inscription 'One of our beers from the North Devon Voodoo range, brewed by the Madrigal Renaissance Brewery.' The brewery logo looked similar if not identical to the pendant found around the murdered girl's neck.

'I'll take a bottle of this Ogun beer back for Dave, if that's OK,' not disclosing the real reason he wanted it.

'Thanks Mum, must be off.'

'Bye darling, come back soon and bring the lovely Kay with you.'

'Will do.'

With that he dashed back out and jumped into the Dart and fired her up. *It's funny how all sports cars are referred to in the female vernacular,* he thought to himself. With wheels spinning he tuned round in one go at the middle harbour junction and wove his way back up to the main road. As he drove back to Barnstaple he was in a good frame of mind. Call it intuition, he thought. *Is there a connection between the victim's pendant, the brewery, and the name of the beer?*

7

On arrival back at HQ, he parked the car and bounded up the steps of the main entrance.

'Good afternoon George. Is Dave in?' he enquired of the desk sergeant as he hurried past.

'Yes sir, you seem to be in a good mood. It's been all on the go here since this morning's grave news.'

'Never better George, never better, carpe diem and all that.'

Rick entered the operations room which was buzzing with a hive of activity from the team Dave had rapidly put together.

'Jeez, Dave, when was the last time we were allocated such resources?'

There must have been half a dozen faces in the room, some of whom had worked with Rick and Dave before, some of them new.

'Whatever we need Guv, the best of the best. Instructions from on high, apparently the chief constable has taken a personal interest.'

'That's all we need; the media will be in a frenzy on this one. We don't want any leaks from within the department.'

'I've set up your office, two telephones, one an extension from the ops room and the other a private line. There are two in-trays, one with latest reports from the team and the other for any messages. One out-tray which Daphne, our secretary will deal with. I've also had Matt set up the investigation board in the ops room and put details of what we know so far on it.'

'Well done, Dave, I've brought you one back from the inn,' he said placing the bottle of beer on Dave's desk.

'Cheers Guv, but it's a bit late for lunch and a bit early for a sundowner,' replied Dave not paying much attention.

'Take a look, Einstein,' said Rick.

Dave picked up the bottle and studied it closely. 'Bloody hell,' he said, 'He is holding a machete with a snake wrapped around him, and the logo looks like the image on the girl's pendant.'

'It also says it's part of The North Devon Voodoo range of beers,' said Rick.

'What are you inferring, Guv?'

'Driving back from the scene of crime I had an intuition that the murder may be part of some occult sacrifice. The Voodoo connection seems to be too much of a coincidence.'

'Voodoo? Here in North Devon?'

'Why not? The practice of Voodoo is not a million miles away from the practices of witchcraft in the middle ages. I'll let you know that Bideford has an unusual claim to fame, in that it was the last place for anyone to be convicted of witchcraft in England. Three local women were hanged on the 25th August 1682 at Heavitree just outside Exeter.'

'Yes, but that's history, I though the witch hunter trials had died off by the end of the 17th century.'

'They had, but witchcraft just went underground. Nowadays, Freemasonry, Wicca and Druidism are worshiped openly, and their respective traditional ways regarded as part of our heritage and culture.'

'There's a huge chasm from there to sacrificial ceremonies,' said Dave, pulling a face.

'I wouldn't be so sure. There've been several cases of murder where the perpetrator has, in their eyes entered into a 'sacrificial pact with the devil' that bear similarities to that of the murder on the Head. There have also been deaths involving consensual and non-consensual sadomasochistic sexual acts. Another disturbing trend has been the incidence of 'honour killings' among the Asian immigrants from Uganda.'

'Right, I'll get a copy of the bottle's labels up on the information board. Moving on, what have we got on the potential murder weapon?'

'Kay believes it is a thick heavy blade. The hand was severed in one fell swoop from above, and the cut is not precise as if it were made by a surgeon's scalpel. It was more likely made from something like a meat cleaver, machete, or an axe.'

'That's quite a wide range, Guv. A meat cleaver suggests a butcher or abattoir worker. There can't be many machetes about, apart from belonging to a gangland 'soldier,' and you are probably talking about city street crime in Plymouth for that, or it belonging to an antique collector of tribal weapons. An axe? Really? There must be thousands out there unless we are talking about a large heavy one used by woodsman and the like.'

'I agree Dave, none of whose owners are likely to be members of a witches or voodoo cauldron. They are more likely to be intelligent, middle class or at least artisans, but you never know.'

Rick looked at him quizzically, 'What about that camera we confiscated down on the beach from that Felicity what's her name, the journalist. Has anyone taken a look at the film inside it to see if there are any relevant photos of something we have missed?'

'Ah, yes, the forensics boys in the lab have had a look in the dark room. The ones taken before she noticed the body are mostly typical seaside scenic shots you would find in any promotional article or holiday brochure.'

'What do you mean, before she noticed the body, I thought she said she only noticed what was going on after Nige was on the scene.'

'Apparently not. The touristy photos suddenly stop, indicating when she saw the body.'

'Are the photos time stamped at that point on the film?'

'Yes, it was 6.50 a.m.'

'Well, that's before Gram Parsons phoned Nige at 7.15 and probably even before Gram went down to the beach. That's not what that young lady told Nige! What do the ensuing photos show?' Rick asked sharply.

'Quite a lot of shots of the body and the surrounding beach.'

'Right, let's have a look at the prints, Dave.'

Dave pulled out the prints from the large envelope they were delivered in from the lab and spread them out across Rick's desk.

'Has anyone looked at these in detail?'

'Not yet Guv, nobody thought they would reveal anything more than was already observed on the scene by us and SOC.'

'Detail Dave, detail. Find a couple of magnifying glasses for you and me to take a look, and whilst you are there, grab a couple of mugs of coffee. Not that muck the canteen supply us. I've bought some tins of Colombian arabica ground coffee and a cafetiere press. You'll find them in the kitchenette cupboard.'

Whist Dave was getting the coffee and the magnifying glasses

Rick lay back in his chair, lit up a cigarette and reflected as to where they were in the investigation and the way forward. He knew that the first 48 hours of any murder case were crucial. In this case, despite making great strides, something at the back of his mind was telling him that this was going to prove to be the most challenging case in his career so far. The murder will provoke great public and media interest and no doubt pressure will be brought to bear from the chief constable down to solve it quickly.

Dave returned shortly after with two steaming mugs. Rick could smell the aroma of coffee drifting across the ops room even before Dave got to his office despite the pungent smell of cigarette smoke.

'Aah, that's much better, proper job Dave,' as he took his first sip. 'Now let's have a look at those photos.'

On the face of it they were just close up shots of the victim taken with a long lens from a distance of about two hundred yards. However, there were a couple that caught Rick's eye.

'Take a look at these.'

'What have we got, Guv?'

'Look, she was also wearing an ankle bracelet, it must have come off by the time Ethan and the SOC boys got down there. Where is it?'

'It wasn't found, probably got washed away on the tide.'

'If it's gold or silver it couldn't have gone far, get a team of blue beats to search that area of the beach again working away from the high tide line.'

'Will do.'

'Now what else have we got?' asked Rick, sitting back in his chair and closing his eyes in thought.

'Matt and Adam are making house to house calls in Hele, paying particular attention to those down at the Bay. It shouldn't take them too long as there are only 150 houses and cottages plus the hotel and the caravan site. I've already instructed PC Worthy to stop any holiday makers from checking out until Matt and Adam have taken their statements. The tide timetable is up on the board, as are the weather conditions last night. There was a full moon and the tide turned to incoming shortly after midnight.'

'What about Hillsborough Head and the nature reserve?' enquired Rick.

'I've mustered a large search party and sent Theo up to co-ordinate. Oh, and you are right, the head herpetologist at Exeter Zoo has identified the snake tattoo as a copperhead viper.'

'More references to death, Dave. As I said, Cleopatra was known to have committed suicide with the help of one. I suspect it's more a statement of undying love rather than a suicidal cry for help, but I can't yet fathom it out.'

'Well, she certainly didn't commit suicide Guv. Maybe she had it done when she was feeling suicidal as a gesture or even a cry for help following a breakup with a loved one, as in the case of Anthony and Cleopatra. Although in Anthony's case he committed suicide first, believing that she was already dead, didn't he?'

'Bloody hell Dave, I'm impressed! You are a deep thinker sometimes. That's a bit too complicated in our case. Anyway, this young lady's education level my not have extended to Shakespeare. On balance, she probably just went into a tattoo parlour seeking an erotic tattoo climbing up her most intimate parts, saw the copper viper had similar colouring to her hair and thought it was perfect.'

'Yeah, you are probably right, as usual.'

'Keep 'em coming. A good detective should always think out of the box. Right, well done, first thing tomorrow you and I are going to pay the Madrigal Renaissance Brewery a visit.'

8

Tuesday 26th

The Madrigal Renaissance Brewery turned out to be a successful small-batch artisan brewery owned by two brothers, Jonathon, and Justin Dukes. The brothers had been born and brought up by their parents in Tiverton. Jonathon, the younger brother, had attended the local secondary modern school and left when sixteen years old with virtually no academic qualifications. He learned his craft as an apprentice brewer at the St Austell brewery in Cornwall. He started as a junior, carrying and fetching malt and barley, progressing to become a fermentation operative and lastly trained as a junior brew master. He left St Austell to return to North Devon as master brewer at The Wizard's Cauldron, another microbrewery in Combe Martin.

Justin was the brighter one, passing his eleven plus exam to go to Tiverton Grammar. He was top of his class and sailed through his A Levels gaining four straight A's. His headmaster put him forward to go up to Oxford University to study economics and business studies. Justin passed his entrance exam and interview with flying colours and was awarded a scholarship. He gained a first-class honours degree and subsequently made a name for himself in investment banking in London and now ran a boutique venture capital fund, raising capital for startup companies and management buyouts.

One Christmas, at a family gathering at their parent's house, the brothers were chilling out in front of the open fire in the snug, drinking an ale from the Wizard's Cauldron brewery and listening to madrigals of canzonas of the renaissance period being sung by The Royal Choral Society.

Justin had a penchant for vocals of unaccompanied secular chants, particularly from the Medieval and Renaissance periods. Jonathon just had a penchant for mystical indie rock music and real ale.

'What's this one Jonathon, another one of your creations?' enquired Justin supping his brother's latest offering.

'It's called Cardinal Sin,' said Jonathon, 'They wouldn't let me call it Devil's Brew.'

'Oh, you and your fanciful references to the occult and the weird and wonderful. If you weren't my brother, I would swear you were a warlock.'

'Well, there's a thought. I'll tell you something, artisan craft beer is the way of the future. I've been to a few of those CAMRA real ale conventions and the potential is huge. People, particularly the older and younger generations, are looking for something different. The older ones remember when beer tasted like cask beer and the younger ones, apart from the taste, think it's cool to drink real ale.'

Justin took a large swig of beer and held his glass high, looking thoughtfully at the clear amber liquid inside.

'Do you know, you are right. How d'you fancy indulging your creativity and we start our own artisan brewery? I'll raise the capital, but we'd be equal shareholders, because you'd create the beers and their names.' He sat back in his chair with a huge smile on his face and continued, 'Susie went to Richmond Art School, so she can help you with the label designs and can also do the office work.'

Jonathon was astounded. It was always his dream to start an artisan brewery of his own, but Justin had never really showed much interest in beer other than quaffing his share at a rugby match with the lads.

'That sounds great! I love it, but we do all the work! What would you be doing?' Jonathon replied mocking his brother.

'Cheeky bugger,' replied Justin. 'I'll be creating the business plan, raising capital, and negotiating supply contracts. I'll also be front of house selling and visiting pubs and other outlets and hopefully negotiating wholesale deals with leading supermarkets.'

It was Jonathon's turn to smile. 'Huh, is that all?' he said, upon which they both burst out laughing.

And so, the catalyst for the birth of Madrigal Renaissance Brewery was born. As luck would have it, three months later the owners of the Wizard's Cauldron called time on their operation and Justin bought the assets of the business from the administrators for a knock down price. They looked round for suitable premises. Justin was keen that it must have some form of industrial heritage. They found just the thing; a three story former silver mine's engine house that had been converted to a large workshop on the ground floor with accommodation above and outbuildings. It was located on the southern pastures of Silver Mines Farm in Combe Martin.

The engine house had been sympathetically restored. It was now a Grade 11 listed building, and the brothers would have to apply for change of use of the workshop into a brewery. When they had inspected the property before buying it, they also looked around the yard and outbuildings. Some of the buildings were almost derelict but could easily be renovated. In one there was still evidence of when it operated as a silver mine. An original 19c smelter, too large and too heavy to move was still there.

'It's just brilliant' said Justin, 'so much history.'

'Look,' said Jonathon, 'There is even some galena still scattered about the place,' as he picked up a chunk of ore. 'See, you can see the silver lode running through it. Susie will love it. If we can gather enough ore, we can buy a small smelting vessel and produce our own silver trinkets.'

The property came with deeds going back to the 14th century but the silver mine had long been closed. Combe Martin used to be famous for silver mining with the first documented evidence of a royal mine in 1292. There was sporadic working in every century up to the nineteenth, including a short-lived bonanza during the reign of Queen Elizabeth I.

The ore that was mined was mainly galena. Lead sulphide, with an unusually high silver content. After the ore was brought to the surface it was smelted and refined to yield lead and silver. The last known mining was in the late 19th century and many of the mines and outbuildings had remained derelict ever since.

'How long will it take to set up, Jonathon?'

'Not that long, I reckon two to three months after we get the keys. Do you think you can get permission for change of use within that time?'

'Nothing ventured, nothing gained little brother. I will make the owner an offer he can't refuse today. Once we've exchanged contracts I'll apply to National Heritage for change of use.'

Within three months the brothers had moved the equipment from the old Wizard's Cauldron Brewery in Hele into the larger new premises on the lower floor of the converted engine house. Justin had decided to take the upper floor as his own private accommodation.

Jonathon then started brewing their first beer based on a formula that he had brought with him from the Wizard's Cauldron, enhanced by his own little bit of magic, tweaking the formulae, and adding mugwort. It became an instant success winning several accolades at beer fairs and was awarded CAMRA's Best New IPA 1966.

Devil's Brew became a bestseller throughout the West Country and Justin negotiated a wholesale contract with one of the national supermarkets.

The whole setup was, however, a major bone of contention to Sam Billings, the previous owner of the Wizard's Cauldron, who accused Jonathon of stealing his formula of Witches Brew. It wasn't the only thing that Jonathon had stolen from Sam; his wife Susie was Sam's former secretary and mistress.

9

It was late afternoon by the time Rick and Dave pulled into the yard of the brewery. The undisputable smell of hops, barley and yeast was in the air. Rick thought it smelt like the first time he had entered the public bar of a pub in his teenage years. The affable Justin, mid-thirties, well groomed, dressed in a crumpled beige linen suit, pale blue open neck shirt, sandals with no socks, greeted them.

'Nice motor gentlemen, I can tell you have a taste for tradition.' Justin's red Porsche 911 was parked outside in the yard. 'That's what we are offering you here, tradional ales with a bit of magic thrown in. My brother Jonathon is the brew master, and he has a batch of his latest creation, Beelzebub, brewing, but I can offer you a taste of Purple Heart.'

Rick and Dave looked at each other as Rick produced his warrant card,

'Detective Inspector Richard McCarthy and my colleague Detective Sergeant Elliot. We are here in an official capacity not to sample beers, although I am sure Dave might buy a case whilst we are here. And you are?'

'Oh, I see. Sorry, yes, I'm Justin Dukes, co-owner with my brother Jonathon. How can I help you?'

'We are investigating a murder; a young lady was found washed up on the beach down at Hele Bay this morning.'

'I'm sorry to hear that, but how does that affect us here at

Madrigal?' asked Justin.

'Well, here's the thing,' said Rick. 'She had copper coloured red hair, not dissimilar to the colour of your snakes draped around the Ogun image and she was wearing a silver pendant that bears a remarkable resemblance to that on your beer labels.' He held back the full details in respect of the tattoo and the severed hand.

With that, Jonathon strolled in from the factory. He looked the antithesis to his older brother. Long unkempt hair, beard, wearing a Black Sabbath T shirt, faded blue denim jeans, and a pair of Converse All Star trainers. 'Beelzebub' is bubbling along nicely,' said Jonathon laughing, 'adding a bit of mugwort seemed to do the trick.'

'Jonathon, these gentlemen are from the police investigating a murder,' said Justin.

'Ooh, err, will the murderer hang then, not upside down I trust?' On seeing the bewildered faces before him, quickly adding 'a reference to The Hanged Man tarot card' he said laughing.

'Enough jokes Jonathon, this is a serious matter. I do apologize for my brother's insensitivity Inspector.'

'It's Detective Inspector' retorted Rick. 'I would like to know where both of you were between the hours of 10 o'clock last night and two o'clock this morning.'

'That's easy' replied Jonathon, 'I was here at the brewery all night mashing up the ingredients for Beelzebub.'

'Can anyone vouch for that?' asked Rick.

'Yeah, old Chugg my assistant was helping me.'

'What about you Justin?'

'I left here at around seven then went down to The Hele Bay

Hotel for a meal and a drink with Jim Derbyshire, the owner. I left there at about eleven and drove home alone.'

'Can anyone verify that?'

'I don't know, I live alone on the top floor of the engine house. My car would have been garaged in one of the outbuildings, so I suppose it was possible that old Chugg either heard me or saw me come back.'

'What about you Jonathon, did you see or hear your brother come home?'

'Sorry Inspector, I can't help you there.'

'Who came up with the name Ogun?'

'I did,' replied Jonathon. 'We used to brew a beer called Witches Brew at the Wizard's Cauldron Brewery, so we launched our first beer as Devil's Brew. It sold so well we decided to create a range of beers called North Devon Voodoo. Ogun is one of the Voodoo Gods, the God of Justice.'

'And the design and artwork?'

'That would be Susie, Jonathon's wife. She creates all our artwork, working with Jonathon after he has come up with the names,' said Justin.

'What about the machete in the image?'

'If you do your research Detective Inspector you will see Ogun depicted on many images with crossed machetes and snakes reflecting their historical use in carrying out voodoo justice.'

Rick threw a glance at Dave who had also not missed the connection to the victim.

'And what about the logo design?'

'That would be me' replied Justin. 'I was looking for something that represented the whole ethos of what we are trying to convey here at the Madrigal Renaissance Brewery. The image is an ancient one connected to Erzuli, the Voodoo God of Beauty. Susie then came up with the idea of selling silver pendants embossed with the image. The connection to the old silver mines where the brewery is now located also appealed. I really don't see what a body on the beach has to do with us though.'

Justin was getting flustered at all the questions, but Rick ignored him.

'Lastly, do you know of anyone who has a grudge against you or the brewery?'

The brothers looked at each other initially shaking their heads.

'Oh, come on, let's not waste each other's time, there must be someone who begrudges your success.'

'Sam Billings is not a fan,' answered Justin. 'He's jealous that we're making a success where he failed. Bloody man keeps accusing me of buying the assets cheap off the administrator, well to the victor the spoils and all that. When he is in his cups and blind drunk, he also accuses Jonathon of stealing his formulae and his mistress.'

Rick could not help to note the animosity between Justin and Sam Billings, possibly not without reason on Sam's part.

'Oh, yes, and who might that be?'

'Susie, Jonathon's wife. She used to be Billing's secretary.'

Jonathon piped up trying to divert the conversation away from Sam Billings. 'Jim Derbyshire isn't a happy bunny either. He bemoans the fact that we are selling our beers direct to the public at the brewery on open days.' He reckons it's taking trade away from The Hele Hotel.'

'That's a minor issue Jonathon,' said Justin.

'Maybe,' retorted Jonathon, 'But Jim is holding a bitter grudge, and he can be very vindictive.'

'OK, that's all for now,' said Rick. 'We'd like to take away a sample of all the different beers that you currently produce. Sergeant Elliot will pay you for them.'

Rick turned and started to walk towards the exit. As he reached the door he turned back and asked, 'Oh, by the way, just a thought, I am not familiar with Beelzebub, is that another one of your Voodoo gods?' knowing full well who Beelzebub was.

Jonathon laughed, 'Ha, got you there. Beelzebub is named in the Old Testament of the Bible as the Prince of the Devils.'

'I thought it must have some atheist connection judging by your warped sense of humanity.'

Jonathon rose to the bait. 'I'm not an atheist I just don't worship your version of God!'

With that Rick turned back and walked out of the door to the car park. They put the case of beers in the boot of the Dart and started the car to set off back to Barnstaple. As they were leaving, a car turned into the brewery yard causing Dave to brake sharply.

'What the heck, bloody idiot,' exclaimed Dave.

'Leave it Dave, we have enough to deal with without getting embroiled on a dangerous driving charge.'

The driver was Jonathon's wife, Susie Dukes.

As she entered the brewery she said, 'Who was that in the flash car? A prospective customer? I taught him a lesson!' she said laughing. 'I turned a bit too fast into the yard and made him brake sharply.'

'You idiot, didn't you notice the bell on the front bumper?'

snapped Justin.

'You mean it was the police in a flash sports car?'

'It's a Daimler Dart, the latest car, usually only given to high speed traffic patrols, but in this case to an aspiring detective inspector of Barnstable CID.'

'Apparently a young woman's body was found washed up down at Hele Beach this morning,' added Jonathon.

'What's that got to do with us?' enquired Susie, dreading what the answer might be.

'He asked about our North Devon Voodoo beers, Ogun in particular. The murdered girl had copper coloured red hair and was wearing one of our pendants,' replied Justin.

Susie then stared at Jonathon, saying in a loud voice 'What did you tell them?'

'Nothing, Susie. Honestly, I told you that was over a long time ago,' he replied tersely.

'What's all this about? asked Justin, 'Not another one of your flings?'

'Nothing you should worry about, just keep your nose out of it,' retorted Jonathon.

Susie was seething. She turned to Jonathon again and shouted, 'Well, you had better get your story straight, it won't take them long to identify her and make the connection back to you.'

'What do you mean, story?' demanded Justin.

'It wasn't just any old fling, Justin,' said Susie. 'The girl might turn out to be Samantha, Sam Billings daughter, she had natural red hair.'

What Jonathon had never told her, or anyone else come to that, was that Samantha also had a small tattoo of a snake on her right buttock.

'Jesus Christ, Jonathon, whatever have you got yourself involved in? First his mistress, then his daughter? You are unbelievable! Could you never keep your pecker in its cage,' exclaimed Justin almost shaking in rage.

'It was nothing, nothing at all, it was just a wild fling last summer. I gave her one of the pendants as a love token.'

'Bloody hell man, what kind of idiot are you? You're nearly old enough to be her father for Christ's sake.'

'She came on to me, I wasn't the first to give in to her whiles, nor the last,' replied Jonathon rather sheepishly.

Justin stood silently for a moment, turning his back on his brother and taking in deep lungfuls of air in an attempt to calm himself. 'Well, I can just imagine Sam Billings' reaction if it is his daughter. He will be distraught with grief obviously, but knowing Sam as we do, he will be out for revenge, that's for sure. Let's hope that lust for revenge isn't pointed this way.'

Justin turned to leave. 'Enough of that, will Beelzebub be ready for the launch at the Tiverton show next weekend? The president of CAMRA will be attending.'

'Yes, big brother,' replied Jonathon sarcastically, 'I'm having a pre-launch tasting among some of our most discerning customers tonight. Depending on their feedback, I'll make any tweaks to the formulae and brew the show batch overnight with old Chugg.'

'Good man, now let's put aside all this nonsense about Samantha Billings.'

10

As they pulled out of the lane that led down to the Brewery, Rick looked across to Dave who was driving, 'What do you make of that Dave?'

'They're both hiding something, although I suspect not the same thing judging by their respective body language.'

'Did you notice how Jonathon reacted to me accusing him of being an atheist?'

'I did, and I wonder which God he worships. A pound says it's whoever the Voodoo God of Creation is. It could of course be all bravado.'

'That's true. Justin seems to be too laid back to me given the serious nature of our investigation. That was until Sam Billings was mentioned. He seems to take Billings' resentment of their success personally. Their alibis are also a bit shaky. You had better have a word with old Chugg. Let's hope he is still in command of his faculties and remembers something. There's not much more we can do today. It's going to be a working weekend I'm afraid, can you check out their alibis in the morning?'

'No prob, what will you be doing?'

'That depends on what Kay's preliminary report has to say. Before you clock off can you make sure we have the findings of the search up on Hillsborough Head for the morning's briefing.'

'Will do, I will also make sure we have anything from the search of the beach and the house to house calls in Hele.'

'Good man, Dave, we have covered a lot in a short space of time. Let's keep the momentum up and nail the sick bastard who did this.'

Dave parked the Dart, and they went up the steps of HQ two at a time encouraged by the day's findings.

'I had better brief the chief, I expect he is lining up a press conference,' said Rick.

He was right, there would be no early night for him either, the chief had lined up a press briefing to go live on the early evening news on local BBC Radio at six fifteen. As Rick feared, he was the unlucky one chosen to give it.

Chief Superintendent Ponsonby-Green was an 'old school,' Etonian. He was middle aged having come up through the uniform ranks and had never served in the CID. He was known as a stickler for the rules and sucking up to the chief constable of the Devon and Cornwall Constabulary, a post that he aspired to before he retired; a post his father Sir Peregrine Ponsonby-Green, had held before him.

He was seated behind his large oak partner's desk, the walls of his office adorned by photos of him shaking hands with various dignitaries including the Prime Minister, Harold Wilson.

'Come in McCarthy' he bellowed as Rick was being shown in by his secretary, followed by a condescending command of 'sit' in a clipped accent hardly moving his lips. Rick sat down facing directly across the desk and felt like a cross between a naughty schoolboy summoned to the headmaster's study and a pet dog.

'Now, I don't have to tell you the importance of solving this murder quickly McCarthy, do I, hmm?'

'No, sir.'

The chief continued: 'There's been immense media interest from the dailies to TV and Radio. The chief constable is breathing down my neck asking for daily briefings, eh what,' he said with a twitch, 'so where are we with this?'

Rick held his cool, he had little regard for the old school style of policing where advancement often meant not what you know or had achieved but who you knew. He carried with him a deep seated mistrust of the old school establishment, that was still prevalent in both the police force and the armed forces of the country. His mind raced back to when he had researched the army history of his birth father whilst at university. There was no doubt in his mind that his father was sacrificed by the an 'old school' establishment of the likes of Ponsonby-Green in the Spanish Civil War, for the 'greater good.'

The English government had desperately wanted to buy time to re-arm in response to the growing influence and power of Nazi Germany under Chancellor Adolf Hitler, and curried favour with the Spanish nationalists without formal recognition.

The covert operation led by his father was a failure. He was betrayed and lost his life in the name of international politics, when it became clear that regime change from a republican to a nationalist government led by General Franco and supported by the Nazis was inevitable. From that day forth Rick carried an anger inside him and was distrustful of the establishment. He swore that one day he would expose the truth.

Rick went through the motions of briefing the chief, with the full knowledge that when he solved the case the chief would take the credit. If he failed, he would be made the scapegoat.

After the briefing he went back into the operations room to give Dave the good news. They now had one hour to prepare Rick's statement. As he entered, Dave was unpacking the case of beers they brought back from the Madrigal Renaissance Brewery.

'Guv, you need to see this,' he said in a combination of excitement and astonishment. Rick walked over to Dave's desk and could hardly believe what he was looking at. There it was, another bottle of beer sitting there, the label said it all, it was in the North Devon Voodoo range called Baron Samedi, God of Death.

'I don't believe it, or luck. We may be on the way to solving this murder much quicker than we thought,' said Rick.

It wasn't so much the Voodoo connection but the choice of Voodoo gods being used to name the beers.

'Right, let's keep this to ourselves for now, we don't want to rush to any conclusions.'

He decided to ring Kay to see if there was anything relevant that she had found so far that he should know about in preparing the press statement. Kay was just about to leave the mortuary and head off home as she had completed the post-mortem of 'Jane Doe – severed hand.' There she was, thinking that she could knock up a seafood linguine for supper to have with a nice cold bottle of Blue Nun, when the telephone rang. *I bet I know who that is* she said to herself.

She picked up the phone and answered, in an exaggerated Devon accent, 'Barnstaple Quick and the Dead Restaurant, how can I help you,' sniggering to herself, knowing full well that it would be Rick just checking in.

'Hi Babe,' replied Rick. 'You know, you are unbelievable, but I love you, truly madly, deeply. One day it won't be me on the phone at this time of day and you'll be up the creek without a paddle.'

'Hello gorgeous, are you heading home? I thought we'd have a cosy night in and forgo the quiz night down at The Kings Arms.'

'That sounds great to me, but I have to give a press statement at 6.15 and just wondered if you've anything relevant that we should go public on at this stage ? It's going out live on local BBC radio.'

'There's me thinking you were on your way home to ravish me over the kitchen table as I prepare supper.'

'I wish! You'll just have to hold onto that dream for an hour or so.'

'Ok, I'll keep you to that. The girl, and I say girl, was aged between sixteen and twenty years old with natural flaming red hair. She died between 12.00 midnight and 2.00 a.m. Her right hand was severed in one blow from a heavy cutting object, maybe a meat cleaver or a machete.

There are signs of multiple vaginal and anal sexual activity, maybe rough sex, rather than rape. She had taken drugs, either willingly or forced. I am waiting for the toxicology report.
I can't be sure of cause of death until then, but she didn't drown, her lungs weren't full of sea water. There are some signs of bruising around her neck but that could've been caused by the rough sex. I still think she died of poisoning or chocked on her own vomit because of ingesting those drugs.'

'Thanks Kay. I reckon I can be home by 7.30.'

'Ok, I'll just have to keep till then. Good luck with the press statement. I'll switch on the Radio in time for the six o'clock news and swoon over the dulcet tones of my brown eyed handsome man,' she said, laughing.

Six o'clock soon came round. The BBC crew had arrived earlier and set up their entourage of outside broadcasting personnel. Rick had prepared and run his statement by the chief superintendent. They decided to keep it to the minimum but include the reference to the girl's age, hair colouring, the tattoo, and the pendant. He would make no reference to the severed hand.

Representatives of both local and national newspapers were present. Local civic dignitaries also turned out, anxious to reinforce that North Devon was an area of outstanding natural beauty with a low crime rate. Tourism was a major income generator for the area.

At 6.15 Rick gave his statement to the press live on the BBC Radio news. The BBC continuity director gave the countdown. 'Three, two, one and live on air.'

'Good evening, my name is Detective Inspector Richard McCarthy. This morning, at approximately 7.00.a.m. a young woman's body was found washed up at Hele Bay Beach, near Ilfracombe. She is aged between sixteen and twenty years old, 5ft 5 ins tall, slim build with natural red hair. She has a tattoo of a snake on her upper right buttock and was wearing a silver Erzuli pendant.

Her cause of death is not yet established but we are treating it as a case of murder and not accidental. If anyone recognizes or knows who this young lady is or saw anything suspicious on Hillsborough Head or down at the Hele Bay beach between the hours of 10.00p.m. last night and 6a.m. this morning, please contact Barnstaple Police HQ on 01234 131313. Somebody somewhere will recognize this girl. All calls will be treated as confidential and police protection offered where necessary. Thank you, I will take relevant questions.'

The local crime reporter of the North Devon Gazette, Alex Craven, who was known for his tenacious investigative journalism, immediately raised his hand and directed a question to Rick.

'Detective Inspector McCarthy is there any truth in the rumour that this young lady had a hand severed?'

'I cannot answer that question at this stage, there is evidence that she fell from a great height, possibly from the top of Hillsborough Head, and tumbled down the rocky cliff face into the sea below.'

'Is it true that you visited the Madrigal Renaissance Brewery this afternoon and questioned the Dukes brothers?' piped up another journalist.

'I am not at liberty to discuss any further matters of the case that might prejudice our enquiries,' replied Rick, his hackles rising.

'Thank you ladies and gentlemen, that will be all today,' intervened the police press officer.

There was a deadly silence in the room followed by murmuring amongst reporters of these astonishing revelations. They were eager to dash to telephones to phone in their reports to their newspaper news desks. Leaving the podium, Rick could hardly contain his anger. Bursting into the operations room he shouted out across the room,

'How the bloody hell did Alex Craven and that other goon of a reporter glean sensitive inside information of the case?'

Nobody answered.

'Well, if I do find out it came from within this room for a backhander, I will make sure that you are booted out of the force in disgrace. Do you hear me?'

'Yes Guv' came the subdued reply in unison.

'I said, do you hear me?' Rick barked across the room.

'Yes Guv,' came the louder response.

'Yes, what?'

'Yes, Sir.'

'And don't you forget that this is now a high profile case, we need to solve it and solve it quickly. Anyone slacking or not up to the task, I can have you back on the beat or on traffic control in a heartbeat.'

Back in Hele Bay, tucking into an early evening meal of homemade steak and kidney pie with all the trimmings, and listening to the six o-clock news on the radio with his wife, Eileen, was Sam Billings.

The familiar sound of the BBC news introductory music was followed by the newsreader Bob Danvers-Walker reading the news. After reporting on the day in Parliament and the Government's statement regarding the Liverpool and London dock strikes, he announced that they were going live to the North Devon Police HQ in Barnstaple for a press statement relating to a body washed up at Hele Bay beach that morning.

Sam Billing's ears pricked up, and his wife Eileen put down her knife and fork and looked at him with some trepidation. When Rick got to the description of the young girl that had been murdered, Eileen shrieked, 'Noooooooo,' fell to the floor displacing the tablecloth and sending their meal flying all over the dining room. Sam turned the radio off, picked his wife up and attempted to console her. Eileen, however, was inconsolable, crying out, 'No, it can't be, please God, not our Samantha,' as tears flowed, cascading down her cheeks like the torrent of water of a riffle on the River Exe. Her chest and breasts were heaving, her heart going two to the dozen sending it into atrial fibrillation.

It was obvious to Sam that it was their daughter and that he had to remain strong for his wife's sake. He settled Eileen down, poured her a brandy, and then telephoned the number given out by Rick on the radio.

The chief superintendent appeared in the ops room and congratulated Rick on his handling of the press statement, he also thanked everyone for their unstinting efforts whilst reminding them of loyalty and keeping all matters relating to the case within the team. May I remind you all that the wartime slogan 'Walls have Ears' equally applies to this case.'

The telephones in the room burst into action sounding like a cacophony of chicks in their nests, calling out for their mothers to bring them food. A number of callers kept coming up with the same name, Samantha Billings. Some callers were her close girlfriends, others were anonymous, possibly past boyfriends or lovers.

Within minutes, the call that they were all waiting for came in. It was answered by Tom, one of Rick's team who, after taking down the caller's details, realized the significance of the call. He immediately put his hand over the telephone's mouthpiece and called out across the room.

'Sir, it's Sam Billing on the line.' Having got Rick's attention he said to Billings, 'Detective Inspector McCarthy will speak to you sir.'

Rick got up from his desk, rushed out of his office and picked up the phone.

'It's Detective McCarthy here Mr. Billings.' Silence. 'Mr. Billings are you still there?'

It was all Sam could do to hold in his emotions saying in a trembling voice,

'I think it's our daughter Samantha.'

'What makes you think that Mr. Billings?'

'The description fits that of Samantha, and the tattoo. It's her all right.'

'I am so, so sorry Mr. Billings. Is your wife with you?'

'Yes, as you can imagine she is in a terrible state of shock.'

'Right, I shall be with you as soon as I can, meanwhile I shall arrange for PC Worthy and a family liaison officer to come round immediately. I'll just hand you back to PC Davison to take down your address.'

Rick waited for Tom to put the phone down, then reflected with some sadness and turned to the team. 'It looks like we have the identity of our victim, Samantha Billings. Does anyone know her?'

'You mean Sam Billing's daughter?' asked Matt.

'That's her.'

'I think my younger brother may have gone to school with her, didn't her dad own the Witches Cauldron Brewery that went bust?'

'Yes, that's her, where is your brother now Matt? Perhaps he can give us some background information on the girl.'

'Oh, he's long gone, there's not much skilled work down here in these parts. He got an apprenticeship up in the dockyards in Plymouth.'

'Anyone else?'

Tom, the old timer of the team, who was not long off of retirement, answered, 'Yes Guv. When I was still on the beat up at Ilfracombe my daughter Christine went to school with Samantha Billings. It grieves me to say it, but she was a wild child then and we encouraged Chrissie to have nothing to do with her. You know how cruel kids can be, they called her the 'school bike' as she had a reputation of going with the older boys behind the bike sheds for a ride, if you get my meaning. Anyone could ride her. She smoked, most kids try it at that age, only Samantha was smoking marijuana and also into ecstasy pills.'

'Thanks Tom, that may be useful background information on the life she was leading. OK, Dave, let's you and I go and see Mr. & Mrs. Billings. Meanwhile can the rest of you continue to keep taking any calls, noting the caller's name and contact number if they identify themselves and any relevant information however small or far-fetched.'

Rick and Dave left the ops room and made their way down the stairs and out into carpark where the Dart was parked.

'Right Dave, drive me to the Billings house in Hele.'

11

Sam put down the phone in the hall, paused momentarily to gather his senses, and then went back into the kitchen to console his wife. He didn't really know what to say so said the first thing that came into his head.

'Someone will be here soon love. Nige is coming round with a bereavement counsellor.'

'I don't need a bloody bereavement counsellor,' Eileen shouted. 'Is it her, Sam? Maybe it's someone else who looks like her,' she stuttered in a timid croaky voice and forlorn hope. What little make up she wore was now smudged, with mascara running down her cheek in rivulets of uncontrollable gushing tears and dropping like the early morning rain onto the kitchen table, leaving dark stains on the wooden surface.

'I don't know for sure darling, but we must prepare ourselves for the worst.'

Eileen burst out sobbing again, bent double with the uncontrollable tears.

'Why Samantha, why us?' she cried.

Sam felt helpless, it seemed that whatever he said there was nothing he could do to pacify her.

It took Dave only 30 mins, weaving in and out of the evening's rush hour traffic with the Dart's blue lights and bell ringing all the way. It was now dusk with the sun going down behind them on the western horizon. As they drove out of

Ilfracombe, Rick glanced left and looked at the towering sight of Hillsborough Head in silhouette against the fading light.

The Billings' house was a detached whitewashed chalet bungalow in Hele, set in a generous plot back from the main road at an elevation overlooking the village and the Bay. The front garden was landscaped and well maintained with a palm tree and other Mediterranean plants. Rick thought that despite the closure of The Witches Cauldron brewery, Sam Billings had not done bad for himself over the years. Dave pulled into the driveway and parked up alongside an almost brand new Range Rover. As they got out of the Dart Rick cautioned Dave.

'It looks like we now have the victim's name, so just be on your guard and not reveal too much. Mr. Billings will no doubt start asking a lot questions.'

PC Worthy, Nige, was already there together with the family liaison officer, Constable Jenny Clarke, who fortuitously lived locally and was off duty at the time she was called out. Constable Clarke had already consoled Mrs. Billings who by now was calm and rational but every now and then the tears began to flow again.

Jenny was well trained, and sadly had experienced the situation before. She was calm, caring, and genuine. She came over as any mother's daughter, offering all the support Sam and Eileen might need in the immediate future. They had all moved by this time into the front sitting room.

As Rick and Dave entered, Rick glanced at the family photographs adorning the mantel shelf. There, staring right back at him was a recent photograph of the victim, Samantha Billings. Rick introduced himself and Dave. He followed protocol and asked the standard set of questions, when was the last time they saw Samantha etc. He then asked them if Samantha had any boyfriends which drew a barbed reaction from Sam.

'That girl, I told her no good would become of her. She was always flirting, especially with older men, ever since she was fourteen, right up to when she left home after leaving school. She got a job at the Hele Hotel; God knows what she got up to there or in the clubs in Barnstable with all of them drugs flying around.'

'And who drove her away, just like you did with Linda?' Eileen shouted at her husband.

Unknown to his wife, Sam Billings had abused his daughter Samantha from the age of eight. One night he had slipped into her bedroom and into her bed to give her a cuddle. She loved it. She was cuddling Daddy. He was cuddling her not Mummy. Mummy only told her off, hit her, often banning her to her tiny bedroom whilst her older sister could do no wrong.

Gradually the 'cuddles' became more than that, and he taught her what grown-ups did when they loved each other. It was what he and Mummy did, and she was now nearly grown up at 10. He also told her that it was because he loved her as much as he loved Mummy that it was only fair that he showed his love for her, but that she mustn't tell Mummy as she would get jealous and hit her. It must be their own little secret. Eileen Billings was never to learn of Samantha's abuse by her husband.

By the time Samantha was thirteen and past puberty, she craved love and attention. She was pretty, had developed small pert breasts, and had been schooled over the years by her father that sex was the way men showed they loved her. As she wanted to be loved so badly, she therefore craved sex.

It was with Derek Chambers, her English Teacher at

secondary school, who she had first had a one-off quickie. She had been sitting outside the Hele Hotel waiting for her dad when 'Mr Chambers' came out alone. She had flirted with him at school before, she thought he was 'gorgeous' looking. He stopped to talk to her, then sat down on the bench next to her. Samantha didn't hesitate in showing her love for him by unbuckling his denim jeans and sitting astride him on his lap. It was over in a trice.

Derek hadn't thought it wrong, certainly not rape, after all she came on to him. She was obviously not a virgin and knew exactly how to turn a man on and knew what she was doing. If anything, she was more skilled at showing him a good time than any of the prostitutes he had sex with down in the brothels along the quayside of Barnstaple. She loved it as much as he did, giggling as she climbed off him. It was the beginning of her wild teenage years.

'She was a good girl really;' said Eileen, 'She was just a 'Fallen Angel' that got in with the wrong crowd. She is at peace now in the arms of the Lord,' she mumbled.

'She should have gone on to college like her older sister, not throw herself at any Tom, Dick or Harry whether they were married or not,' Sam retorted.

'She was our daughter Sam!' shouted Eileen, still sobbing.

Samantha's older sister Linda had left home at the earliest opportunity after passing her A levels at 18 and had gained entry to The London Veterinary College. She vowed never to return home. She could never forgive her father for abusing Samantha and had confronted her sister about it, but Samantha just shrugged her shoulders and said she liked it and that he loved her. Linda felt guilty, guilty that she had not spoken up when he had tried it on with her when she was younger He had backed off after she had threatened to tell her mother. Guilty that he soon turned his attention to Samantha who was younger, prettier, and more vulnerable that she was.

Linda was the intelligent one, passing her eleven plus exam, going to the grammar school and destined for higher education and a professional career, whereas Samantha's best assets were her good looks and charm when she applied it. Sam got in with the wrong crowd and left school at 16 with few academic qualifications, leaving home at the earliest opportunity. Her father continued to sexually abuse her right up to the time she left. After leaving she had a choice of either getting a menial job at the local glove making factory or working in hospitality and tourism either in a shop or as a barmaid, waitress or housekeeper at the many bars, pubs, clubs, and holiday lets.

After the tension in the room calmed down, Rick arranged for Sam to go to the Mortuary in the morning at 10.00a.m to identify Samantha's body. Jenny had arranged for the Billings' GP to call round to give Eileen something to calm her nerves. He elected to prescribe one of the modern benzodiazepine drugs, the so called drug of choice, 'mothers' little helper', Valium.

Rick bid Sam and Eileen goodnight and left them in the capable hands of Nige and Jenny. Life would never be the same again for Sam and Eileen Billings.

As Dave drove them back to Barnstaple, he half turned to Rick and said, 'God, I hope that I am never put in such a position. I can understand fathers, even mothers, brothers and sisters taking revenge and killing whoever did that to their child or sibling.'

'That's what I am afraid of Dave. Billings seems to be taking it too calmly for me. I hope he hasn't got something like that in mind. Maybe he has an idea of who might have done it.'

It was now gone 9.00 p.m. as they drew up at Kipling Terrace in Bideford and Rick bade Dave goodnight,

'Goodnight Dave, I suppose it will be a fish and chip supper for you tonight. I'll see you at the usual time in the morning. Another day another dollar as they say the other side of the Atlantic.'

'Good night Guv, not the best of days but at least we now know who the victim is and a bit about her home background.'

As Rick walked in, he was handed a large Jack Daniels with ice by Kay. Next to his love of real ale, in particular Imperial from the Exeter Brewery, he had an acquired taste for Jack Daniels, his preferred 'short.'

'I heard the Dart coming down the road. I guess it's been a tough day for both of us. Seafood Linguini OK for supper? I picked up the clams, mussels, and prawns down on the quayside on the way home.'

'Sounds great, have we got some decent plonk to go with it?'

' Blue Nun or Mateus Rose?'

'The Mateus Rose I think, but don't expect me to make another table lamp out of the bottle!'

Later that evening, while eating supper, Kay confirmed the main findings of her autopsy report. Leaving aside the fact that the deceased had suffered multiple wounds from the cliff fall, the most heinous physical and sexual abuse, was asphyxiated, and had her right hand severed, Kay was more than ever convinced that the girl, or Samantha as they now knew, had died from poisoning. They would have to wait for the toxicology report to confirm her suspicions and if she was right, identify the poison or poisons involved.

After supper and clearing away the dishes, they both curled up on the sofa and relaxed with a second bottle of Mateus listening to one of Rick's favorite jazz albums by Miles Davis, '*King of Blue.*' It was their way to forget the horrors of the day for a moment. That night they made love, slowly, tenderly and drifted off to sleep with the music of Dinah Washington playing softly in the background.

12

Friday 29th

The following morning the newspapers, both local and national, carried the story of the murder. One of the nationals, The Daily Chronicle, had the scoop of a close-up photo of the murder scene on the front page showing the girl's body lying at the water's edge with her right hand missing and the headline, *Mutilated girl's dead body washed up in sleepy Hele Bay, North Devon.* It had been taken by Felicity Wainright with her pocket camera. So much for the agreement Rick had reached with her when he confiscated her main Nikon SLR camera, not knowing that she had another.

The photos had also been syndicated and appeared in various newspapers abroad including Le Monde in France and Der Spiegel in West Germany.

When Rick arrived at HQ, the chief superintendent was already in and summoned him to his office. The chief was livid, almost incandescent with rage.

'I've had the chief constable, the Police Complaints Commission, the Women's Rights Movement and God know who already on the telephone this morning. How the hell has this happened McCarthy, hmm?'

'She was coming down from Hillsborough Head onto Hele Bay beach, sir, at the same time as when the girl's body was discovered by a dog walker. I questioned her and confiscated her Nikon SLR camera. She must've also had a pocket camera on her. I thought I had an agreement with her that she wouldn't publish the story, let alone any photographs in exchange for a scoop if we discovered anything major or made an arrest' replied Rick.

The chief shouted at him. 'Since when do the police make bargains with potential witnesses, McCarthy, eh?' His voice reverberated all over the top floor where his office was located.

'There is no excuse sir, but in CID we sometimes must bargain with informers and the like in order to get a result.'

'Well, it's not my way of policing. You had better get a result on this one McCarthy, and quickly, otherwise you might find yourself back in uniform looking after the traffic squad,' he said, waving his hand dismissively. 'Now get out of my office and don't come back until you have something good to say.'

'Yes Sir, of course, you have my word.'

Rick turned round and departed like a naughty boy who had just been caned by the headmaster for something that he hadn't done.

As he walked back into the ops room, you could have heard a pin drop.

'Ok, enough said, you probably heard the chief from down here. I don't ever want to go through that again so let's get on and solve this bloody crime.'

Dave went off to see old Chugg to verify Justin and Jonathon Dukes' alibis.

Later that morning at the pre-arranged time, Sam Billings attended Barnstaple Mortuary to identify the deceased as his daughter Samantha. Kay was waiting for Rick when he arrived at the mortuary.

'Cheer up chicken' she greeted him, 'You look as though

you have seen a ghost.'

'Sorry babe, you know that I hate it here. These places are never the best place to spend any length of time in. Despite everyone's attempts to make them more socially acceptable with vases of imitation flowers, prints of local artwork, and a visitor's chapel for those that felt the need, they are cold, desolate, and morbid. Apart from giving me the shivers it is a stark reminder of the business we are both engaged in. Dead bodies.'

Sam Billings arrived on time. He was on his own and looked lonely, sorrowful. He was met by the mortuary manger, Clive Jones, who introduced him to Rick and Kay. 'Detective Inspector McCarthy you have already met, and this is Kay Stone the senior forensic pathologist who performed the postmortem. There is no easy way of doing this Mr. Billings. Shall we go through, or do you need a bit of time to compose yourself?'

'No, let's get it over with.'

'Yes, that's Samantha,' Sam confirmed looking harrowed but calm with the loss of his only child. He turned and said, 'We are supposed to outlive our children, aren't we? How could this have happened down here in Devon? She was a bit of a wild child running with the hippy set, but she never deserved this. Promise me inspector that you will get the evil bastard that did this to my Samantha.'

'I am trained to never make promises Mr. Billings, but I can assure you that I will never give up until we have brought the person or persons responsible for murdering your daughter to justice.'

'So, you think it may have been more than one person involved? Tell me inspector, how did she die? Was she interfered with?'

'I'm sorry Sam, do you mind if I call you Sam, but I'm sure that you must appreciate that I'm not at liberty to reveal any more at this stage. We'll keep you informed of our progress.'

Kay escorted Sam out of the building. On returning she said to Rick, 'I have dealt with scores of identifications, but something bothers me. He was too calm and collected if you ask me.'

'My thoughts entirely. It was as if he was going through the motion of identifying her. For someone faced with his murdered daughter he was remarkably calm, making comments and asking questions. We shall have to keep our eye on Sam Billings, he may be involved in her murder or have revenge in mind.'

'We have the toxicology reports back,' said Kay. 'I had a look earlier on. My suspicions were right, she did die of poisoning. There was an excessive amount of LSD in her blood, not enough to kill her but there were also various herbs in her stomach including mugwort, cuckoo pint, monkshood, hemlock, and bella donna all of which are poisonous plants.'

'Hm, mugwort, that's interesting. I believe it's used in the fermentation process when brewing certain beers.' *Curiosa and curiosa* he murmured to himself.

'Why, is that important?'

'It could be; the beers being brewed at the Madrigal Renaissance Brewery use mugwort in the fermentation process. They are called their North Devon Voodoo range, and one of them is called Ogun God of Justice. It features an image of him holding a machete.'

'Sounds too much of a coincidence to me.'

'You're probably right but we have to follow up all leads.'

'Well, I am about to wrap up here. I thought I might pop over to Croyde later, the surfs up and I thought I might take a break and do a bit of body boarding. Some of the old gang will be down there surfing and having a barbecue lunch with a few beers on the beach.'

'You know how to make me jealous, Kay. You go and enjoy yourself and say hello to the guys and girls from me.'

Rick decided that he would walk back to police H.Q. After the stifling heat of the summer the air was now cooler, a sure sign of the equinox with summer on the wane and autumn on its way. He left the mortuary, which was attached to the North Devon Infirmary and walked up Litchdon Street in order to cross The Square and proceed over the Taw Bridge.

The walk enabled him to clear his head. *I'll show that prig of a chief superintendent what real policing is about. Justice for Samantha Billings and closure and comfort for her distraught parents, he* thought to himself. *What did Eileen Billings call her? 'A Fallen Angel?'*

He was not a religious person despite being brought up in the Christian faith, but Eileen Billings was. Rick pondered, *A Fallen Angel as I recollect from RE lessons and Sunday School were angels that were either expelled from heaven or had sinned. Such angels also encouraged other humans to sin.*

He stopped on his way to grab a coffee, a double expresso, from a newly opened coffee bar that had imported and installed one of the latest Gaggia coffee making machines from Italy.

Wow thought Rick, feeling the buzz of the strong coffee. *Just what I need to clear my head and focus on the day ahead.* He finished his coffee and despite the temptation to order another got up and left. As he crossed The Square, he lit up a Camel and walked past the Albert Memorial Clock Tower. Looking up he could see a familiar face coming the other way. It was his predecessor, the retired Chief Inspector Bill Walker. As he approached Rick greeted him, 'Good morning, Bill, how's retirement treating you?'

'Bored out of my mind Rick, I'm tripping over the old lady all the time in the house, and I never was much of a gardener. I've taken up fly fishing, much more my scene, casting a fly out to catch a wily trout instead of a wily criminal. How goes the Hillsborough Head murder enquiry?'

'It's a tricky one, you know the form, lots of circumstantial evidence, a few 'red herrings' and difficulty nailing down hard physical evidence.'

Bill responded, 'Word down at the police social club is that some kind of cult is involved.'

It never surprised Rick how word got around in the police fraternity, mostly gossip but sometimes a little gem comes out of it.

'Really? Anything interesting Bill?'

'Well, you know I am not one to gossip, I just keep my ears to the ground. Have a word with ex police sergeant, Jack Johnson. He seems to move in strange circles and is a good source for the word on the street. You'll find him down at the social club most evenings by all account. He also likes a game of poker now and then at the Tumbling Dice Club.'

'Thanks Bill. I can't stop but we must have a pint soon. Give my love to Marge.'

'We must do that, but remember, don't be a stranger. Some of the lads would be only pleased to see you down at the social.'

Rick continued his walk back to HQ thinking, *Jack Johnson, yeah, I remember him, one of the old school sergeants before my time. His reputation is still revered by some. As I recall he served his time on the beat before being promoted to sergeant. He was warned more than once of his over aggressive methods of questioning a suspect. Some said it was nothing short of intimidation and sometimes assault. How things have changed. However, he got results.*

13

As Rick entered the ops room invigorated by the walk back from the mortuary, the team looked up not quite knowing how he was going to react following his earlier encounter with the chief super. They soon found out; Rick was still buzzing.

'Right, I don't need to repeat the chief's words, but they were plain spoken and not very pleasant. Where are we at, Dave?'

'I've been back up to the brewery to see old Chugg to check out the Dukes' alibis.

Old Chugg, Jeremiah Chugg, has been in the brewery trade man and boy as a labourer and then 'masher.' He was now in his sixties and still lived alone in Hele, not far from the now demised Witches Cauldron Brewery. He travelled backwards and forwards to the Madrigal Renaissance Brewery on his old 1953 Velocette motorcycle, which was parked in the yard with a his white 'Stirling Moss' style, cork lined crash helmet dangling from the handlebars.

'What did he have to say about the brothers' alibis?'

'He was working that night, and he can confirm that Jonathon was working with him. He did say that Jonathon popped out at about 10.30 p.m., but he wasn't sure of the time he got back. It was certainly around midnight as he takes a break about then for a cuppa and a pastie, which he warms up on top of the copper vessel used to boil up the mashed 'wort.' He said Jonathon sauntered in just as he had finished eating.'

'That tends to let him off the hook for Samantha's murder Dave. 'What about Justin?'

'That's where Chugg's account differs from what Justin told us.'

'Go on.'

'He confirmed that Justin left just after 7.00 p.m. He had to go out to one of the outbuilding to get more barley and saw Justin driving away. Unfortunately, he has no recollection of him getting back and said that he would never think of looking in the outbuilding that garaged Justin's car. He did say however there were no lights on in the upstairs apartment when he went out for his midnight cuppa.'

'OK Dave, I'm not sure if any of that helps us or not at this stage. Anything else to report?'

'Ethan dropped in his photos of the crime scene and will talk to us about his findings and observations later on. The house-to-house enquiries carried out in Hele by Matt and Adam revealed little, they are a tight insular bunch up there and may be hiding something. However, interviews with the staff at the Hotel and pub are very revealing.'

'Don't tell me. Samantha Billings was having an affair with a member of staff.'

'Not quite, she had had an affair with Jim Derbyshire, the owner, but broke it off a few months back on the pretext of the age difference between them.'

'Well, well,' said Rick.

'That's not all, one of the barmaids and best friend of Samantha, Sharon Roberts, who shared digs with her in one of the caravans, said Samantha had also had a fling with Jonathon Dukes at the same time.'

'My, my, a nice little menage-a-trois in sleepy Hele.'

'Did this Sharon say how Derbyshire reacted when Samantha said it was over?'

'Not very well. Apparently Derbyshire was used to getting his own way with women and there had been complaints to the housekeeping manager about the way he treated the housemaids. He had tried it on with several, even to the point of firing one in tears as she rejected his advances. It was her word against his that he attempted to rape her in one of the guest bedrooms. Matt has taped off the caravan awaiting your inspection before calling in SOC.'

'Anything else?'

'Yes Guv,' piped up Adam.

'One of the holiday makers said that they saw Samantha strolling hand in hand and embracing someone on the beach just before 11.00 p.m. last night. They recognized her from working behind the bar in the Hotel. They looked back ten minutes later, and the couple were nowhere to be seen. Also, another one of the chambermaids was parked up at Larkstone car park making out with her boyfriend that night, and she saw Freddie Fairbrother, the owner of Freddie's Bar and Grill in Ilfracombe, leaving the carpark at the western foot of Hillsborough Head, at about 1.00.a.m.'

Rick called across the room to Matt and Adam, 'Good work boys, but I want you to go back and get formal signed statements from the relevant member of staff at the Hotel and the holidaymaker who saw Samantha down on the beach with someone. Find out if she would recognize the person and show her a photo of Jonathon Dukes. Dave and I will be there shortly to take a look around the caravan that Samantha was living in, and to talk again to Sharon Roberts.'

'OK Guv' they replied in unison.

'Has anyone anything else to report?' he asked, looking around the room. Anything from the search up on Hillsborough Head? And yes, I'll have one of those,' pointing to Dave's coffee.

'I'll let Theo fill us in on progress of the search up on the Head,' replied Dave as he nipped to the kitchenette to get another mug of coffee for Rick.

Theo Clarke was another one of the up-and-coming stars of the team. Handsome, bright, tenacious, Cambridge rugby blue, a man after Rick's heart.

'OK Theo, what do we have?'

'Right,' said Theo slightly nervously. 'In short, a minefield of evidence. The boys are still up there sifting through ashes, combing the bushes and heathland, even abseiling down the cliff face looking for any evidence both there and on the rocky promontory below. It looks like she was definitely murdered up there alright. We have found a makeshift table or altar and a charred hand together with remnants of burnt clothing in the ashes of a fire. We have sent them to forensics for a match to the victim.'

Theo walked over to the evidence board and pointed to photos taken of their findings.

'In fact, we have also found a burial pit of all sorts of bones, both human and animal, that goes back years. It show signs of them being severed from different parts of the bodies. There is also evidence of different poisonous plants as well as hallucinatory drugs such as speed, ecstasy and the latest LCD heart shaped pills doing the rounds in the clubs.' Theo cleared his throat and continued.

'We didn't find the weapon or object that severed her hand;

however, we found a torn piece of black cloth with a label stitched on it on a gorse bush near the cliff edge. We also found a PH meter on the coastal path that crossed the Head, and it was not far from a clearing used for whatever took place up there. It's a vintage portable model made by the Analytical Instrument Company. It doesn't show any definable fingerprints, but they are used to measure acidity or alkalinity in liquids and most telling, are used in the brewing industry.'

Everyone in the room looked at each other. The reference to brewing kept coming up.

'The forensic boys are looking at the piece of black cloth to identify the type of material, what garments it is used for and anything else to try and trace suppliers and therefore customers who bought such items.'

'Good work, Theo. Thank the team and buy them all a beer or whatever is their tipple, in their downtime. Keep a small team up on the Head and also start searching Larkstone car park on the Ilfracombe side of the cliff. The chances are that the perp or perps parked there and ascended the Head from there.'

Rick walked over towards the evidence board and continued, 'I know it's a big ask Theo, but can you also get a team looking at the quay where the trawlers are moored in Ilfracombe Harbour, then along the coastal path past Larkstone and continue up to the Head.'

A junior on the team, P.C. Faye Steventon, caught his attention.

'Have you considered that another female might be involved, sir?'

'Why do you ask that, Faye?'

'It's just that, all the emphasis so far seems to me to be

predicated by the perp being a man because of the nature of the crime. However, it struck me, call it feminine intuition, that no respectable girl would be on Hillsborough Head willingly at that time of night, nor would she have such a provocative tattoo, particularly where it is on her body.' Faye looked around at her colleagues rather self-consciously, hoping she wasn't just making a fool of herself.

'Then there is the evidence of use of drugs leading me to the conclusion that she was probably a good time girl, promiscuous, and could incite jealousy amongst both men and other girls. Perhaps we should not only take a close look at her boyfriends, but also at the girls she ran with.'

'Good thinking Faye, it had occurred to me about jealous lovers but not the female angle.' Rick's enquiring mind was immediately triggered, *what if Sharon Roberts is involved in this in some way? Jealousy can be a terrible disease, especially if you are jealous of someone who has something you think you ought to have yourself.*

'Can you talk to all her other friends who phoned in. Also go and talk to the staff at Freddie's Bar and at the various clubs she went to in Barnstable. Who did she go with, who sold her drugs etc. Can you then visit all the tattoo parlours both locally and in Barnstaple to find which one gave Samantha the tattoo and what they know about her. Similarly ask them about any other females aged between sixteen and twenty-two who have had an erotic tattoo in the last year and whether they knew Samantha.'

'Yes Sir,' replied Faye, pleased that her suggestion had been accepted and taken seriously.

Rick felt a sense of pride that he had such young, intelligent, enthusiastic, ambitious members on his team. They would all go far in his eyes, either with the Devon and Cornwall Constabulary or elsewhere. He wouldn't be surprised to see one of two of them with the Met or The Flying Squad at Scotland Yard in London in the future. Adam in particular reminded him of himself as a rookie when he first joined the CID.

'What do we do first, Guv?' asked Dave.

'We should go and take a look at the caravan that Sharon Roberts was sharing with Samantha and find out what else she has not shared with us so far. We have enough circumstantial evidence to interview Jonathon Dukes. We will deal with that later, leaving Jim Derbyshire and Freddie Fairbrother for another day.'

On arriving back at Hele Bay, they were staggered at the number of people there. The car park was nearly full, and Tracy was doing a roaring trade at the café. The crime scene was no longer taped off, and any evidence not already discovered within the tide line had been long washed away.

'Take a look Dave. True crime is a growing business. Who said crime doesn't pay? There are now TV shows recreating past crime investigations, magazines devoted to it, and the sale of other paraphernalia such as replica police notebooks, mini cameras, fingerprint kits. The once niche genre of storytelling that spun real-life crimes into entertainment is becoming a national obsession. Apparently, if we believe the media, we're all a nation of crime experts now.'

Sharon Roberts' caravan stood out in the caravan park above the beach with blue police tape secured around it. They soon found the acting manager of the Hotel who had the keys to the caravan to let them in.

At first glance it looked like any other young girl's cramped bedsit. The beds untidily made up; posters of pop stars stuck up on practically every available wall and make-up strewn on a makeshift dressing table. Running the length above each bed, was a small shelf. Above Samantha's was a photograph of her Mum and sister. Rick noticed there was not one of her father but there was another which took him by surprise, it was one of her, arm in arm with Jonathon Dukes.

In the small refrigerator was some nibbles of cheese and other comestibles together a number of unfinished bottles of wine, no doubt a perk of the leftovers from people dining at the Hotel.

Rick went outside for a cigarette, whilst Dave conducted a search of the caravan. Wearing surgical gloves so as not to disturb any forensic evidence, he reached under Samantha's bed and found a heart shaped trinket box decorated with red roses and butterflies. He took it outside to show Rick.

'What have you got there, Dave?'

'It was under Samantha's bed, tucked well out of view.'

'Open it up then, let see what treasures are in there.'

The box contained the usual number of cheap decorative trinkets but amongst them was a silver heart shaped locket containing another photo of Jonathon Dukes.

'It looks like it was more than just a fling with Jonathon. We need to talk to Sharon about their relationship.'

There was something else that took Rick by surprise, and he hadn't seen it coming. It was a medical discharge note from a private clinic. Samantha had had an abortion when she was sixteen years old, not long after she'd left home.

Rick's mind went into overdrive. *Who was the father of the unborn child? Is this what she needed to confide to whoever she met on the Hele Bay beach the night she was murdered? If it was Jonathon it was way before his time, but she clearly still loved him and maybe felt there was no one else she could trust.*

There was nothing more to be done, Dave would get the SOC boys to give the caravan a thorough going over just in case he'd missed something.

They locked the caravan up and went into the Hotel to return the keys and to seek out Sharon who was on duty at that time. She was just about to finish her shift and joined them in the hotel lounge, which fortuitously was empty at that time of day. The lounge had seen better days, a well-worn patterned Axminister carpet, dark red velvet curtains and torn chesterfield sofa. It looked more like a seedy nightclub than an inviting holiday hotel lounge with a beach view.

'Sharon, I know this is difficult for you, being Samantha's closest and best friend as I understand it, but we need to ask you a few questions about her.'

'That's OK, anything that will help you catch her murderer.'

'On the night she was murdered did she say anything to you about meeting someone down on the beach at about 10.30 p.m?'

'Yes, she went to meet Jonathon.'

'And she never came back?'

'No. That wasn't that unusual, and I thought she had just gone off with him. She still loved him you see, despite him calling it off once he'd met Susie.'

'What was so troubling her that she arranged to meet him that night?'

'It was about Freddie Fairbrother. He wouldn't take no for an answer, he kept pestering her and threatening to tell everyone she was an easy-going slut who would go with anyone.'

'I see, and was she?'

'No! She did go with Freddie but only the once as far as I know. We had a laugh when she told me that his you know what, was only the size of a tiny lollypop. She still held a flame for Jonathon and hoped that one day he would leave Susie and come back to her.'

'One last thing Sharon, did you know Samantha had an abortion when she was only sixteen?'

Sharon was shocked, she thought that she was the only one that knew.

'How on earth do you know that?'

'We found the medical discharge letter from the private clinic in her trinket box.'

'Yes, I knew. Samantha came to me in tears when she knew she was pregnant, that was when we decided to set up home together in the caravan. She never wanted the child; even worse she was paranoid and revolted by the thought. I had some money left to me by my late grandmother, so I paid for her to go to this clinic for an abortion.'

'Does anyone else know?'

'Not that I know of, but she may have told Jonathon.'

'Do you know who the father was?'

Sharon paused, as if to consider whether she should reveal who the father was.

'It was her father, Sam, he had been abusing her for years.'

This time it was Rick and Dave who were visibly shocked. *This case gets darker and darker* thought Rick. *Her father! God that girl must have suffered so much in her relatively short life.*

'Thanks, Sharon, I know that must have been difficult for

you.'

They left Sharon in peace. She had lost a lifelong friend who had been troubled all her life. Samantha had been used and abused, and she did not deserve to die for it.

14

Jonathon Dukes arrived voluntarily with his solicitor an hour after they had got back to the office. They were escorted to an interview room and met by Rick and Dave. Dukes was advised that the interview was being conducted voluntarily and that he was not being arrested or charged with anything, but that Detective Sergeant Elliot would be taking notes that may subsequently be used in court. The interview commenced at 12.00 noon.

'Can you please state your full name for the record?'

'Jonathon Tristan Dukes.'

'Mr. Dukes, can you please tell us where you were between the hours of 10.00p.m. on Thursday 29th and 2.00.am. on Friday 30th.'

'I have already told you that, I was working at the brewery all night and left at about 7.00 a.m. the following morning. Old Chugg, that is Mr. Jeremiah Chugg, my labourer at the brewery can confirm that.'

'That's where we have a problem Mr. Dukes. You see we have already spoken to Mr. Chugg, and he says that you were working that night, but disappeared for an hour or so from about 10.30p.m. and got back around midnight.'

Jonathon fidgeted in his chair and swallowed hard.

'That's just not true, old Chugg gets a bit confused as to timing when he has had a few glasses tasting the brew. I did pop out at about 10.30 p.m. to get some fresh air away from the intoxicating air in the brewery and have a smoke, but I was back in by 11.00.'

Jonathon's immediate blatant lie had not gone unnoticed. *This is not starting well for Dukes,* thought Rick, *let's see what more lies he tells as he digs himself into a hole.*

'Well, that's not quite right is it Mr. Dukes, because another witness saw you down on Hele beach at about 11.00 with a Miss Samantha Billings, holding hands and kissing.'

Jonathon became more agitated. 'Ok, I own up, Sam and I had a fling a while back and she asked to meet me that night as something was troubling her. It was actually a bit more than just a fling inspector, and it was serious at the time, but I broke it off when I met Susie, my wife. At the time Samantha took it badly but said that it was just a bit of fun and that it was just all about the sex. Later on, I realized she had only said that out of pride, and to spite me, and that she had actually fallen in love with me. Maybe if I had known it at the time, we could have made a go of it, and she would still be alive today. We have remained good friends ever since though.'

Rick sat back in his chair and paused before saying, 'And what might have been troubling her, Mr. Dukes?'

'Samantha told me that she had also had a fling with Jim Derbyshire, which incidentally I knew all about, but also that Freddie Fairbrother had kept coming on to her and wouldn't accept her saying no to his advances. She said that she only went with Freddie the once because he told her of his lair up on the Head. He told her he only took special girlfriends up there for rampant sex, and he persuaded her to go and see it. She was so gullible and said the sex was futile, it was all 'wham bam thank you mam' and over in a trice.'

It was hard for Rick not to smile at such pathetic revelations from a mature married man. Keeping a straight face and looking Dukes in the eye, he continued:

'And how did you feel about that? Her telling you it was only a bit of fun and all about the sex. Did it make you angry enough to kill her?'

'You mean the girl washed up was Samantha?'

'Oh, come now Mr. Dukes, you must be aware of the press statement issued last night. It must have been staring you in the face, her red hair, the tattoo on her right buttock and the locket.'

Jonathon took a deep breath, sitting back in his chair and looking up to the ceiling for inspiration. 'Ok, I did meet her, but I did not kill her,' he replied in a raised voice. He was rattled now and starting to panic.

'What time was that?'

'It must have been about 10.45.'

'Until when?'

'Around 11.30.'

'That's a long time for just a chat, did you have sex with her?'

Jonathon was too quick with his answer, 'No, I told you it was over some time ago.'

Rick thought he was lying.

'Where did you go after meeting her down on the beach?'

'We went our separate ways. Samantha said she was going back up to the Hele Hotel, and I drove back to the brewery.'

'You didn't take her for a climb up Hillsborough Head?'

'No! Why would I do that?'

'You tell me Mr. Dukes; I'm asking the questions.'

'No, I did not.'

'Did you see anyone else as you left?'

'No, it was dark of course, so there could easily have been someone else down there in the shadows of the café and toilets.'

'Could they have got there by coming down the path from the top of the Head?'

'I suppose so.'

'I understand mugwort is used in the fermentation of some of your beers,' continued Rick.

'Why yes, it's used in brewing all of our beers, but what has that got to do with this enquiry?'

'Everything or nothing Mr. Dukes. You see, traces of mugwort have been found at the scene of the crime.'

Jonathon's heart was now pounding at such a rate you would have thought he had just run a marathon. It was so loud he was sure everyone in the room could hear it.

'But it grows in the sandy grasslands and edges of fields all over North Devon,' retorted Jonathon.

'You are quite right, it does, but not on Hillsborough Head Mr. Dukes.'

'One last thing. Do you use a PH meter in brewing your beer?'

'Yes. How on earth can that have any significance?'

'Can you tell me the make of the meter you use?'

'It's an old handheld portable Analytical Instruments model.'

'Quite rare then?'

'You bet.' Jonathon just couldn't resist bragging about his brewing prowess. 'I bought it at a Breweirana auction in Exeter, way back when I worked at the St. Austell Brewery.'

'You see, that's another thing Mr. Dukes, that very same

model of PH meter was found halfway up the Head on the coastal path.'

'Well, I must have lost it when walking one day. I have previously walked the whole North Devon coastal path for charity. Maybe I had it with me and dropped it.'

'So, you haven't missed it?'

'Now you come to mention it, I wondered where it had got to. We have been using a more modern one of late.'

'Hmm,' murmured Rick.

With that Rick thanked Dukes for coming in and terminated the interview.

'You mean that's it, no further questions?' enquired Jonathon.

'That's all for now, you are free to go. We know where to find you if we need to follow up on this interview.'

Dukes and his solicitor were escorted back out of the building. As they got into his car, the solicitor said, 'It doesn't look good Jonathon. They have a lot of circumstantial evidence, and no doubt they have a lot more that they are not yet revealing. They appear to be building a case against you for the murder of Samantha.'

'But I am innocent!' shouted Jonathon.

Back in the ops room Rick decided that he would try and catch Jack Johnson that evening.

'Oh Dave, before I forget, I met Bill yesterday when I was walking back from the mortuary. He suggested that we might have a word with Jack Johnson?'

'That old reprobate, why do you need to see him?'

'Just something Bill said. Apparently, the talk amongst the old squad is that Jack reckons the murder may have something to do with an occult of some sort.'

'Well, we can find him most nights down at the social.'
'OK, no time like the present.'

15

Rick and Dave sauntered into the social club at about 6.30pm.

'Allow, allow,' cried out Geoff Chambers from behind the bar. 'Good evening, sir, we don't see your likes down here too often. Has Dave finally persuaded you to mix with the has-beens and have-nots of the force?'

'Good evening to you too, Geoff,' Rick said with a smile. 'How are the Grecians doing these days?'

Geoff was an ardent supporter of Exeter City football club, known as The Grecians after the city's history. There is an annual re-enactment of the Siege of Troy in the St. Sidwell area of the city, as the residents there identified themselves with the Greeks and lived outside of the city walls.

'Middling, sir, they could do with a new center forward. Ever since they sold Harry Renshaw to our rivals at Plymouth, we've lacked a decent goal scorer up front.'

'One day, eh Geoff, have you seen Jack Johnson lately?'

'You're in luck, he usually comes in on a Friday evening, as do a lot of the regulars. He should be in soon. Now what can I get you?'

'I'll have a pint of Imperial and Dave will have a shandy as he's driving.'

Dave looked at Geoff and raised his eyebrows as if to say *Aren't I the lucky one?*

It was early and there weren't too many old blues in the club. One or two recognized Rick and just nodded, and a couple were in the corner playing cribbage as if it were the world cup final. A cry of twenty-nine went up, 'gotcha yer you bastard,' all in good friendly banter.

They took their drinks and went through into the games room where Rick challenged Dave to a game of bar billiards. Another couple were playing 301, double out, at the dart board.

'Loser pays for the drinks, OK?' said Rick.

'I know you; you can be a right hustler. I suppose you were your university champion at the game?' replied Dave as he reached for the balls.

Rick just smiled, 'Ok then. I'll give you a 100 point start.'

He still won the game with ease just as Jack Johnson appeared and sauntered over.

'Geoff tells me you are looking for me. Working an old case of mine then?'

'No, nothing like that Jack, I just want to pick your brains on the latest murder enquiry.'

'Oh, you mean the poor girl up on Hillsborough Head.'

'Yeah, that's the one. Here, let me buy you a pint and we can find a quiet corner for a chat.'

Dave took the hint and got another round in and ordered himself a pint this time. Rick and Jack sat at a corner table well away from earshot of the early crowd at the bar.

'Jack, Bill Walker suggested that I have a word with you about the case. Have you heard something?'

'Nothing specific, but I do know there are some loonies in these parts that are into the occult. Voodoo and the like.'

'How do you know that, Jack?'

'Because some time back I was asked to join them.'

Rick was taken aback; this was a bit of a showstopper. 'You were asked to join? How come?'

'Well, you must know that I had a reputation of being a bit of a rough diamond and didn't always play by the rules.'

Rick smiled, almost laughing at the suggestion, such was Jack's reputation. He sat back on the hard wooden chair and raising his glass in acknowledgement said, 'they still talk about you today. It's not like the old days eh.'

Jack smiled too, thinking *it certainly isn't*.

'I was never much of a churchgoer. When my wife Mags, who was a churchgoer and devout Christian was dying of cancer, all the vicar did was to tell her to pray to God for forgiveness of her sins and then 'He' will welcome her to his flock. I thought he was a total waste of time and no help at all.' He took a slow drink of his pint. Rick said nothing, sensing there was more to come.

'One evening after she'd passed, I got pissed and lippy over a game of poker with a few of the lads and started going on about the hypocrisy of the Church. I used words like, burn them all for all I care, and send them off to their fucking precious heaven. All that wealth. They are one of the biggest landowners in the country and what have they ever done for us? Nothing.'

'Well, there was someone at the poker game, who in the interval took me to one side and asked me if I wanted retribution for Mags' passing. Too right, I said, not really knowing what I was saying.'

It was Jack's turn to sit back in his chair, pensively looking around the room. Taking a deep breath and a sip of his beer he continued, 'He started telling me about a group of friends who felt the same way as me, a sort of brotherhood if you will. I met him a few times and he enlightened me to the ways of alternative religions. Anyway, to cut a long story short he eventually asked me if I was interested in joining a local cauldron of Voodoo worshipers of which he was a member.'

Rick couldn't wait to find out who it was. 'Jack, I can assure you, you could have done nothing to prevent this horrendous murder even if you had joined them. Who was it who was grooming you to join?'

Jack hesitated for a moment. 'It was Jim Derbyshire. I'm sorry I should have come forward, but I was so ashamed that I was dearly tempted to join them. I never gave it too much thought until your press announcement on the radio. We all listened in here, down at the club. It was then that I started to have thoughts about what Derbyshire had told me about Voodoo worship, including debasing promiscuous young women for personal gratification. Boys will be boys and all that. I then bumped into my old boss Mr. Walker and shared my thoughts with him.'

So, Jim Derbyshire is a member of the cauldron, thought Rick. *We need to know a lot more about him. Was he up on the Head that night?*

'Is there anything else you can tell us?'

'He wouldn't tell me who else was involved but said that the leader, the warlock, was a man of high esteem and lot closer to all of us than I could ever imagine.'

'What did he mean by that?'

'I don't know but I suspected he is a leading light in the community, maybe somebody in high office or authority.'

Rick slipped a couple of quid over the table to Jack.

'Thanks Jack, get yourself another drink, you have been a great help. Stay out of trouble.'

Jack slid the money back. 'That's OK sir, another time. You need everyone's help to nail whoever murdered that poor girl.'

'Once a copper always a copper, eh Jack?'

Jack laughed, 'I wouldn't go that far, sir.'

Rick and Dave got up, leaving Jack to finish his pint. As they passed the bar Rick put the two pounds into the police benevolent collection box, and another pound over the counter telling Geoff to buy a round of drinks for the lads later in the evening.

'Cheers sir, come again anytime.'

16

Saturday 30th

Rick had slept on what Jack Johnson had told them about Jim Derbyshire, and his perception as to who the warlock might possibly be. He had racked his brains all night, even in his dreams, searching for names of people in high public office. Several options kept coming to mind, not for any reason of suspicion but just the positions they held in the community. The mayor, councilors, the coroner, magistrates, doctors, solicitors, accountants, even the chief constable. The list was endless.

At the morning briefing Rick decided to keep details of his and Dave's meeting with Jack Johnson to themselves for the time being.

'Good morning team, well done everyone so far.'

'It's not looking too good for our Mr. Jonathon Dukes, is it,' piped up Dave looking over his shoulder as he poured himself a cup of coffee.

'I agree there appears to be a lot of circumstantial evidence against him, but something doesn't quite add up. It's all too easy at this point. I suspect that someone else maybe trying to frame Dukes or at least was party to Samantha Billings' murder. We need more prima facia, hard, physical, and forensic evidence as well as establishing opportunity and motive.' He then turned to look at the team before him. 'Anything from Ethan and his scene of crime team from down on the beach?'

Matt stood up from the windowsill he had been perched

on, saying, 'I believe he is wanting to tell you himself when he brings in the crime scene photos. He said something about, 'You'll love this one Guv, a real showstopper,' when I passed him in the corridor earlier on.'

It wasn't long before Ethan turned up. He laid out the photos which confirmed all they already knew.

'Good work Ethan, now what's this about a showstopper you have been holding back on?'

Ethan coughed once, as if he were embarrassed, so unlike him. He blurted out, 'We found a newly discarded packet of used Durex in the dry sand and pebbles, with two sets of fingerprints on it. Samantha Billings and another unidentified one.'

'Fuck me,' muttered Dave, to more sniggers from the team.

'That's not surprising, we already know that Derbyshire was having an affair with Samantha,' said Rick.

'Maybe,' said Ethan, 'But here's the thing, the fingerprints are not Derbyshire's. In any case why would he have sex on the beach when he owns the Hele Bay Hotel?'

'How do we know it was newly discarded Ethan?'

'The packet is dated 0967/0870 indicating a shelf life of 3 yrs. from this month. So, whoever was on the beach having sex with Samantha had to have bought them this month. We found the packet just below the high tide line. The last high tide was the night before the murder at around 2.00 a.m. On the night of the murder, it was much lower. From where we found the Durex packet if it were there the night before it would have been carried out on the outgoing high tide. It figures that the packet was used and discarded the evening of the murder.'

'Wow, you are wasted in SOC Ethan, have you thought of transferring to CID?'

'Not really Guv, this is as good as it gets for me.'

'Ok, we only have Derbyshire's fingerprints on record due to a caution he received by the MET some time back. It is more than likely that the prints belong to either Jonathon Dukes, in which case he is lying about whether he had sex with Samantha on that night, or they belong to Freddie Fairbrother.'

'But we've no evidence to suggest that Freddie was on the beach that night,' piped up Matt.

'True. Anyway Dave, I think it's time we had a chat with Mr. Derbyshire. You know what to do.'

Dave left the briefing and set off for the Hele Bay Hotel to bring Jack Derbyshire in for an interview. An hour later the telephone rang in the operations room.

'DI McCarthy' answered Rick.

'It's Dave. Derbyshire has gone missing. Nobody has seen him since last evening about 10.00 p.m. He told his receptionist that he had some urgent business matters.'

'Hold on the line Dave, I'll send Theo over to take witness statements. He can ask around if anyone else has any knowledge of his whereabouts or where he was going.'

'Will do.'

Rick called Theo over and told him what Dave had reported. He instructed him to get down to the Hele Hotel to assist.

'Right Matt, it may be early days, but just in case, put out an APB on Derbyshire, then look at his police file and see if anything comes to mind. I want to know anything and everything about his past.' Rick was buzzing now. *Had Derbyshire done a runner?*

'Adam, get yourself out there and visit Derbyshire's known haunts, starting at the Madrigal Renaissance Brewery. The rest of you continue the existing lines of enquiry.' Turning back to the phone, 'Any more news Dave?' enquired Rick.

'Not much, he appeared to be on edge and the receptionist apparently heard him shout out. 'That bitch, she doesn't know what she is talking about,' as he stormed out of the Hotel.'

'OK Dave, Theo will be with you soon.'

As Rick started to get up from his desk the phone rang again on another line. 'Just hold on for a minute, Dave.'

'DI McCarthy.'

'It's George, sir, a mature male body has been found by a stable lad at the Samson Smithy and Livery stables in Berrynabor. He was found in the stable yard first thing this morning under a pile of horse manure.'

'Shit! Another murder is all I need,' said Rick under his breath, thinking *you imagine you are getting somewhere on a case and then you get kicked in the bollocks, or in this case shat upon.'*

'OK George, can you inform Kay and the SOC team, I'll meet them there. Also get PC Worthy up there to cordon off the immediate crime scene and ask him to take a statement from the stable lad.'

'Right away, sir.'

'Dave, are you still there?'

'Yes Guv.'

'It could be a coincidence, but a dead body of a mature male has turned up under a pile of horse manure at Sampson Smithy and Livery Stables in Berrynabor. Could it be Derbyshire? Get yourself over there and take charge, I'll be with you as soon as I can.'

'There was me thinking that he might be guilty and topped himself rather than face justice, but he wouldn't have buried himself under a pile of horse shit,' said Dave.

'Now then Dave, you are starting to sound like George, pre-empting our enquiries.'

'Sorry Guv, it's just getting to me a bit. We've been going at it nonstop over the past few days.'

'Tell me about it! Statistically, as you know, most murders are solved within two weeks or else they drag on for months, sometimes years. In the case of female victims, we also know nearly 50% are most likely killed by a spouse, partner, or ex-partner or by another family member, so these have got to be top of our list. I'm not sure whether this helps us or not, but if we include past lovers and family members, statistically it's almost a 50% chance that Samantha's murderer falls into this category.'

'That's very interesting' said Dave, 'I never knew that. If that were the case it would include Jonathon Dukes, Jim Derbyshire, Freddie Fairbrother, Sam Billings and his wife and her older sister Linda.'

Rick sighed and stressed, 'We must keep up the momentum if we are going to crack the Samantha Billings case. Admittingly we could have done without this one, but I've got a feeling in my bones, if you pardon the pun, that they must somehow be connected. Right. Off you go to Berrynabor. I'll meet you there.'

17

It was nigh on noon before Rick reached the Smithy at Berrynabor. It wasn't difficult to find. Just another sleepy old village, inland from Combe Martin. He stopped off at the village shop and post office and bought a pack of sausage rolls, half a dozen doughnuts, six cans of Coca-Cola for the team, and an extra Mars bar for Dave.

On arrival, as Rick climbed out of the Dart, Dave came bounding across the yard out of breath.

'You OK, Dave?'

'Just a bit short of puff, I shall be as fit as a fiddle by the time this investigation is over, what with walking up Hillsborough Head several times.'

'Not if you keep stuffing yourself with bacon sarnies and Mars bars,' Rick said with a grin.

'OK, point taken.'

PC Worthy had taped off the stable yard area and was taking the stable lad's statement. Kay and the SOC team were already busy examining the scene of the crime.

Rick handed over the sausage rolls and doughnuts to Dave to share out, taking one of each and a can of coke for himself.

'You sure know how to show a girl a good time,' called out Kay across the yard.

'Well, you should know. How are you getting on?'

'We've only just started. I'll let you know after my preliminary investigation.'

'Right, what's the score, Dave?' enquired Rick casting his eye around the yard and smithy. The pile of horse manure and straw was in the far corner of the yard.

'It's Derbyshire all right. Nige identified him. The stable lad had finished his early morning chores of feeding the resident horses and cleaning out their stables. He then hosed the stables out and laid some fresh straw before shoveling up the manure and used bedding he'd removed, piling it onto the already steaming mound in the far corner of the yard. It was when he started to turn the mound with his pitchfork to enable better composting that he struck something soft but solid, struggling to pull out the pitchfork.

His immediate thought was that he must have stabbed a buried sack of oats or something. He then carefully removed the top layer of manure and, holy moly, uncovers the body. Understandably, he threw up his breakfast thinking he must have killed a vagrant or such like, although why on earth a dosser would cover themselves in horse shit, anybody knows. Perhaps he was pissed and thought it was just soiled hay.'

Rick commented, 'I'm surprised the body wasn't found until this morning.'

'Well, the livery closes at sunset, the horses are then fed, watered, and bedded down for the night. So, by the time the stable lad had finished and said goodnight to Jed the blacksmith, it would have been about nine o'clock. Other than the occasional neigh or snort by the horses, all would have been quiet after ten.'

'Hmm. According to the receptionist, it was just after ten last night when Derbyshire stormed out of the Hele Hotel.

Presumably, he was off to meet that bitch who doesn't know anything.'

'Who is she Dave, and what doesn't she know?'

They left Kay and Ethan to get on with it whilst they made a reconnoiter of the yard. They had a word with Jed the blacksmith, which proved to be more difficult than Rick would have imagined. Jed was profoundly deaf caused by all the years of hammering hot ironwork and horseshoes. He wore two hearing aids, but Rick still had to shout and keep repeating himself to get through to him. He noticed that it was easier when facing him as Jed had learned to lip read, but he still struggled with some of the softer and higher frequency words.

'I'm usually in my bed by ten,' said Jed. 'I'm knackered after a day's work and dead to the night once I fall asleep. I'm up at the crack of dawn, pumping up the brazier to get the fire back up to temperature and I usually put some bacon and eggs to fry on my long-handled iron skillet. You can't beat blackened crispy bacon.'

'So, you never heard or saw anything in the yard between 10pm and dawn?'

'No siree,' replied Jed.

Having decided that Jed had nothing more to offer, not even some of the crispy bacon that sounded delicious, Rick and Dave walked back across the yard to the crime scene.

Rick lit up a Camel and Dave munched on a left over sausage roll while they waited for Kay to finish her preliminary inspection of the deceased. Ethan would be there the rest of the day looking for evidence. After a satisfying drag, Rick stubbed out the cigarette and looked across at Kay and Ethan. Kay raised her open palm and fingers to indicate she needed just five more minutes. When she had finished, she got up, took her gloves off and came over.

'What do you think Kay?'

'Well, the stable lad will be pleased to know that the victim was already dead prior to being stabbed in the chest by him with the pitchfork. There are no other signs of trauma that I can immediately see. No signs of being hit by a blunt instrument or strangulation, so once again I must conclude that I think he was poisoned. There are some dark stains on his trousers suggesting he may have soiled himself, not unusual as the urethra and sphincter shut down at the time of death.'

Kay collected her evidence samples and put them in her 'doctors' bag. She then took off her body suit and head covering and put everything away in the boot of her car. Turning back to face Rick she said, 'I'll do the full postmortem as soon as we get him back to the mortuary and send off tissue samples to the path lab for toxicology, marking it urgent.'

'Thanks Kay, see you tonight.'

Rick then turned his attention to Ethan who was still examining the area surrounding the mound of manure.

'Anything you can tell me, Ethan?'

Ethan looked up. 'A couple of things so far sir. He had one of those silver cross pendants stuffed into his mouth. Attached to the chain dangling out of his mouth was a label with the inscription Romans 12:19.'

'Any of you Bible punchers here know what Romans 12:19 says?' asked Rick, looking around the yard.

'It says, *Vengeance is Mine says the Lord*, you philistine,' answered back Ethan, whose father was a Methodist lay preacher. He continued, 'There are two impressions on the horse manure, one a small boot, maybe size 5 or 6, likely to be female. The other is much larger, a shoe of 10 or 11, could belong to Derbyshire. We'll take photos and plaster casts of both back with us and set about identifying them.'

'Ok, Ethan, over to you and the SOC boys. Keep at it. I'll see you back at the ranch later this afternoon.'

'OK, Guv, I'm sure if I keep digging, I'll find more interesting evidence, but I won't spoil my entrance for later.'

'Are you referring to having to dig through all that horse shit Ethan?' Asked Dave with a grin, to more sniggering from the team.

'Dave, haven't you heard of the old adage 'Where there's muck there's brass?'

'Always the theatrical Ethan, always the theatrical,' said Rick. He concluded that there was nothing more to be done on site, so they decided to take a look at the access points to the smithy. They walked back out of the yard the way they came in. Nothing out of the ordinary struck them. They retreated about two hundred yards and then noticed a bridleway from the road on the right leading off up to Berrynabor Downs.

A further two hundred yards or so they came across a farm gate on the left. It was closed but not locked, with a battered old tin notice fixed on it saying, 'Private Road No Access to Strawbridge Farm.'

'Where's his car Dave? He must have driven somewhere to meet 'that bitch.' My guess is it's not too far away from here and whoever he met had a part in his murder. When we get back, get hold of an Ordnance Survey map of the area, and find out where both the bridleway and this track lead to.'

With that, they both strolled back to the smithy, Rick puffing away at another cigarette and Dave just thinking about a fish and chip supper.

It was late afternoon before they got back to HQ. Rick was ensconced in his office when he looked up from his desk. Just as he was thinking about wrapping things up for the day, Ethan came breezing in as if he had won the pools.

'Alright Ethan let's be having you; you look like the cat who got the cream.'

Ethan couldn't wait to reveal his further findings. 'Kay was right. He probably was poisoned; I found a phial of Ketamine among the pile of horse dung.'

'Well, well. Can you enlighten us any further?'

'I have spoken to Kay who confirms that Ketamine is a dissociative anaesthetic used medically for induction and maintenance of anaesthesia. She will tell you after the post-mortem whether Derbyshire had Ketamine in his blood.'

He continued excitedly, 'I've also spoken to the drugs squad, and they told me it's used in hospitals by anaesthetists for most day surgery procedures and by veterinary surgeons who use it to sedate large animals, such as horses or cows. It cannot kill you, unless consumed in large doses, but could if ingested with another poison. It is also used as a recreational drug and can be readily bought in the clubs down in Barnstaple. Dissociative drugs can lead to distortion of sights, colours, sounds, self, and one's environment. It is the choice of druggies as it doesn't have the same come down affects as MDMA, or 'hippy crack' as it is known.'

'Thanks Ethan, good job as usual. Now, before anyone runs riot with the idea that Kay killed him, there are several other possibilities.'

The room burst out with laughter.

'Seriously. Good detective work. You rule out no one until proved otherwise. In this case I can vouch for Kay's alibi.'

More laughter.

'Let's hold fire until we have the full post-mortem and toxicology report.'

Rick walked over to the evidence board and studied it for a few seconds. Turning to the team, he pointed to the board, 'Whoever the murderer is must know the working of the smithy and stable yard well, so, who of our prime suspects rides horses?'

'I don't know about prime suspects but Susie Dukes rides,' said Faye.

'Susie Dukes? What do we know about her?'

Theo, who was always keen to lead, started the appraisal. 'She is married to Jonathon Dukes, one of our prime suspects who owns the Madrigal Renaissance Brewery with his brother Justin. She is Sam Billings ex-mistress and designs all of the brewery's artwork including the Voodoo series of beers. Last but not least, she rides horses.'

'She is a good looker too,' piped up Dave, 'maybe she is riding more than a horse in this sex craved community.'

More laughter from the team.

'An interesting point Dave. I'm sure you meant the point in all seriousness,' said Rick, followed this time by stifled laughter.

'Maybe by murdering Derbyshire she was trying to divert our attention away from Jonathon Dukes,' said Theo.

'My thoughts entirely,' replied Rick.

'Theo, this one's for you. Find out all you can about Susie Dukes. You know, her background, what was she doing before she met Sam Billings, how did the affair with Jonathon Dukes start, previous lovers etc.'

It was approaching the end of the afternoon for what used to be a normal working time of the day. Rick needed time off to both relax and at the same time assimilate the evidence so far. He particularly needed to think of the implications of Ethan's revelations.

He went back in his office and called Dave in.

'How's the background search on Freddie Fairbrother coming on?'

'Best call Theo in on that one, he's the one doing all the work.' Dave called to Theo across the ops room.

'Theo, stop fantasising about Faye and get into the governor's office, now.'

A sheepish Theo appeared in Rick's office doorway.

'Hah, so you do have a thing for her then?' asked Dave. It had become a rumour among the team for some time now.

Theo blushed, giving the game away.

'So, have you done anything about it, does she know? The sooner you do, the sooner you get back to 100% focus on the task in hand, son.'

'Stop teasing the boy, Dave. You were his age once and no doubt smitten by some lass.'

'Come on in Theo, don't let Dave pressurise you in doing something you don't want to.'

'The problem is Guv, I do like her a lot, and don't know where to start?'

'Just take your time. How about just asking her out for a drink or for a coffee after work. In the meantime, can you just fill us in on your enquiries into Freddie Fairbrother.'

'Thanks Guv. Fairbrother has always been something of a Jack-the-lad. He is intelligent though, seen to be a good businessman. He went to school with Linda Billings, and as we know, he tried it on with her younger sister Samantha but was rebuffed by her as inadequate in the sex department.

His father is in the hospitality trade, owning the Tumbling Dice Club and Casino in Barnstaple. It was only natural that Freddie followed in his footsteps and his father set him up in Freddie's Bar and Café down on the harbourside in Ilfracombe.

He could always look after himself, took up boxing, a bit like Dave, but in his case, he was a natural.' He said with a grin, glancing at Dave. 'He won the All-England Boys, Junior Middleweight Championship, turned pro at 18 and was a contender for a Lonsdale Belt as the British and Commonwealth title holder. He had to retire in the sixth round in his final warm up fight with a busted hand with broken carpel and metacarpal bones. He was never the same afterwards and soon retired from boxing. Some say it was a fix and his trainer was investigated for binding Freddies hand too loose before putting his boxing gloves on them.'

Theo shuffled from foot to foot. 'There was also a rumour in the boxing club that Freddie's father had won a lot of money on that fight, betting on Freddie's opponent. Freddie was the out and out favourite, never having lost a professional fight. The odds for his opponent were 8 to 1, and some say that old man Fairbrother bet £500 on him to win.

Freddie has no police record or cautions. He is a bit of a gambler, no doubt taking after his father, and plays poker, often at his father's club. He is rather good at it by all accounts as he often wins large amounts of money and isn't afraid to collect debts owed to him personally. Jim Derbyshire was known to be one of his poker playing buddies.'

Interesting, thought Rick thinking of his conversation with Jack Johnson.

'He was raised as a catholic but known to be an atheist.'

Oh, is he? Another link to Derbyshire and possibly the cauldron.

'Thanks Theo, keep up the good work. Now go and ask that girl of yours out.'

The next day was Sunday, the team had been hard at it for five days solid and deserved a much needed and welcome break. He knew that he did. *The thought of a few beers and some prime time with Kay put a smile on his face. Topsham, that's where we'll go, not too far down on the Exmouth estuary, good food, what's not to like.*

A big cheer went up as he announced it. It was the little things like this that endeared Rick to the team. Work hard and play hard, was one of his mottos from his Rugby playing days. Using the old World War 1 analogy, he wanted team players who would 'die in the trenches' for him and vice versa.

After wrapping up the ops room at around 5.00, he left a contingent of volunteers to man the fort on shifts until Monday morning.

18

Rick called Kay before he left for home and told her the good news. She squealed with delight as he asked her to book a room at one of their favorite hideaways, The Globe in Topsham.

'I've carried out the postmortem and sent the tissue samples off to the path lab. I'm afraid as it's Sunday tomorrow we probably won't get the toxicology report until Monday afternoon. I'll fill you in on the postmortem as we drive down to Topsham. You are going to love this one!'

By the time he got home Kay had booked The Globe and thrown some overnight weekend clothes into a soft carpet bag ready for the day off. As luck would have it a local four-piece jazz quartet, Prohibition, was playing at the Inn on an 'open mike night' for any aspiring jazz singers.

A quick shower and change of clothes into casual weekend gear and they were off in Kay's VW Karman Ghia sports coupe. Topsham was only sixty miles away and they were there well in time for dinner at 7.30 p.m.

Topsham is a quaint estuary town on the banks of the River Exe almost midway between Exeter and the mouth of the river at Exmouth. It has a rich maritime and architectural history dating back to Roman times. Its position, offering a sheltered harbour to seagoing trade, enabled it to thrive as a port, a centre for both fishing and shipbuilding. There are many Dutch-style houses in the town dating from the time when it was an important cotton port. Many of the houses are built using Dutch bricks brought over as ballast from the Netherlands where the wool and cotton from Southwest England had been exported.

The Globe, where Rick and Kay stayed whenever they came down to Topsham, was a 16th century Inn. After a period of genteel decline, the town was now at the beginning of a resurgence as a destination for artists and musicians, drawn by its solitude, nature reserves and high luminescent quality of light. Magnificent sunsets often lit up the estuary, emblazoning everything with magical colour. Rick and Kay liked its bohemian feel, and when time permitted often came down for its annual music and food festivals.

Kay drove them, handling the Karman Ghia expertly like it fitted her like a glove. Her love of fast cars came from her father, Frank Stone, a former regional sports car racing champion. Kay had spent many a happy hour helping her Dad work on his beloved Austin Healy 3000 as she grew up, or at the racetrack in the pits, cheering him on. Her favourite job was holding out the comms board, giving him vital info on his race position and when to come into the pits for tyre changes.

Rick couldn't wait to hear the results of the autopsy. They hadn't even got to the outskirts of Barnstaple and onto the Exeter Road before he enquired. 'Come on then! What's the big revelation you hinted at on the phone?'

'Well, I'm fairly certain he was poisoned.'

'Is that it? said Rick sounding disappointed and irritated.

'Keep your pants on' said Kay trying to calm Rick down. 'Or in the case of Derbyshire, he didn't.'

Rick looked at her wondering what on earth she was getting at.

'I don't know how I missed it first time round, but the soiling of his trousers was not just from urine and faeces, there was also blood. He was castrated, the whole reproduction tackle cut off.'

'Jesus' said Rick. 'This points to a revenge killing, not a diversionary tactic.'

'What happened to his tackle?'

'More likely fed to next door's pigs on the other side of the fence, they eat everything.'

'Any other revealing evidence?'

'Yes, he had a branding no bigger than a shilling under his armpit. Around the rim is the word Bondye and it has an A inscribed in the middle of it.'

'A Voodoo connection if I am right,' concluded Rick.

They continued their journey down to Topsham. It was a beautiful evening and there was little traffic, making it a very pleasant ride from North to South Devon. On the way they passed through the hamlet of Chimera. Rick commented on the strange name, 'I wonder how it got that name?'

As a forensic pathologist Kay was sometimes called upon by the archaeology department at Exeter University to identify bones found on an excavation. Some years back she had been called to the department's summer dig at Eggesford Barton, on the banks of the River Taw. Whilst on the dig she heard the strange story of how the local hamlet of Chimera got its name.

'Apparently, way back in the 17th Century up until after the English Civil War, the hamlet was a village called Lower Chawleigh' she replied. 'A local soothsayer, 'Mad' Maddie Micawber was arrested and charged with being a witch during the puritan witch hunts. She was tried and found guilty at Exeter Assizes and burnt at the stake in the grounds of Exeter

Castle. On the day of her cremation, a vision was seen by several locals in Lower Chawleigh of Maddie turning into a fire breathing monster in the form of three animals, a lioness, a goat, and a snake. A so-called chimera from Greek mythology.

The rumours of Maddie's illusion spread, and mysterious fires broke out in various village buildings associated with the church. The local puritan priest condemned the acts as that of the Devil whilst villagers fled in their droves to the larger village of Upper Chawleigh. From that day forth the village of Lower Chawleigh was known as the sparsely populated hamlet of Chimera.'

'Wow,' remarked Rick. 'You should be selling tickets for tours of spooky archaeology sites in Devon. Have you got any more in your closet?' he laughed.

'It's only a myth, Rick, an illusion.'

It took a few minutes for it to sink in as they continued to wind down the lanes towards Exeter. Suddenly Rick cried out, 'Eureka,' causing Kay to brake sharply and almost swerve off the road.

'What now?' asked Kay in a raised voice.

'Of course,' said Rick. 'Chimera is a myth, an illusion, a mirage, call it what you will.'

'So?'

'The murders Kay, what if they too are an illusion?'

'Are you losing it, how can a murder be an illusion? We are supposed to be having a relaxing night away so you can get away from all of that for a night and a day.'

'Sorry darling, it's just that the murders are real all right but what if the evidence has been staged? An illusion if you like, to get me and the team to think that the murders must have been committed by one of the Dukes' family, either by Jonathon, Justin, or Susie, or by two of them, or even all three acting together. What if it is none of them?'

'My word, you do have a warped mind,' said Kay getting impatient behind a slow-moving car whose driver refused to drive above 35 mph on an open road. 'Have you always had the ability to think outside of the box?'

'You may be right. Dad always said that from an early age I took after 'Mad' Dickie, my birth father. He was apparently always looking at the alternative, the downside, and in his case having a plan B. Dad said those are the characteristics that earned him his VC, so perhaps I inherited the ability?'

'Well enough of that, you really know how to chat a girl up on a date, don't you,' Kay replied sarcastically, teasing him.

'That's it, I promise, no more talk about the voodoo murders. That can all wait till I'm back at the ranch on Monday. Let's just go and chill, have a nice meal then some jazz. You never know I might just get up and croon away to one of our favourites. Your request of course.'

The rest of the journey was uneventful with no more 'shop' talk.

As they arrived in Topsham the sun was going down over the estuary with sunset fast approaching. The fiery orb of the sun looked as though it was drowning in the waters below. The sky was ablaze with a blend of reds, oranges, and yellows which were being mirrored in the calm water, and the wavelets of the incoming tide were tinted vermilion, with underlying streaks of blue. The dark waters and the luminous sky made the horizon look like a meeting of two worlds – the known and the unknown.

Rick and Kay were speechless looking at such a magnificent and breathtakingly beautiful sight. Having parked the car, they just stood, hand in hand and in silence looking across the estuary. It filled their souls and reminded them just why they loved Devon so much and Topsham in particular. They entered the gnarled old oak door and signed in at Reception.

Having unpacked what little luggage they had for the overnight stay they went straight down to the bar for drinks before dinner. A pint of Imperial from the Exeter City Brewery for Rick and a Dubonnet and gin cocktail for Kay.

Dinner consisted of a mouth-watering starter of prawn cocktail. The local prawns had been caught that day in the mouth of the Exe, and homemade Marie Rose sauce was swirled withing the shredded fresh lettuce. This was followed by Steak Diane, flash fried at the table with shallots and button mushrooms, and a peppercorn sauce served with sautéed potatoes and spinach from the kitchen garden. The choice of wine was limited. Rick chose the chianti served in a flask half covered with a wicker basket.

Later that evening the Prohibition Jazz Quartet set up in the main bar and started playing jazz classics. As the evening went by, they invited aspiring jazz singers up to join them to perform audience requests. After Rick had downed couple more pints of Imperial, Kay persuaded him to get up and sing.

Rick needed little persuasion as he stepped up on the makeshift stage. He asked Prohibition to play Charlie Parker's version of *'All the Things You Are.'* The song had been written by Oscar Hammerstein and Jerome Kern and recorded by Frank Sinatra, but nothing compared to Charlie Parker's version in Rick's eyes, even if he was a bit biased!

By the time he had finished singing the final refrain '*You are the angel alone that lights a star, the dearest things I know are what you are, all the things you are, are mine*' Kay, and half the audience were fighting back tears. Rick stepped down from the stage to rapturous applause.

Rick was in his element and Kay was simply happy to see him relaxed and away from the stress of a major murder enquiry. They stayed till the end of Prohibition's set and even danced cheek to cheek to the final song '*Blue Moon.*' As Rick thanked the quartet for their performance, the lead trumpet player came over and said, 'Rick, my boy if you ever decide to give up the day job give me a call, we could use a lead singer for our gigs.'

Rick could not help but raise a smile. 'If only you knew Denzel if only you knew,' Rick replied, thinking life in a jazz band sounded idyllic at the moment the way the case was going.'

That night he and Kay both slept well after making slow passionate love with the curtains drawn wide open. The room was basked in moonlight from the full moon reflecting on the dark estuary water. Tomorrow could wait.

In the morning they took a leisurely stroll along the quayside hand in hand, watching the crab and lobster boats go out before they returned to The Globe for a sumptuous breakfast. Rick thought of his Dad going out if the sea conditions were right. Sunday was just another working day for the commercial fishermen. A full West Country fry up for Rick was ordered, and smoked salmon and scrambled eggs for Kay. It was then time to set off back to Bideford.

As they were loading the car with what little luggage they had, they met Denzel, the Prohibition trumpeter. 'Don't forget that job offer is still open Rick. We've got a big gig coming up at Taunton, and next year we are off to the Montreux Jazz Festival. If not, see you down here next time.'

'It's mighty tempting Denzel, but I've got a murderer to catch!'

'Yeah man, well someone's gotta do it,' he laughed.

The day was their own and they were in no hurry, so they decided to go into Exeter and have a look round the cathedral, the Sunday market, and the many independent shops in Market Street.

They both knew the cathedral well from university days and never tired of its grandeur. The present building was completed by about 1400, and has several wonderful features, including an early set of misericords, being part of the hinged seats in the choir stalls, the longest uninterrupted medieval stone vaulted ceiling in the world and an astronomical clock.

They sat for a while in a pew in front of the main altar and took time to reflect on life. Although they were both not practising Christians, they believed that they lived life in accordance with Christian values. Before leaving they lit candles in memory of both sets of parents.

Rick's weekend was made when he found a rare copy of an early Miles Davis LP in the market, titled '*Young Man with a Horn*,' recorded on the Blue Note Record Label in October 1953. Kay was also delighted at finding a pristine vintage Hermes handbag. Rick smiled to himself. The handbag cost Kay ten times the cost of his Miles Davis L.P.

After a light lunch in The Ivy, an art deco bistro on the High Street, they set off for home arriving back at Bideford late afternoon.

19

Monday 31st

Rick woke after a good night's sleep and felt more refreshed than he had since the beginning of the murder enquiry. He got up, washed, and shaved, then quickly got dressed ready for a new day at 'the office.' Despite the overwhelming circumstantial evidence, he was convinced more than ever that the evidence as presented so far surrounding the murder of Samantha Billings, was in effect an 'illusion.' It was an attempt by the murderer or murderers of the voodoo cauldron to draw attention away from them and frame Jonathon Dukes.

If that was the case, Dukes could not have been up on the Head that night. If so, who was the mystery man that took her up there of her own accord? *Freddie Fairbrother came to mind.*

Rick's mind was racing, and he couldn't wait to get back to HQ. By this time Kay had stirred from her slumber. She too had slept well. Sitting up in their king size bed she called over to Rick, 'Hey, handsome, what's with you this morning? It's only half past six.'

Letting the bed clothes fall from her shoulder revealing her breasts she said provocatively, 'Are you sure you wouldn't like a lie in?'

'Any other time Babe, the double header last night will keep me going for now,' he replied with a wide grin.

'Well, that's a first. I have never known you to refuse an early morning quickie before.'

'You are gorgeous, and I adore you to bits, but my mind is racing two to the dozen about these murders. In any case, Dave will be picking me up any minute, and even I couldn't manage it by then!'

Kay laughed. 'Away with you then, nothing quite as exciting for me today. I have a corpse from an unexpected death of a planning officer at the Town Council to deal with today. It may turn out as a case for one of your colleagues if the rumours of bribery are true.'

With that the entry phone buzzed. It was Dave.

'I'll be right down, Dave.'

Rick bent over the bed and kissed Kay on the lips then on each breast. 'See you tonight, Babe, have a good day.'

'You too, knock 'em dead!'

They both laughed at the significance of her witty remark.

Rick leapt down the apartment block stairs and out to Dave waiting in the Dart.

'Morning Guv, couldn't sleep?'

'On the contrary, I can't wait to get started. I have a few new angles that I want the team to look at.'

'Oh yeah? Anything you want to share?' said Dave as the Dart's engine roared into life and they sped off.

'I don't want to keep repeating myself, but I will say it again, I don't think Jonathon Dukes is our man.'

'Really? Well, that is a revelation! Have you been on the sozzle all weekend?' Only Dave could talk to the 'governor' like that, such was the bond that had built up between them since Rick was promoted to detective inspector and Dave appointed as his sergeant.

As they drove into the HQ car park the clock of The Albert

Clock Tower in the town square could be heard chiming 7a.m. across town. The desk sergeant of the night shift was taken aback as Rick and Dave entered the building. He was lounging back in his chair drinking a cup of coffee and reading the Racing Times.

'Have you got a tip for the big race at Exeter this afternoon, Simon?' asked Rick.

'Sorry sir,' he replied, quickly dispensing with the paper, and sitting upright. 'It gets a bit quiet in the early hours.'

'That's OK sergeant, understood, now what about that tip?'

'Funnily enough, there is a locally trained horse called Cool Jazz fancied at 10 to 1 in the 3.30 at Exeter this afternoon, and I thought of you.'

'Too good to miss, Simon. Here, can you put a fiver on for me?'

'Are you sure sir? that's nearly a third of a week's wages for the average PC.'

'Call it a sixth sense, Simon.'

'I'll have some of that too,' said Dave, 'Put me down for two quid.'

Word soon got round the building and before you could say 'Jack Robinson' all of Rick's team and nearly half of the rest of the building's personnel were in on the bet.

Just as Rick and Dave got to the stairs Simon called out after them. 'They've found Derbyshire's car sir; I have left a message in your in-tray.'

Rick put his hand up to acknowledge.

'Thanks Simon.'

Rick and Dave walked up the stairs and entered the ops room alone. There was an eerie silence as they switched on the lighting. The team were not expected for another hour or so.

'OK Dave, make some strong coffee and come over and join me. Let's you and I bounce around some ideas, some based on the evidence so far, and in addition, some off of the wall, or straight out of the left field as the Yanks would say.'

'Sounds like a good idea to me, Guv.'

Dave made the coffee and drew up a chair at Rick's desk. He had found some stale biscuits in the kitchen.

'I get the hint' said Rick sniffing at the biscuit and bending it. 'I'll send Faye out for some bacon sarnies when she gets in. Now let's have a recap of the evidence so far. Where is that note about Derbyshire's car? Ah yes, here it is.'

He read for a minute and then looked up. 'Apparently, a couple of ramblers found the car yesterday whilst out walking. They thought it odd that it was tucked away behind the hedgerow near the car park up on Haggington Hill. It's been taped off with 'Police Aware' stuck to it awaiting our inspection before being towed away to the police compound.' He sat back in his chair, cradling his coffee.

'After the team briefing, I suggest that you, I and Ethan go and have a look. Get hold of him as soon as he comes in and ask him to send the SOC boys over there in advance.'

As they waited for the others Rick filled Dave in on the results of Kay's postmortem, causing Dave to reel back before replying, 'Fuck me, or in his case, he couldn't even if he wanted to. And he wasn't dead at the time? I wouldn't wish that on any man.'

They went through everything that Matt had put up on the evidence board.

'What do you think Dave?'

'Well, it seems the evidence for Samantha's murder all points to Jonathon Dukes having committed it, unless it is a clever attempt to frame him for it. The Derbyshire murder could be by the same person or persons to draw our attention away from them. Or it could be revenge for Samantha's murder, or for some other unrelated reason.'

'You don't think they were carried out by the same person?'

'They may be linked, but I just don't buy it,' replied Dave.

Rick continued, 'What about Jim Derbyshire's role in Samantha's murder? We know that not only was he a member of the cauldron, but also one of warlock's acolytes. If we can prove that he was there at the time of Samantha's murder, we would have had a good case for charging him with at least conspiracy to murder if there was intent on sacrifice, murder alone or with others, or at the very least manslaughter if her death were accidental arising from her abuse and severing of her hand.'

Dave sat thinking, then posed the question, 'Could his murder have been by another member of the cauldron, possibly by the other acolyte because Derbyshire's actions actually killed Samantha, or are we talking about two killers still on the loose? Are the murders linked somehow either by person or by motive?'

They sat in silence. Rick was still thinking of Freddie Fairbrother, but he did not want to share what Jack Johnson had told him with the rest of the team until Theo had found out more about Fairbrother. Hopefully, more evidence linking him will be found.

'Dave, you will make a good detective inspector one day. I'm not convinced that Jonathon Dukes murdered Samantha, but he may have been present of course. We need to find out a lot more about Freddie Fairbrother's involvement. We also need to know more about Voodoo and their heinous practices.'

'What about Ethan's father?' said Dave. 'He is a Methodist lay preacher, maybe he can enlighten us.'

'Good thinking, set a meeting up with him. Ethan can introduce us, and his presence might encourage his father to reveal more than he normally would.'

Just then the team started to drift in. Luckily for Dave who was starving by now, Faye was the first to arrive. Before she could take off her coat, he was up asking her to pop out to the café down the road and get some bacon sarnies.

'I'll have double bacon and a fried egg in mine, what about you, Guv?'

Rick just smiled and shook his head at the sheer capacity Dave had for eating.

'Make mine a regular one please Faye, brown bread for me and get yourself one on me whilst you are there,' he said, giving her a pound note.

'Brown bread? You can't have a bacon sarnie with brown bread, that's sacrilege,' piped up Dave. 'It has to be white with lots of HP sauce.'

'Sacrilege it may be, but it's a lot healthier than that 'plastic' white stuff you eat.'

After tucking into his brown bacon sarnie and waiting for all the team to arrive, Rick called them all together.

'Right team, I trust you all feel as invigorated as I am after a day off to recharge your batteries. We now have a second murder, that of Jim Derbyshire. As you know, Derbyshire was found dead, murdered, up at a smithy in Berrynabor on Friday morning. His car has since been found abandoned not far away up on Haggington Hill. Dave and I will be going over there as soon as the team meeting has finished. I will attempt to recap on the evidence so far; please interject if I miss anything, anything at all however trivial it may seem to you.

A silver cross pendant was found stuffed into the victim's mouth and attached to it a label with the words, Romans 12:19, 'Vengeance is Mine'.

Rick paused, allowing the information to sink in, then continued; 'The postmortem suggests that he too may have been poisoned and we will know more when the forensics report is done by the path lab this morning. However, in this case we suspect that Ketamine was used. A vial containing Ketamine was found at the crime scene. Kay is almost certain that another drug was also used with it to kill him. The drug squad will tell you only too well that Ketamine is used as a recreational drug, but it is primarily used as an anesthetic by anesthetists for patients undergoing surgery in hospital, or by veterinary surgeons to subdue large animals such as horses and cows.

What you won't know, other than Dave, is that Derbyshire was castrated by the murderer, either prior or post dying. This suggests that the motive was a revenge killing.'

The room was deathly silent, everyone listening intently. The men cringing at the thought. Rick continued. 'Now, what do we know about Jim Derbyshire's murder? We know that not only was he a member of the cauldron, but he was also one of warlock's acolytes. Is there anything in his past that would suggest a revenge killing? Could his murder also have been by another member of the cauldron, or are we talking about two killers on the loose? Are they linked somehow either by person or by motive? Matt, you have been looking into Derbyshire's background. Anything more to report?'

'Yes Guv. As we know, we have been told by staff at the Hele Hotel that Derbyshire considered himself a 'ladies' man and put himself, or more specifically his pecker, about a bit. As well as being one of Samantha Billings past lovers, there is a rumour that he has also had a fling with Susie Dukes in the past.'

'Now that is interesting, it looks like Dave's intuition was right in a perverse sort of way.'

'Nothing perverse about me Guv,' piped up Dave, to sniggers by the team.

Matt continued, 'Derbyshire came down from London to North Devon after having made a lot of money in the music industry. He bought the Hele Bay Hotel and Caravan Park in 1965. He has a record of a caution for an assault on a young girl in a club in Barnstaple in 1966. Based on the premise that there is no smoke without fire, I contacted the Met in London to see if he had any prior record with them.' He looked around the room to see if everyone was listening to him. They were, so he continued:

'A helpful PC searched their archival database and found out that Derbyshire was questioned and arrested in the case of the rape of a young girl in London back in 1964. I spoke to a Detective Chamberlain who made the arrest. Derbyshire was released after the prosecution office instructed the Met that they had to let him go for lack of physical evidence, but Chamberlain was as certain as he could be that it was Derbyshire, and that he was guilty.'

'Well, well,' said Rick.

'That's not all, the victim's name was Linda Billings; she was a student at The London Veterinary school.' A gasp went around the room. Was that Samantha's sister? Raped by Derbyshire?

'Oh yeah, this sounds too much of a co-incidence, and I don't believe in co-incidences,' said Rick. 'Derbyshire had kept that quiet; he must have felt someone walked over his grave when he found that he had moved to where she had grown up with her parents and sister.'

'I think you are right Guv; the very same, Linda Billings is Sam Billings' eldest daughter and Samantha's sister.'

'Great intuition Matt, find out what happened to Linda after she went to the London Veterinary College. Where is she now?'

'Ok you lot, you've been fed and watered. Time for reflection. We still don't know how Freddie Fairbrother might fit into this. We do know he was a former lover of Samantha Billings, and he was spotted at the Larkstone car park at the time frame of Samantha's death, so he is a person of interest.

Theo is investigating his background, and as well as the general investigation, Faye is looking into Samantha's background. Theo, go careful in Fairbrother's case. We don't want to ruffle too many feathers at this stage.'

20

Linda was a straight A student at the London Veterinary College. She was engaging, well-liked by her contemporaries and soon made a circle of new friends. It was a time to forget the past horrors of her father and make a new life for herself. She got a job behind the bar at the student Union Club and also took a part time waitressing job at a local café to make ends meet.

Linda embraced the life of a student in London during the swinging sixties. A life of partying, safe sex and rock and roll. 'Work hard and party harder' became the rallying cry of her fellow top students.

Saturdays became the highlight of the week. Out with the girls, wandering down Carnaby Street looking at all of the outrageous clothes that Rock and Pop stars and many of their devotees were buying. Coffee in one of the 'Coffee Bars' that had sprung up everywhere, their favourite being the 2i's in Old Compton Road. They might visit the V&A or the Tate to view the latest exhibition in the afternoon. Then back to their student accommodation in the halls of residence at the college campus in Camden to chill out and recharge their batteries before a night out.

Those nights out usually meant a bite to eat at the café she worked at, then drinks down at the Mean Fiddler in Harlesden or the Windsor Castle pub in Maida Vale to see which pop acts were appearing later that evening. If they were lucky, they might see one of the up-and-coming R&B or Rock groups trying out a new set before appearing at more renown venues such as The Marquee Club in Oxford Street. Later that evening they would move on to the Marquee hoping to see such acts as The Rolling Stones, The Yardbirds with Eric Clapton on lead guitar, or The Who.

They had recently seen a new R&B phenomenon who had just come over from New York, Jimmy Hendrix, who made the guitar sing like no-one else. Linda was convinced that he would go far but come to a sticky end such was his outrageous persona. Sometimes they ventured further out to the Crawdaddy Club at Richmond, or Eel Pie Island in Twickenham, favourite venues of The Rolling Stones.

It was when serving drinks in the student union bar in her final year that Linda heard of a new club, Shadowland, that had opened up in Camden itself. *That sounds good,* she thought to herself, *I must get the girls out down there for a mid-week treat sometime.* As luck would have it, the following week a poster appeared on campus advertising The Small Faces appearing at Shadowland for one night only the week after next, tickets at the door.

The only one of her friends interested in going was Fiona, a bit of a wild child and the daughter of an Earl. The place was packed, drinks were flowing and the smell of marijuana thick in the air. The crowd went wild when the band struck up their current hit, *Itchy Coo Park* with its innuendo of getting high on drugs.

It was just gone midnight when Fiona decided she was going back to the campus. She needed to prepare some notes for her early morning tutorial on Concurrent Immune-Mediated Anaemia and Thrombocytopenia in Animals. *Oh joy*, she thought to herself knowing where she would rather be at this moment. Linda stayed on, dancing away to the hypnotic sound of the band.

It was not long after Fiona had left that the person who sidled up to her almost as though he had been watching and waiting for the opportunity, spoke. Over the top of the noise Linda heard a voice.

'High, I'm Jim, the owner of the club. What do you think, am I onto a winner?'

At first Linda thought he was referring to the club, little did she realise Jim's real intentions. They danced together for a while before Jim invited her to his VIP lounge, saying the band would be joining them after their set.

Linda had had a few drinks by now but was not drunk and was certainly in control of her senses, so she agreed. After all, meeting the band was an opportunity not to be missed, so she went to the lounge with him. Jim put on the Stones '*Let it Bleed*' album on his stereo deck and cracked open a bottle of champagne. After pouring them both a glass he invited her to join him on the sofa. When giving evidence later she said he was full of himself, acting like a big shot movie producer inviting her to his 'casting couch.'

Linda's suspicions started to rise. She could see where this was going and got up to leave.

'Whoa there, young lady, come to Jim and let's party.'

'I don't think so Jim, thanks for your hospitality but you're not my type.'

That was a red rag to a bull as far as Jim was concerned. He was used to girls throwing themselves at him in the hope of meeting some of their pop idols. He grabbed hold of Linda and threw her onto the couch.

'No, I don't want this,' she cried out as her mind flashed back to her father's abominable act with her and her sister Samantha. Jim wouldn't take no for an answer. He pinned her down, ripped open her top and grappled at her jeans. Linda struggled and shouted, 'No' again.

Jim punched her in the stomach so as not to leave any marks on her face, shouting at her, 'Shut the fuck up you cock-teaser, and you won't get hurt,' as he undid and pulled down her jeans and panties.

Thankfully, it was over as quickly as it had begun. Linda was now shaking and crying as she got up, pulled her jeans and panties up and shouted, 'You bastard, one day you will pay for this.'

Jim just laughed, 'Now get out, cry-baby. Grow up you tart! It's the swinging sixties, everyone's at it.'

Linda was distraught but somehow made her way back to the campus. Despite the late hour, it was now gone 1.00 a.m., she knocked on Fiona's door. Fiona was still up studying for her morning tutorial. She answered the door to be met by Linda who just burst out crying.

'Good God Linda, what's happened?' After getting her a brandy, kept in her eyes purely for medicinal purposes of course, Linda calmed down and told her Jim, the owner of the club, had raped her.

'Oh my God, we must telephone the police right away.'

A Detective Constable Chamberlain, together with a female police officer turned up half an hour later and took Linda's statement. They didn't require a medical examination, nor did they ask if she had visible bruises or torn clothing to corroborate her story, but they made it clear on her statement that she had gone up to Jim's private VIP lounge, and had drunk his champagne, willingly. Jim Derbyshire, the owner of the Shadowland club was arrested. He was subsequently given a caution but let go on the advice of the Crown Prosecution Service due to lack of evidence. It was his word against Linda's.

The episode changed her life forever. She was offered counselling and met a counsellor from the All-Saints Church in Camden.

Linda completed her studies and qualified as a vet. She changed her name by Deed Pole shortly thereafter to Sarah Cooper.

She became a 'Born again Christian' and regularly attended bible studies, becoming a fervent activist for the rights of rape victims. The stress she had suffered meant her appearance had changed and she had lost a lot of weight. She was previously curvy with long flowing auburn hair, now much slimmer and with her new name, she decided to have a different hair style too. The glorious thick auburn locks had to go, and were replaced by a short pixie style, bleached a pale blonde.

It was during a public meeting advocating a change in the law surrounding rape cases that she met Sir Mortimer Clarke who was a guest speaker at the event. They got married the following year and moved down to North Devon. She had never told Sir Mortimer of her past.

21

The shrill of a phone interrupted the team briefing. It was Chief Superintendent Ponsonby-Green's secretary saying that the chief wanted to see Rick immediately, the emphasis being on immediately.

'I have every confidence in you Rick, but I'm under pressure from the chief constable, and we need to nail this one. The media frenzy is beginning to get out of hand.'

'It's frustrating, sir, and it seems we are taking one step forward and two back as if some unknown supernatural force is watching every step we take, but we are making progress. I remain convinced that Derbyshire's murder is linked to that of Samantha's.'

Rick returned to the ops room and reconvened the team meeting: 'The pressure is really on guys. The media are starting to come up with their own conclusions. The chief said the headline on the Daily Mirror front page this morning was *Magic Casts its Spell in North Devon*. So, Ethan, what do we know about the piece of black cloth found at the Samantha Billings murder scene up on Hillsborough Head?'

'It's a blended wool cloth used in making ceremonial cloaks for the likes of university fellows and professors, barristers, civil dignitaries etc. There is an outfitters, Ede and Ravenscroft in Exeter, that makes and sells them. As you can imagine identifying who may have purchased the cloak that this piece belongs to is nigh on impossible. However, as luck would have it, the fragment torn off included the label which identifies the type, size, and year the cloak was made. It was made last year and is a 2xx size, almost certainly for a large male. What makes it unusual is that this type is made with a full hood.'

'Right, if we narrow it down to persons who were the subject of some form of ceremony, perhaps celebrating an achievement, prize or appointment to high public office, we might find a match.' said Rick.

'Adam, get down to Ede and Ravenscroft and see if they can provide a list of who purchased such a robe in the past.' Adam was another junior member of the team, having joined the force as a graduate entrant at the same time as Faye. He was delighted to be given a task to do on his own. A chance to prove himself.

'OK team, keep pushing on, keep focused, any findings that can't wait for the next ops meeting don't hesitate to contact either Dave or myself. Anyone got anything else to say or raise?'

Faye couldn't resist herself, saying, 'Is it the latest fashion to wear different coloured socks, sir?' which drew laughter and a lightening of mood in the room.

Rick looked down and laughed. 'Well, I did get up at sunrise! I must have grabbed a couple of loose ones in my sock drawer, but now you mention it, I think I might stay that way. A sort of good luck charm, what do you all think?' The team didn't know whether Rick was joking or not.

Rick's luck held; unknown to him Cool Jazz came in a winner later that afternoon at the Exeter races. It must have been the socks.

Rick, Dave, and Ethan left the ops room to head off to

the Haggington Hill car park and take a look at Derbyshire's car. Dave had already established what, where and when the car was bought. As they got in the Dart to set off, Dave was driving, Rick was in the passenger seat, so Ethan had to sit sideways across the back bench as it didn't allow for any leg room. Dave looked over his shoulder at a disgruntled Ethan with his arms around his knees, and smiling, said 'We're in luck to some degree Ethan. Derbyshire's car is a white Ford Corsair, purchased new from the Ford Main Dealer, Taw-Ford, in Barnstable on the 1st of the month, so hopefully there will be little historical contamination of evidence.'

On arrival they found the SOC boys had already examined the interior of the car and were now searching the surrounding area.

'Anything from inside the car?' Ethan asked Perry Jackson, his deputy.

'Surprisingly, a fair bit, considering the car is virtually brand new. There is evidence of a struggle in the car and the victim being dragged across to the passenger side, presumably unconscious. Here, let me show you. There are mud smears across both seats, and some coins on the floor which must have fallen out of his pocket in the process.'

'Any signs of who the attacker might be, Perry?' asked Rick.

'Possibly a short female. The driver's seat has been adjusted, brought forward. Derbyshire was a tall man, but not too heavy that he could not have been dragged by a woman. There is no way he could have driven the car with the seat in that position though. We are dusting for prints, but don't hold your breath, the attacker wore gloves, surgical gloves if I were to guess. One other thing we found was a horseshoe near the car, it's marked

SS14, probably from the Samson Smithy.'

Rick smiled, 'That's a lot more than we have previously had to go on, so well done Perry.'

He left Ethan with Perry and his team and walked back to where they had parked the Dart, waving at Dave to join him. It was a lonely place at the best of times, with a panoramic view down to the coastline. You could make out Hele Bay and Ilfracombe looking westwards, and Combe Martin and the coastline eastwards all the way up to Lynmouth and beyond.

Turning to Dave, Rick said, 'I can see why the murderer chose this place to meet. I shouldn't think you get many people up here after dark save for the odd courting couple. It puts a different perspective on how Derbyshire was taken to Samson's Smithy. It looks as though he met his murderer up here, possibly a woman, and was then driven there in his own car by him or her. The murderer then dumped his car back here where it was found, so he or she, more likely she, must have either parked nearby or had ridden up here to meet him where their horse possibly lost a shoe. Let's have a look ourselves before we go, but Ethan will have to widen the search for any further evidence.'

They didn't find anything obvious; it was like looking for a needle in haystack, a job best left for SOC.

Dave suddenly had a thought, 'I know it was late, sometime after 11.00p.m and dark, but we're not far off of the main Hele to Combe Martin main road. Maybe some passing motorist saw something.'

'Good thinking, Dave, get a radio and TV request put out. I want it featured on every news report throughout the day and evening.'

Meanwhile, Ethan had arranged for Rick, Dave, and himself to go and see his father at 3.30 for afternoon tea. His father, Jeremiah was the lay preacher at the Marwood Methodist Chapel. The Methodist movement started in Marwood in 1806, with the first service held at Blakewell Farm. In 1828 funds were raised to build the first chapel, superseded in 1872 when the present chapel was built alongside it, incorporating an auditorium with two north and south transepts. The old chapel was converted into a private residence and was now the home of Pastor Jeremiah James and his wife Eve.

The village of Marwood was only a few miles north of Barnstaple off the Braunton Road, and they arrived at Ethan's parent's house promptly at 3.30. Pastor Jeremiah warmly greeted them. After, shaking hands and clasping his father, Ethan introduced Rick and Dave.

'Father, may I introduce Detective Inspector McCarthy and Sergeant Elliot.'

'Gentlemen, welcome to our humble abode, and do come in. Eve has prepared a simple afternoon tea and will join us later after our discussion.'

Jeremiah led them into the snug which also served as his office, reading room and private chapel. Above the entrance door on the stone lintel was carved the Wesleyan doctrine of personal salvation: 'God's Grace Free in all and Free for All.'

John Wesley was an English cleric, theologian and evangelist who was one of the founding fathers of a revival movement within the Church of England, known as Methodism. The first recorded date of the movement was a pamphlet published by Wesley and his group of fellow believers known as 'The Oxford Methodists' in 1732.

The snug was simply furnished with of an oak desk and chair, two old worn leather armchairs each side of the fireplace, an oak bookcase and side table with a facing kneeling prayer chair. The planked oak floor was covered with a threadbare rug.

Above the desk was a tapestry sampler sewn by Ethan's younger sister Ruth in 1953, when she was eight years old. Sadly, Ruth died of meningitis when she was nine. Ethan was only eleven years old at the time. The sampler depicted the 'Rule of John Wesley.' It was beautifully sewn and mounted within an olive wood frame, a nod to Jesus Christ himself.

Wesley's Rule seemed rather poignant to Rick.

Do all you can,
By all means you can,
In all ways you can.
In all places you can,
At all times you can,
To all people you can,
As long as you ever can.

On top of the side table was a photograph of Ruth receiving her confirmation, and a simple candleholder with a white candle that had been continuously alight and replaced since her burial. Adorning the wall above it was a painting of Christ the Redeemer on the Holy Cross.

'Please be seated and share a glass of elderflower cordial with me.'

Rick and Dave sat in the armchairs and Ethan squatted on the prayer chair. Pastor Jeremiah passed them each a glass of elderflower cordial and raising his glass, remarked. 'Ah, our elderflower. Freshly picked from the fields surrounding our main chapel, steeped with water from our own well. Delicious, I'm sure.'

Rick and Dave gratefully received them.

'Thank you, Pastor, it's such a refreshing drink,' said Rick.

'Now what can I do for you inspector? Ethan tells me you would like an insight into the practice of Voodoo?'

'As you know Pastor, a young girl was washed up dead in Hele Bay last Wednesday. We believe that she was murdered up on Hillsborough Head in some form of sacrificial ceremony. Evidence suggests it may have been some form of devil worship, possibly Voodoo. It occurred to Dave that as a preacher, in your theologian studies, you would've become aware of Voodoo and might be able to offer us an insight into their beliefs and evil practices.'

'That I can, but I must warn you of the dangers you face when probing into their affairs. I have firsthand knowledge that the curses that they inflict can materialize to be true, although I am of the belief that it must be through some physiological sense that the perpetrator holds over the victim. I once attended an exorcise where a young girl, a member of the chapel, was the alleged victim of a Voodoo curse. She was in a trance, her tongue extended, licking her lips, salivating, cursing Jesus Christ our Lord, and using foul language, shouting words of blasphemy such as, 'Fuck me Bondye, spill your seeds of life inside me. I am yours. Kill all non-believers in Voudun.'

Rick and Dave were visibly shocked, not just the language but the fact that a methodist minister had repeated them. The reference to Voudun in her blasphemy did not go unnoticed by them.

'Thank you for the warning Pastor, but please do continue.'

'Voudun, or Voodooism goes right back to the 17th century having been first practiced in Africa as Voudun. It spread in earnest to the Afro-Caribbean regions with the advent of the slave trade. The slaves combined elements of their West African traditions and beliefs with the Roman Catholicism imposed upon them by their masters. Forced to adopt catholic rituals they gave them double meanings, and in the process many of their spirits became associated with Christian saints.'

Pastor Jeremiah crossed himself as he spoke of the Christian saints and continued, 'Voudun refers to a whole assortment of cultural elements: personal creeds and practices, including an elaborate system of folk medicinal practices. It includes proverbs, stories, songs, and folklore. Voudun is more than a belief; it is a way of life to many. It teaches belief in a supreme being called Bondye, an unknowable and uninvolved God of Creation. Voudun believers worship many spirits, called loa, each one of whom is responsible for a specific domain or part of life. For example, unrequited love, you would praise or leave offerings for Erzuli, the God of Love, and so on. In addition to helping, or impeding human affairs, loa can also manifest themselves by possessing the bodies of their worshipers.'

Rick and Dave were listening intently. Pastor Jeremiah continued, 'Followers of Voudun also believe in a universal energy, a soul that can leave the body during dreams, and spirit possession. In Christian theology, spiritual possession is usually considered to be an act of evil, either Satan or some demonic entity trying to enter an unwilling human vessel. In Voudon, however, possession by loa is an epiphany, a life changing experience. In a ceremony guided by a priest, priestess, or in some cross-over wiccan cults the warlock, such a possession is considered a connection with the spirit world. Many of the African spirits were adapted in the New World. Ogou, for instance, the Nigerian spirit of hunting and warfare took on a new persona; he became Ogun the God of Justice and has inspired many political revolutions that oust undesirable oppressive regimes.'

Rick and Dave were mesmerised by Jeremiah's knowledge of a faith considered by Christians to be evil. 'Pastor Jeremiah, I am somewhat astounded by your intimate knowledge of Voodoo.'

'Inspector, one of the first teaching in theologian school is to know thy enemy. Satan is everywhere. I have heard of such a gathering known as a cauldron, the same as in Wicca, practising in North Devon. There has been reports of activity all along the ley line from Lundy Island up to Glastonbury, but this is the first I have heard of it involving human sacrifice. Normally it is of small animals, a chicken or even a lamb.'

'Is there anything that you can tell us to help identify the members?' enquired Rick.

'I have heard that this North Devon cult also worship Wakan Tanka, the spiritual founder of the North American Sioux Indian Tribe, as well as Bondye the Voudun God of Creation. Many of the North American Indian Tribes as well as the Afro Caribbeans in Central America, pay homage and offer sacrifices to Wendigo, an ancient devil, said to be half man, half beast. Anyone showing an unusual hobby involving either the slave trade, or Afro Caribbean or Indigenous North American Indian history, might be of interest.

At gatherings of the cauldron, they would be wearing hooded ceremonial cloaks, white for the celebrants and black for the warlock. All would have an image of Bondye on its back. The warlock would have two acolytes to assist him, similar that in Catholic churches. All three would have a small branding of a circle under their armpits, no bigger than a shilling, with the word Bondye engraved around the perimeter and the letter W for warlock or A for acolyte in the centre of the circle.'

Rick glanced at Dave at the significance of this revelation.

'The warlock is likely to be someone in high public office. They often feel unrecognised and unrewarded for their public service, possibly someone who is also disillusioned or feels let down by the church.'

'Thank you Pastor, you have truly given us food for thought and, unknowingly at this stage, may have helped us enormously in solving this heinous crime.'

'You are both welcome, and indeed would be welcome at the chapel anytime. Now, talking of food of a different kind, I think it's time for tea, please join us in the kitchen.'

Pastor Jeremiah led them out of the snug to the kitchen at the rear of the property. It was a large room that served as both kitchen and dining room, bathed in light from the stone mullion windows overlooking the kitchen garden.

The kitchen area had a large inglenook fireplace at one end of the room with an Aga cooking range. There was an oak dresser and ample cupboard space with a larder. In the centre of the other end of the room was a long three plank oak table and eight chairs for when they entertained the minister and his family, or fellow brethren after prayer meetings.

Eve had laid the table with crockery and cutlery, and two large glazed brown teapots, one of freshly made tea and the other with hot water to top up the tea. Upon the table were dishes of home-made blackcurrant, gooseberry and strawberry jams and a large pot of cream from the local dairy farm.

'Sit down brothers and pour yourselves a cup of tea whilst I get the scones out of the oven,' said Eve, who had put on her Sunday best dress to greet them.

She joined them at the table, placing down a large plate of scones that were plain and another that contained dried fruit. *Hmm they smell delicious* thought Dave, almost salivating at the thought of eating one, or even two.

After a short blessing by Pastor Jeremiah, Eve passed them round, inviting them all to tuck in. They helped themselves putting cream on first followed by jam, the Devonian way, as opposed to jam first followed by cream, the Cornish way. Dave wasn't bothered which way he prepared his, hardly waiting for the others, but followed tradition so as not to upset Eve. In fact, he was first to compliment her,

'Eve, you are a wonder to behold. I've not tasted such delicious home-made jams since my mother passed. On behalf of Rick and myself, not forgetting Ethan, I thank you for your kind and generous hospitality.'

That saw him in Eve's good books as she picked up the plate with only one scone left and offered it to him.

After tea, Rick, Dave, and Ethan bade Jeremiah and Eve farewell and headed back to HQ.

Eve clasped Ethan in her arms and quietly whispered in is ear. 'I love you son, God is all forgiving, come back into the fold.'

Upon leaving, Pastor Jeremiah pronounced 'God bless you all and may he use his powers to help you find the murderer or murderers of this evil act.'

22

As they left Marwood and turned back onto the main Barnstaple Road, Rick was feeling elated. He smiled to himself thinking *we know now that Derbyshire was almost certainly one of the two acolytes who assisted the warlock at the murder scene up on Hillsborough Head. He may not have administered the poison that killed Samantha, but he would be guilty of aiding and abetting her murder.*

The branding found on Derbyshire at the post-mortem meant that they now had a clear identification mark that would be found on the second acolyte, and on the warlock. Pastor Jeremiah's insight as to the probable background of the warlock was also extremely helpful; a person of high public office but feeling unrewarded for their service, or disillusioned with the church, which turned them to Voodooism.

'Please thank your father again Ethan. I'm sure that you picked up on one or two things that he said that could help us immensely in the Hillsborough Head murder enquiry. And, well done to you Dave for suggesting we spoke to the Pastor.'

On arriving back at HQ Rick sensed a mood of joy.

'Cheers sir,' said George at the front desk, giving him a wink as he passed him. This was followed by a round of applause as he entered the ops room.

'What on earth is going on, Matt?'

'Haven't you heard, sir? Cool Jazz won in the 3.30! It came

in at 10:1. Everyone in the team had a bet on it and most of the others in the building too. Rumour has it the chief himself put £5 on. That will get you back in his good books.'

'Oh, I very much doubt that. Solving these murders quickly is the only way of doing that, but yes, 10:1 you say. That's me £50 richer.'

Rick briefed the rest of the team about the meeting with Ethan's father. 'OK, let's stick with these revelations for the minute. Who is the second acolyte and how do we identify him. Any thoughts?'

'He would have been one of the last to leave the murder scene. What about Freddie Fairbrother? He was seen driving away from Larkstone carpark at around 1.00 a.m. by some lovers parked there,' said Matt.

'Good thinking, Matt. We know that he was rejected by Samantha for his lack of manhood. Unrequited love, revenge? How many times have we witnessed that in a crime? How do we prove or disprove it?'

Faye, who was sitting next to Theo on the pretence of discussing some point in their investigation, but more likely was finally arranging a date between them, looked up sheepishly and said, 'We need to be careful of entrapment Guv, I was reading in the police journal of such a case thrown out in court.'

'Wise words, Faye.'

'Undercover observation Guv?' said Dave.

'You are not suggesting that one of the girls goes undercover and sleeps with him are you, Dave?'

'No! Even I wouldn't suggest that!' Dave replied to laughter in the room.

'Where and when are we likely to be able to observe his left armpit?' Rick asked the team.

A flurry of silly answers reverberated around the room, ending with changing room, swimming, GP, hospital. Rick stopped them there.

'You are all missing the obvious,' said Rick.

'Previous or current lover?' spurted out Faye as if she were answering a parlour game.

'Yeees,' said Rick, 'another one up for you Faye.'

'Changing rooms, that's a good one too. Theo, find out what gym or sports clubs Fairbrother belongs too. Maybe football or rugby. We know he used to box, and perhaps he still does. Then come up with a way of either finding a witness, or at a last resort get yourself into the changing room. You could be the janitor, kit man etc or even join the club. I gather you are a bit of a sportsman yourself.'

Theo smiled to himself. *This one is definitely for me.*

'Right what else have we got? Adam, any more news regarding the piece of black cloth?'

'Ok' said Adam rather nervously being the junior member on the team. 'It's the hood that's the issue. Several black cloaks are made and sold by Eve and Ravenscroft but very few of them have hoods.'

'Surely that makes it easier, doesn't it?' replied Rick.

'Well, yes and no. Most are made and shipped abroad to colder climates, so I think we can discount them. Some are made for theatrical, film and TV production costumes. Others are made for friars and the Abbots of a Benedictine monastery, as they are the only order that currently wear black, as opposed to the traditional brown. There is only one practising Benedictine Monastery in Devon, Buckfast Abbey at

Buckfastleigh.'

'I hardly think that an abbot or one of the friars could be our warlock. He would be missed at the monastery as the friars live a secular but regimented life,' said Rick.

Adam continued: 'The list of individual members of the public investing in such a high-quality cloak is minimal, only fifteen in the last year, ten of which were bespoke as a women's fashion item. The five male cloaks were all made for medieval re-enactors. Four of which have been interviewed and discounted from our enquiries. We are still trying to trace the fifth, a Major Barnaby St John Stevens, a former army chaplain.'

Rick glanced at Dave. *Got you*, thought Rick.

'Good work Adam. Follow up on the theatres, film production studios and see if any cloaks have gone missing. Dave and I will take over the hunt for St John Stevens.

Right Dave, back to Derbyshire's murder for a moment, let's have a look at that ordnance survey map of Berrynabor.'

Dave spread out the map on Rick's desk. 'Look at this,' said Dave pointing to the map. 'The farm track is a back entrance to Strawbridge Farm.'

'What about the bridleway?'

'It goes up to Berrynabor Downs and beyond into Combe Martin. It looks as though it was part of an old drovers way. There are two properties shown on the map, The Old Rectory and Silver Mines Farm.'

'Well, well, and who do we know has a brewery on land at Silver Mines Farm? None other than the Dukes brothers. Find out who lives in both The Old Rectory and Strawbridge Farm.'

A phone call to the Land Registry was all it took; Strawbridge

Farm was owned by Sir Mortimer Clarke and the Old Rectory, owned by an Andrew Martin.

'That name rings a bell,' said Dave. 'I saw something in the North Devon Gazette. Now let me think. Yeah, that's it, he's the Mayor of Ilfracombe who recently sold his business of selling everything and anything to do with medieval re-enactments, including books, armour, clothing, and replica weaponry. Apparently, he's a bit of a celebrity on the subject, giving lectures and organising re-enactment fayres and battles. I seem to remember he also advises film and TV production companies on the matter, so he's not short of a bob or two. He probably bought The Old Rectory from the proceeds of the sale.' Dave was excited now. 'I need to double check, but I'm sure there was also something about him donating a sizeable sum to a local history group who are researching something to do with the ley line from Lundy Island to Glastonbury and its effect on witchcraft in North Devon.'

'Did he indeed?' said Rick with some degree of interest and surprise. 'Double check it and let me know. We never saw this one coming Dave, what did Jack Johnson say after his meeting with Jim Derbyshire? That he suspected the warlock is a leading light in the community, maybe somebody in high office or authority. Well, they don't come much higher than the local mayor.'

It was time for another Camel and a deep intake of breath. Things were coming together.

'Find out more about our esteemed mayor. No wait, you've got enough on your plate, get one of the juniors to look into his background. Get them to pretend to be a student journalist from Exeter University and interview him about a piece they are doing on medieval reenactment, or such. You never know he might let something slip.'

After the briefing had finished Dave took Rick to one side. 'What was all that about between Ethan and his mother just as we were leaving?'

'Ah, you noticed it too. She whispered something about God is all forgiving and him coming back into the fold.'

'What a strange thing to say.'

23

Tuesday 1st October

The team gathered for their early morning briefing. Jane had brought in a dozen doughnuts and Adam had made mugs of black coffee. Milk and sugar were on the desk. Anyone wanting tea had to make their own.

Rick opened proceedings. 'Good morning team, we are making good progress, keep up the momentum. We still need a breakthrough, that second burst of energy as we round the final bend and hit the home straight. Ok what do you have to report?'

Matt was first to speak up, telling the team that forensics had come up with information on the shoe prints found by SOC at Samson's Smithy. 'The shoe prints are pretty much what Ethan had surmised. The smaller of the two is from a riding boot size six, indicating that it is more likely to be that of a female, and the larger one is size eleven, suggesting a tall male, and it matches the shoes of Jim Derbyshire.'

'Anything about the horseshoe found near Derbyshire's car, Matt?'

'Theo has been back to the smithy and Jed confirmed that the horseshoe is one of his and is made from a special alloy to make it more comfortable for the horse. They are expensive and usually only bought by owners of valuable horses that are either show jumpers or engaged in point-to-point horse races. Here's the list of his clients who have this horseshoe, size 14, shod on their horses. There are only four.'

Rick looked down and scanned the short list. There, staring out at him, like the eyes of a rabbit caught at night in headlights, were the names of Susie Dukes, Sarah Cooper-Clarke, Giles Faraday the Coroner, and Andrew Martin, the Mayor.'

Rick knew Susie Dukes, Giles Faraday, and Andrew Martin but *who the hell was Sarah Cooper-Clarke,* he thought. It didn't take long to find out as Matt continued:

'Jed told Theo that Sarah Cooper-Clarke was the local vet and married to Sir Mortimer Clarke, a gentleman farmer. They moved down from London only a year or two back and bought the old Strawbridge Farm and stables up on the Downs between Hele and Berrynabor. Apparently, he made his fortune up in the City in one of them new-fangled 'hedge' funds. The only thing I know about hedges is that they surround fields and gardens. I can't see her being involved unless she has taken tips from her old man on the use of a hedging sickle and slashed the victim with it,' which drew laughter from the team.

'Where's Theo by the way?' asked Rick.

'He's out and about trying to identify who the second acolyte is, looking for a person with the Bondye and A branding under their armpit.'

'Does he know the latest info on Freddie Fairbrother's boxing prowess?'

'He does. Theo's a fit lad Guv. I'm sure he can handle himself if necessary. Coincidently he is following up a tip from someone at the boxing club.'

'OK, but you had better send someone down to the club as backup. There are some nasty pieces of work down there who wouldn't think twice about punching the lights out of a copper.'

Theo had joined the boxing club when he found out about Freddie's past history. He had done a bit of boxing at the police training college and spun the yarn on joining that he just wanted to get in shape, without disclosing that he was a policeman. So far, he had got away with weight training, working with a punch ball and shadow boxing. Freddie was a legend at the club with photos of his various achievement adorning the walls.

That morning, Theo had just finished his training session and was taking a shower in the changing room. He was just drying himself off when someone with their back to him reached out of a misty shower cubicle to reach for his towel laying on the rack next to it. As the persons' arm extended to grab the towel, Theo thought that he could make out something under his armpit. A skin blemish maybe, but no as the steam began to subside there was no mistaking it. It was the branding of Bondye with an A in the middle. The person turned round and smiled. It was Freddie Fairbrother.

The last words that Theo heard were 'So now you know, such a shame, the trainer thinks you have promise son.' The dumbbell came down with a thud and Theo fell like a sack of potatoes.

'You idiot Tiny, what did you do that for?' cried out Freddie.

'He recognised you Freddie, I did it for you and the cauldron.'

Freddie knelt down to check on Theo. He felt his pulse, there was none.

'Quick, move him over so that it appears that he hit his head on the bench and smear a bar of soap on the floor a few feet away from his feet. Give me a few moments to slip away. Then go rushing out into the club shouting for help as if you had just gone in and found him on the floor.' Tiny did as Freddie had commanded him.

Sergeant P.C Jones and P.C Evans from the traffic squad were arriving at the club to back up Theo when they noticed the ambulance. They got out of the squad car and rushed over.

'What's going on?' Sergeant Jones asked one of the paramedics.'

'It looks like an accident in the changing rooms. One of the lads appears to have slipped on a bar of soap.'

Sergeant Jones, who went through Middlemoor Police Training College with Theo, rushed into the club fearing the worst. He showed his warrant card and was ushered into the changing room.

'No, no' he cried out. There lying before him was the deceased body of Theo. His police training kicked in as he went back into the boxing hall and made for the main entrance.

'Right, listen up everyone, nobody is to go into the changing room, and no-one is allowed to leave.' Unknown to him Freddie Fairbrother had already slipped out the back entrance. The sergeant then radioed into Command and was put through to the CID operations room. Dave answered the call.

'Dave Elliot.'

'Dave, it's Rory Jones. There's only one way of saying this. Theo is dead.'

'Dead? What do you mean dead? He can't be, has there been an RTA?'

'No Dave, it was me that responded to the call for back-up at the boxing club. Theo was found dead on the changing room floor. It looks like he slipped on a bar of soap and hit his head on a bench.'

'Jesus, no! Not Theo.' Dave was visibly shaken. 'OK' he said, 'D I McCarthy and I will be with you as soon as we can.'

Other members of the team heard one way of Dave's phone conversation with Sergeant Jones. Dave looked across the room at Faye. She knew, call it a sixth sense, some might call it love. She could see in Dave's eyes as he looked at her, it was the one person's name she did not want to hear.

Dave crossed the room to her. 'I'm so sorry Faye, it's Theo.'

Faye was shaking her head in disbelief, saying nothing but staring at Dave with tears welling up in her eyes. She burst into tears, whilst Adam and Matt were visibly shocked. Rick heard the commotion and came out of his office. Adam was consoling Faye as he crossed the room. He knew that that could mean only one thing.

'What's up Dave, it's Theo, is it?'

'I'm afraid so. Rory Jones from Traffic responded to the call for back up at the boxing club. Theo was found in the changing rooms, dead. It looks at first sight as though he may have slipped on a bar of soap and hit his head on a bench.'

'Well, we all know things are not necessarily as they appear at first sight. Get Kay and Ethan down there as soon as.'

Rick went over to Faye who by now had composed herself. 'I'm so, so sorry Faye. It doesn't help to know that Theo was a wonderful young man, destined, like yourself for a great future. Whatever the future holds he will be remembered by everyone of us here and will always be with you in spirit.'

Faye responded in a quivering voice desperately trying to hold back more tears, 'Thanks Guv,' but bursting into uncontrollable sobs, said 'I never had the chance to tell him I loved him too.'

'Right Dave, let's get down to the boxing club. You know the way.'

Sergeant Jones was still holding the fort when Rick and Dave arrived. Ethan and the SOC team had been the first to arrive a few minutes earlier and were already busy at work in the changing room.

Rick introduced both himself and Dave to Sergeant Jones who consulted his police notebook and told them what he found when he arrived at the scene.

'Who found Theo?' asked Rick.

'John Foreman, known as 'Tiny,' on account of his intimidating physique,' replied the sergeant, pointing to a well-built man of over 6ft tall sitting down on a worn chesterfield leather sofa with his feet up, and smoking a cheap brand of cigarette.

'Ok, first a word with the manager.'

'That will be Dixie Davis, he was a champion heavyweight way back in the day when I first started here,' said Dave. 'Let me introduce you.'

Dixie Davis was in his office. He was in good shape for a man in his sixties. He still looked after himself, kept fit and was eating all the right things. Plenty of chicken, fish, vegetables, and salad with the occasional treat of a juicy T Bone steak.

'Dixie, this is Detective Inspector McCarthy.'

'Detective Inspector, eh? I thought this was just an accident.'

'It may well be Mr. Davis, but the deceased was a member of my team and let's just wait for the pathologist and SOC to confirm cause of death, shall we?' Rick didn't like him, didn't trust him. 'Tell me Mr. Davis, has Freddie Fairbrother been in this morning?'

'Why, yes, he was in earlier for a workout, but why do you ask?

'Just curious, that's all.'

Dixie Davis did not believe that for one minute.

'That's all for now, we'll require a list of all members.'

'Of course. You'll find Dave's name on it.'

Rick and Dave then went into the changing room to consult Kay. They both took a moment to stand silently and reflect on Theo's life before asking her how she was getting on.

Kay had finished inspecting Theo's body. It didn't take her long to confirm that Theo had died from a severe trauma to the head causing a massive brain bleed. Death was instantaneous.

'So, it was an accident?' enquired Rick.

'I didn't say that. The trauma could have been caused by him falling backwards and striking the edge of the bench behind him. It could equally have been caused by a heavy wooden object. I think you need to put that question to Ethan.'

Ethan, who had arrived earlier, already had the scene marked out. His first inspection was of the bench.

'What do you think Ethan?'

'This was no accident. There are no signs of Theo hitting the bench. No blood, no hair follicles, nothing. Looking at the crime scene I would say it had been staged to look like he fell. I have examined the shower screen and there are minute particles of blood on it. I think he was facing the cubicle when he was hit from behind and then fell forward not backwards. It looks as though he was facing someone either in or coming out of the shower cubicle.'

'Maybe he recognised him or the cauldron branding under his armpit. Could it have been Freddie Fairbrother? Dixie said he was in the club earlier,' said Dave with some conviction.

'Maybe Dave, maybe.'

'What about the wooden object that Kay believes he may have been struck with?'

Kay intervened. 'It would be rounded by the shape of the wound.'

A search of the changing room revealed traces of blood in a wash basin. 'We'll send the blood to forensics, but my money is on it being Theo's,' said Ethan. 'It looks like the murderer has made a poor attempt to wash off the blood from the wooden object.'

'Right, I want a thorough search by SOC of the entire building looking for this object. If the perpetrator made a poor attempt to clean the object up, maybe he made an equally poor attempt to conceal it.'

Ethan who has a good eye and intuition when inspecting a crime scene was quick to come up with one observation. Racked up along one wall were various items used in training. Skipping ropes, trainers, padded gloves that looked similar to American baseball gloves, chest expanders and dumbbells. It was the dumbbells that caught his eye. He shone an ultraviolet light on them and low and behold one showed up with a minute blood splatter. 'Here's the murderer's weapon,' he said as he bagged the object. 'We'll run a fingerprint test when we get back to HQ.'

'OK, keep at it, Ethan. Dave get someone to take statements from all present and then let them go for now.'

'Will do, Guv,' they said in unison.

As they turned to leave Dixie said 'Good to see you Dave, even in difficult circumstances. You're looking a bit out of shape, get yourself down here for a workout and massage.'

'I might just do that Dixie.'

Rick just smiled to himself as he looked on in disbelief and thought of the quote from one of his favourite John Wayne films, '*That'll be the day.*'

24

Wednesday 2nd

It was difficult to trace St John Stevens who bought a black cloak from Eve and Ravenscroft. His army career showed he was court marshalled in 1958 for a violent sexual assault and rape of an army cadet at the Devonshire regiment's barracks in Topsham. He became a lay preacher and subsequently a supply priest of the Exeter Diocese. In 1960 he was dismissed by the bishop after an internal enquiry found him guilty of a succession of incidents involving children of both sexes when preparing them for holy confirmation. The church excommunicated him.

Since then, he appeared to have vanished. There was no police record of him, nor was he on the 1961 census or electoral register. The Inland Revenue had no knowledge of him, and he didn't hold a current bank or post office account.

'It looks like he is either dead or living a life 'off the grid' Guv,' said Dave after exhaustive enquiries.

'Damn,' said Rick, 'I thought we may have found our warlock. Keep Adam at it until we find evidence of him dying, or that he is out there somewhere. Someone must either know of his whereabouts or is covering up for him. In the meantime, let's you and I concentrate on Derbyshire's murder.'

'How are we getting on tracing Linda Billings?'

'Another dead end so far. She too has vanished. There are no records of her after she completed the course at the London

Veterinary College.'

'Bloody hell. With all these disappearing acts you will have me beginning to believe in voodoo.'

'What if she changed her name, Guv?'

'Why on earth would she do that, other than getting married of course. Of course – she's probably got married, but there must be a record of that. Why is isn't it showing up?'

'People change their name to forget the past, some traumatic event maybe or to re-invent themselves. Perhaps she changed it before getting married, so we have a double whammy. I know someone who was brought up by a family who never adopted him. They only told him when he became of age at 21 and he had to sign legal documents etc in his own name. He decided to change his name from his birth name to their surname.'

'How do you go about that?'

'It's easier than you think. You need a solicitor to draw up a Deed Poll for you to sign and he or she to witness. It then gets published in the London Gazette and 'Bob's your uncle' you have a new legal registered name.'

'Well, it's a new one on me Dave, but maybe that's what's happened to St John Stevens too. Get Adam onto it. Get him to go through The London Gazette records from the time he vanished, and whilst at it, do the same for Linda Billings. Unlikely, but worth a try.'

Rick paused for thought, he had so many hares running in both investigations it took all of his mental prowess to keep track. *Thank goodness for the likes of Dave as my number two,* he thought to himself. He sat back in his office chair, swivelled, and looked out of the window across the rooftops of the town. Beyond the clock tower were views to the River Taw. His mind drifted for a moment. He closed his eyes thinking *Oh for a break to go surfing down at Woolacombe and Croyde with Kay.* Doubts started to creep into his mind. *Am I ever going to solve this one? These two? And now with Theo's, three?*

He tapped out a cigarette from its soft packet, offered Dave one, and lit up. He tried not to smoke in the office but in this instance he felt the need. The cool strong flavour of the smouldering tobacco hit the back of his throat and the smoke filled his lungs. A brief moment of silence and peace wrapped around him as he exhaled, forming smoke rings.

'What's up Guv, you look as though someone has just stepped on your grave.'

'I don't know Dave; we are so close but so far away from solving these murders.'

'And we will. Nil Desperunderum and all that.'

'Nil Desperandum, Dave,' he snorted with a half-smile. 'I know, never give up, and we won't. Not until we have the murder or murderers banged to rights.'

Having taken advice from a local solicitor, Adam arranged for two officers from the MET, to go to the P.R.O. The Public Record Office, in Chancery Lane, London, to search their data base of The London Gazette. They were looking for evidence of the publishing of the change of name of both Linda Billings and Major St John Stevens. It would prove to be an onerous task as The Gazette is printed and published every week on a Friday by Her Majesty's Stationary Office and filed at the P.R.O. on the same day without any indexing of content. However, each issue had a regular section on 'Name Changes.'

In the case of Linda Billings, they started from the day she graduated from The London Veterinary College. In the case of Major St John Stevens, they started from the date of his dismissal from the Exeter Diocese.

Linda graduated on the 30$^{th\,of}$ June 1965. After a few days of painstakingly going through each issue, bingo, they found a record of her changing her name by Deed Poll. It was published on Friday 13th August 1965. There it was, her new legal name of Sarah Cooper. Linda had taken her grandmother's family name. They printed off copies of the entries together with their interim report and had them sent by a dispatch rider to Barnstaple H.Q. for Adam's attention.

Major St John Stevens proved to be a much more difficult task. He was dismissed and excommunicated by the Church of England on the 30$^{th\,of}$ March 1960. The search of the database archive was long and thankless, conducted in the bowels of the P.R.O. building. It was airless with no windows. Fortunately for the two officers involved, a secretary took pity on them and provided them with a fan, copious supplies of bottled water, and a mountain of sugary snacks to keep them going. They looked forward to her twice daily visit to break the tedious monotony of their work.

It would take another 377 issues, and a further ten days later to find that there was no trace of him at all. The only pleasing outcome of the search was that six months later, one of the young officers married that same secretary.

As soon as the report arrived, Adam opened the envelope and read the contents. A mixture of emotions came over him. Elated by the news about Sarah Cooper, nee Linda Billings, but deflated that so far, they were no further forward in finding the Major. He immediately took the report to Rick who was in his office having a well-deserved cup of coffee and cake. It was his secretary Daphne's birthday, and as was tradition she had bought cakes for all of the team.

Adam knocked on Rick's open door and walked in.

'Hi Adam, have you had one of Daphne's birthday cakes? They are delicious. What have you got for me, good news I hope.'

'Good and bad Guv, I have the report from the Met.'

'You had better let me have the bad news first.'

'There is no record in the London Gazette of Major Barnaby St John Stevens of ever changing his name legally. At least, not so far. It could take another week at least if they have to search the data base right up to today's date.

'Damn,' said Rick. 'Well, keep them at it, we have plenty of other fish to fry at the moment.'

'He could still be alive, sir, and living under an assumed name.'

'That's true Adam, but we are no further forward, and we are back looking for a needle in a haystack. What's the good news?'

'Sarah Cooper is Linda Billings. She changed her name legally by Deed Poll on the 13$^{th\ of}$ August 1965, so, Sarah Cooper-Clark?'

Rick almost jumped out of his chair. 'No way! Good old Dave, his hunch was right. Well done Adam for sticking at it, that's what real policing is all about.'

Rick called out into the main ops room, 'Dave, get yourself in here. Now!'

Dave got up from his desk, sauntered across the room, and entered Rick's office.

'What have I done now?'

'What have you done Dave? You may well have just cracked

the case of who murdered Derbyshire, that's all. Listen to this,' said Rick gesturing to Adam.

Adam then repeated what he had just reported about Linda Billings.

'Bloody Nora, Guv. It doesn't prove that she did it, but it certainly is suspicious. She has motive in revenge for the murder of her younger sister. As a vet she has access to Ketamine and surgical instruments, so the means. She rides a horse of fourteen hands that is shod with the same type of horseshoe found at the scene of the murder.' Dave was ecstatic! 'All well and good, but it still doesn't prove that she did it. We certainly have enough to question her under caution. Let's get her in tomorrow morning, advise her to have a solicitor present and caution her.'

25

Thursday 3rd October

Dave had arranged for Sarah Cooper-Clarke to come into HQ accompanied by her appointed solicitor at 10.00 a.m. On arrival they were shown into the interview room and offered tea or coffee. Both declined it.

There was also a jug of water and four glasses on the table. Dave helped himself to coffee, shortly joined by Rick. Dave poured him a cup, black as usual, Rick took a sip. *Ergh, canteen instant coffee again,* he thought to himself almost gagging. *I must persuade them to get one of those new Italian Gaggia Expresso machines that they have down in the café in the main square. If the powers to be won't, maybe I can get the CID squad, including my team to have a whip round.*

The interview commenced at 10.15 and the tape recorder was switched on. All parties stated their full name before Rick commenced proceedings.

'Mrs Cooper-Clarke, or should I refer to you by your birth name of Linda Billings?'

Rick's comments took her solicitor by surprise. Sarah never flinched. He gave her the statutory caution.

'You are here today to answer questions under caution in relation to the murder of Mr. James Derbyshire of The Hele Hotel, Ilfracombe. Did you know Mr Derbyshire?'

'Not personally. We had met at the hotel before I left home and went to college in London.'

'That's odd. We have on record that he was interviewed as a suspect of raping you whilst you attended The London Veterinary School.'

'That's something in the past I care to forget. My name is now Sarah Cooper and since marrying Sir Mortimer, Lady Sarah Cooper-Clarke, although I don't use the title.'

'Were you aware that he was intimately involved with your younger sister?'

'Not specifically. Sam had loads of boyfriends, both before and after I left.'

'Did your sister ever confide in you about her relationship with Mr. Derbyshire?'

'No.'

'You knew he was considerably older than her?'

'Yes.'

'How did you feel about that? Angry?'

'Inspector, can we keep the questions to matters of fact, and not speculate?' intervened the solicitor.

This one's on the ball, thought Rick.

'It's OK,' said Mrs Cooper-Clarke. 'I was neither happy nor unhappy, and as I said, Samantha had many boy and men friends.'

'Promiscuous, was she?'

'Maybe, but that doesn't mean she can be taken for granted, abused and murdered,' she retorted.

Who's angry now, thought, Rick.

'Abused? What makes you think that?'

'OK, Sam had a reputation as being 'easy' from a young age. Right since she was at secondary school at about 14 years old I would say. She did write to me now and again when I was in college in London saying this guy or that guy had tried it on, or sometimes when she went with someone, they expected her to perform certain sex acts with which she was uncomfortable.'

'Was she specific as to who these men were? I am assuming they were all men?' Rick had suddenly remembered Faye's words about not discounting girlfriends.

'No, she was not specific as to who, but yes, boys and men.'

'Why did you leave home?'

'I wanted to go to college and train as a vet.'

'Yes, but why so far away? Why London? Isn't there a veterinary college in Exeter where you could be nearer your family? Did you have a falling out with your family, your father in particular?'

Rick could see from her body language that that question struck home. She started to fidget, and her voice wavered.

'No, I did not,' she replied again without conviction. 'I just wanted to get away and make a new start in life.'

'Is that why you changed your name by Deed Poll?'

'Yes, I suppose so,' she said unconvincingly. 'We were all horsing around in the student's bar one evening bemoaning our backgrounds and slagging off our parents, you know the sort of things students get up to.'

'I don't think I do, Mrs Cooper-Clarke.'

'Someone mentioned that their brother, who was a solicitor, had told her sometime how easy it was to change your name legally. Start afresh. No baggage from the past. I thought about it and decided that's what I wanted to do.'

'Why Sarah Cooper?'

'Oh, that's easy. It was my granny's Christian name and her maiden surname.'

'I hear you ride horses, do a bit of show jumping and dressage.'
'Yes. Do you ride inspector?'
'No.'
'I also believe that you have your horse shod at Samsons Smithy where you are also the visiting vet?'
'Yes, that's right. It's an easy ride for me from home up onto the downs. There is an old farm track all the way.'
'So, I believe.'
'What size is your horse?'
'Fourteen hands, but I don't see the significance of your question.'
'I also believe that you have a certain type of horseshoe for your horse.'
'My, my. You are well informed, inspector. That's right, it is one that is more comfortable for the horse, particularly when jumping fences. More expensive of course, but when one must, only the best for my Bessie.'

Rick paused for a moment, purposely looking through his notes to give Sarah the chance to take in what they had been saying. He wanted to let her digest the fact that he knew a great deal about her. She was playing it cool so far, and mostly keeping control of her feelings. He continued:

'Do you have access to Ketamine?'
'Of course I do, it's a standard anaesthetic in veterinary practice.'
'Have you lost any phials lately?'
'Now you come to mention it, a whole batch of five phials did go missing recently.'
'Did you report it to the police? It is after all used as a recreational drug by some people.'
'No, I didn't see the point. All that aggravation! At first I

thought it was a mix up with the pharmaceutical company that supplies it. Then as time moved on, I suppose I couldn't be bothered. Some kids probably stole it, it's all the rage to take in the clubs in Barnstable. A small dose just gives you a high, your senses become addled, and you lose all inhibitions.'

'You couldn't be bothered?' said Rick rather sarcastically. 'Did you murder Mr Derbyshire?'

'Don't be so ridiculous. I am a well-respected member of the local society. Why on earth would I want to do that?'

'Revenge, Mrs Cooper-Clarke, revenge.'

With that Rick decided that he had no more questions to ask at this stage of his enquiry. He only had motive, opportunity, and plenty of circumstantial evidence but he could not prove intent. He had no option but to let her go and not charge her with Jim Derbyshire's murder.

Sarah Cooper-Clarke was relieved but perturbed at the amount of circumstantial evidence the police had gathered. She needed time to think. *I need to stop this once and for all. It's not my fault that Daddy continued to abuse Samantha after I left. It's not my fault that those perverts Derbyshire and Fairbrother took advantage of her.*

In the Bible Jeremiah 11.20 said ,
But, O Lord of hosts,
Who judges righteously,
Who tries the feelings and the heart,
Let me see Your vengeance on them,
For You have I committed my cause.

Vengeance is mine said the Lord

After she had left the building with her solicitor, Rick and Dave played back the interview tape.

'There,' said Dave, switching the tape off, 'This part where you questioned her about Samantha's promiscuity and asked her if she was angry. She lost her cool for a moment, suggesting a possible motive for revenge.'

'Yeah, I agree with you.'

'And here,' continued Dave as he scrolled the tape forward. 'Where you put to her the question of whether she had a falling out with her father, Sam Billings. Her reply was unconvincing.'

'Spot on again Dave. I would say we have our prime suspect for Derbyshire's murder just where we need her at the moment.'

'Let's start flushing out the others in the frame and see what we come up with. It pains me to say it, but Jonathon Dukes comes to mind again as the Madrigal Renaissance Brewery is just a bit further on up the bridle path from the Smithy, but as far as we know, he doesn't ride a horse.'

'No, but his brother Justin does,' Dave replied.

'Now there's an interesting thought. We haven't considered Justin in any of our scenarios. Could he really be mixed up in all this?'

'You remember when we first went to see them at the brewery? Justin got quite hot under the collar, and he accused Sam Billings of jealousy, saying Sam had accused him of underpaying for the assets of the failed Wizard's Cauldron Brewery. He also only has a partial alibi for the night of the murder. We know that he left the Hele Bay Hotel at around 11.00 p.m but old Chugg does not have any knowledge of the time of his return to the brewery.'

'Yeah, but that alone doesn't seem to give cause enough to be a party to Samantha's murder.'

'What if he is the warlock?'

'Bit of a long shot, Dave.'

'Stranger things have happened Guv. You know he has never married?'

'I can't see what that has got to do with it.'

'Well, you know my warped mind. What if he gets his kicks out of debasing promiscuous young women?'

'You really are a conundrum sometimes. Anyone else but me might consider you to be a bit of a pervert. However, if you think there may be something in it, have a poke around and see if you come up with anything.'

Freddie Fairbrother had gone to ground ever since the incident in the boxing club's changing room. He was holed up in his father's office at the Tumbling Dice Casino, not that he thought that even his father could get him out of this one. As he downed another Jack Daniels, he thought *that bloody fool Tiny Foreman, he never did know his own strength. He won't be able to keep his mouth shut once they collar him, as surely they will in next to no time. A copper, worse a young CID detective.* He downed another and before he knew it had consumed half the bottle.

He felt the whole world on his shoulders, and blamed Jim Derbyshire for introducing him to the cauldron. He never really believed in voodoo, it was just another fantasy as far as he was concerned, an escapism from the persistent feeling of emptiness, unhappiness, and hopelessness that had become a regular part of his day.

At the time, he felt there was no more pleasure or joy in

life. His boxing career and dreams were over. His self-esteem shattered by Samantha Billings' rejection. He became confused over his sexuality and felt revolted and depraved after he had got drunk and had a one-night stand with a lad he didn't even know the name of. He just met him in a bar. He couldn't even remember which bar.

Once he was in the cauldron, there was no going back. Initially it was a revelation as far as he was concerned. He felt wanted, part of a brotherhood. It was exciting, thrilling. As part of his initiation as one of the warlock's acolytes he had to prove himself by bringing a young promiscuous girl to the ceremony that fateful night.

He never thought that Samantha would lose her life that night. He had no idea that one of the cauldron would be in such a trance that he would chop her hand off, although he subsequently suspected that the warlock was only too aware of what was going to happen. He thought it would be like previous times, where they picked up promiscuous girls down at the clubs and pubs, spiked their drink with roofies and enticed them to go up the Head at night to 'party.' Once they were up there, the cauldron would ravage them, teach them a lesson, and they were left too traumatised to go to the police.

In any case they were so drugged up they would find it difficult to even remember where it happened let alone identify anyone involved. The girls were usually 'dumped' somewhere up on Exmoor.

That night he had arranged for a fellow celebrant to take him to Hele Bay where he knew that Samantha was working an evening shift in the Hotel. He waited under cover of darkness and observed her making love to Jonathon. Already high on marijuana his revulsion and appetite for revenge on Samantha grew.

After Jonathon left her on the beach he sauntered over making some excuse that he had been drinking with a friend up at the Hotel Bar and had strolled down to the beach to take in the sea air. After sharing another spliff of marijuana with her, followed by a couple of Fierce Little Heart pills, one thing lead to another and he persuaded Samantha for 'old times sake' to climb up the Head to their old secret place for sex.

As he sat in his Dad's office he worked his way through the remaining half of the bottle of Jack Daniels, becoming increasingly more morose and morbid. His mind was in turmoil. *It's only a matter of time before McCarthy comes for me. At best I'll get fifteen years for aiding and abetting, at worst a minimum of twenty for murder. I can't do that, it would be worse than hell, worse than my miserable life at present.*

26

Friday 4th

The day started off quietly. Rick began to think that the investigation was heading for the doldrums, nothing was happening. How wrong he could be.

Dave had just finished a phone call when he came into Rick's office looking contrite.

'Don't tell me you have something on Justin Dukes.'

'I couldn't have been more wrong, Guv. You would just not believe it if it didn't come from me,' Dave replied as though he was the fountain of all knowledge.

'Go on then Einstein. Hit me with it,' he said sitting back in his chair.

'He appears to be whiter than white, very much the country squire, a devout catholic and pillar of society. He is chairman of the regional CAMRA organisation, a member of the Round Table and a magistrate of all things. He is engaged to Lord and Lady Blandy's daughter, Fiona, and is an active supporter of her charity for distressed and abused women.

Moreover, he rides a 16 hand horse, a big bugger by all accounts, with a totally different compound of horse shoes to that found up at Haggington Hill. Apparently he rides in point to point cross country races.'

'You have got to be kidding me?'

'No, my sources are impeccable.'

'That changes everything. I suppose he could still be our

warlock, but what motive does he have for either murder? Other than plain conjecture, we have nothing to suggest that Justin Dukes participated in either murder. I propose we eliminate him from our enquiries, at least for now, and concentrate on the leads that with already have.'

Rick continued, 'How are Kay and Ethan getting on examining the dumbbell from the boxing club?'

'Kay has matched the blood to that of Theo's and Ethan has managed to lift a couple of fingerprints which are running through the data base. There seems no doubt that it is the murder weapon.'

'Ok, let me know if Ethan comes up with a name.'

Later that morning Ethan appeared having been hard at it in the forensics lab.

'Good morning. Have you got something for us?' asked Rick.

'Two sets of prints on the dumbbell. John Foreman's and Dixie Davis.'

'Thanks. Given that Foreman openly admits to finding the body and Davis was in his office at the time, my money's on Foreman as Theo's killer. We may not get him on a murder charge, but we surely will get him on manslaughter.'

Dave, go and arrest him and take Faye with you. Don't ask me why, but it might give her some sort of satisfaction, if not closure. Also get Sergeant Jones from traffic to meet you there. Tiny Foreman might put up a fight.

Whilst Dave was away, P.C. Olivia McJade, a police cadet seconded to the team for work experience, drew Rick's attention. She had been given the task of interviewing Andrew Martin, the Mayor, by Dave.

'Hello Olivia, how are you getting on being at the forefront of a murder enquiry? Does it encourage you to think of a career in CID?'

Olivia was nervous and in awe of Rick, such was his reputation. She had first come across him, not that he would have noticed her, on the police cadet training course where Rick, or Detective Inspector Richard McCarthy as he was introduced to the audience, gave a lecture entitled 'Modern Day Murder Enquiries – Always Expect the Unexpected' and she had found it riveting.

'Good morning, sir,' she replied, 'I am loving it, if I am allowed to say that.'

'Loving is good, anything else?'

'It's a real eye opener sir, the pressure, the pace, the twists, and turns. I am amazed at the capability of the team, the ability to think outside of the box and not just accept the obvious.'

'Do you think it is for you? Are you up for it?'

'Oh yes sir, the first opportunity I get.'

'Well, you have a long way to go, let's see what you are capable of.'

Olivia proceeded to report on her interview with Mayor Martin.

'As luck would have it sir, I managed to get an interview with the Mayor early yesterday evening. He gave me five minutes before having to leave for a council meeting.'

'Anything interesting?'

'I can see why he became the Mayor. He has charisma, and I would say he was a borderline narcissist in as much he was full of himself. That may have been because he considered me just a 'university hack.'' She smiled, having enjoyed playing the role. She had really wanted to go on the stage, or at least be involved with the theatre in some way, but she was very bright and her parents persuaded her to pursue a career that actually paid a regular wage.

'Most of what he had to say was already in the public domain and not very newsworthy, but he was keen to tell me of his local charity work and his involvement organising historical re-enactments throughout the southwest. I pressed him as to whether any of these events involved beheading. One of the most prominent that he was keen to talk about was the capture and execution of Sir Thomas St Leger at Exeter Castle. on the 13 November 1483. St. Leger had faithfully served Edward IV in both a military and administrative capacity for years.

Edward IV died suddenly on 9 April 1483, leaving behind a twelve-year-old son, Edward V, who was Sir Thomas's nephew by marriage. However, Richard III ascended the throne not Edward V.'

Rick sat back in his chair, smiling, enjoying the history lesson. He liked history and was impressed by this young lady. Olivia, who was still standing, took a deep breath and continued.

'St Leger had been unshakably faithful to Edward IV and, like many others that rebelled against Richard III, was distressed at Edward V having disappeared from sight after having been deprived of his crown. The rebellion failed, leading to St Ledger's capture and demise. He was beheaded without trial.'

Rick allowed Olivia's enthusiasm to get the better of her with such a long description of the fate of Sir Thomas St Ledger. Besides, he never knew the full story of St Ledger's demise and was interested.

'The Mayor even showed me a replica of the axe that would have been used. That's when it hit me.'

'It hit you?' said Rick, faking concern.

'No, not the axe, sir,' Olivia laughed. 'What if Samantha Billings' hand had been chopped off by an axe, not a machete or a meat cleaver? Maybe even the axe he showed me? One thing the team have taught me is to think out of the box. Well, with all the circumstantial evidence surrounding Jonathon Dukes and the voodoo Gods, has our thinking been clouded by the thought of Ogun's machete being the weapon?'

'How old are you, Olivia?'

Olivia was a bit taken aback by Rick's question.

'Eighteen, sir.'

'So, you qualify as a fully-fledged PC this year?'

'Yes, sir.'

'As soon as you have done your initial compulsory time on the beat, six months I think it is, put in for a transfer to CID and I will back your application.'

Olivia couldn't believe what Rick was saying.

'Yes, sir, thank you sir,' she said blushing, her eyes filling with tears. 'Was my interview with the mayor and my report, OK then?'

'Outstanding. I can't say at this stage whether what you have found out is relevant to our investigation, but it has certainly given me food for thought.'

'Thank you, sir, ' almost curtsying as if he war royalty.

Olivia went off proud as a peacock. She had no doubt in her mind that CID is the career that she wanted. She thought to herself *Mum and Dad will be proud. If I end up anywhere near as good as Detective Inspector McCarthy I'll feel immensely fulfilled.*

Dave returned later that morning slightly bruised and battered sporting a cut lip and a black eye.

'Oh Dave, sorry mate, but someone has to do it.' said Rick smiling and trying hard not to laugh.

'You should've seen the other guy.'

'I take it Tiny Foreman resisted but is now safely in custody charged with the murder of Theo?'

'Yeah, you were right, he did resist arrest. It took all of Rory Jones and me to subdue him. We allowed Faye one swipe after he was cuffed, I think she found it kind of cathartic if that's the right word.'

'That'll do Dave, is she OK?'

'Yes, she's good, despite her young age and being a bit of a titch, but she is already mentally tough. I gather she is also doing some martial arts and self-defence training courses. She'll go far, that's for sure.'

'Another one of your proteges has given me the run down on her interview with Martin, the mayor.'

'Oh yes? Has Olivia found out anything interesting?'

'Get her to go through her report with you, but the most significant revelation was that when he was bragging about the re-enactment events that he puts on, he showed her a replica axe that they use for beheadings. She was one step ahead of me by suggesting that we may have been blindsided by all the voodoo connections to think that it must have been a machete that was used to cut off Samantha's hand. What if it was a medieval style axe, moreover the axe that Mayor Martin showed her?'

'Blimey Guv, it's almost frightening. She is only eighteen, another one destined for a career in CID.'

'Don't fret Dave, I am a great believer in having talent,

particularly young talent working for me. They add a different perspective and drive you on. Their success is our success. Keep them coming, that's what I say.'

Dave left Rick's office to go over to see Olivia. Matt knocked and came in; he had information on the search for Major Barnaby St John Stevens, the disgraced army chaplain who went off the radar in 1960. Unlike the search for Sarah Cooper-Clarke, the search through the PRO for him yielded nothing regarding a possible change of name by deed poll. Matt still believed that he must have moved on under an assumed name. His tenacity had finally paid off.

'Matt. How is another one of my rising stars? I'm having a very encouraging morning, Come on in.'

'Good morning, Guv, although it's a bit late for that. I've been waiting to see you.'

'I know, it's been a busy morning too. Well, you're here now, so what can I do for you?'

'Major St John Stevens, Guv.'

'I thought we had put him on the back burner as there has been no sign of him since 1960?'

'He has turned up in Plymouth, arrested by the local plod for an act of indecency, going by an assumed name of Captain Roger Jennings DSO. He has been working as a lay preacher at St John The Evangelist church, in and among the soup kitchens and men's hostels for distressed seaman. The Plymouth boys ran a check on him and found that a Captain Roger Jennings had died in Exeter in 1959.'

'How on earth did they trace him back to these parts and his real name?'

'They ran his photo by the Exeter diocese, who recognised

him. They told them that he was a man of interest to us in a murder enquiry, and they are holding him in custody in Plymouth for 48 hrs.'

'Right, off you go then. Go and interview him. I'll have a word with my counterpart at Plymouth to arrange for a CID sergeant to accompany you at the interview, but it's your shout. Draw some money from the cashier in case you have to stay overnight. And well done.'

27

Saturday 5th

Matt caught the early morning 6.30a.m. train from Barnstable to Exeter and then caught the 7.15a.m. Penzance bound express train to Plymouth. The section from Exeter to Plymouth was part of the Great West Railway's London to Penzance Cornish Riviera route. The train on that day was pulled by the King George V steam locomotive in its immaculate, shining green livery. It was one of the last steam trains running before the changeover to diesel locomotives.

It was not long after sunrise that the train pulled into Exeter Station. The sight and sound of it as it rounded the northern goods yard bend, with smoke billowing from the chimney, steam hissing out of the cylinders as the brakes were applied, and the rising sun reflecting off of the brass livery was a sight to be behold. It looked like a giant behemoth appearing out of the early morning mist.

On the journey Matt kept going through his notes on Major St John Stevens and working out how he was going to approach the interview. He constantly reminded himself that it was a big call for the Guv to trust him on this, and he didn't want to screw it up.

The train arrived on time at 8.30 allowing Matt plenty of time to get a taxi to Plymouth Police H.Q. He reported promptly to Sergeant Jack Hingham at 9.00 a.m.

'Well Detective Constable Matt Smith, if your detecting abilities are as good as your time keeping then I am well impressed.'

'Good morning, sergeant. Our governor, D.I. McCarthy believes that good timekeeping and dress code are part and parcel of good detection. It's all in the mind apparently.'

'Well, his reputation goes before him so who am I to argue. Come on, let's get you settled with a cup of tea or coffee. Have you had any breakfast?'

'That's kind of you but I managed to get a bacon roll in the buffet car on the train.'

Sergeant Hingham led Matt off to the CID room and introduced him to the team as one of Rick's proteges. They sat down over a cup of coffee and discussed what each other knew about Major St John Stevens.

'Quite a character then our Major St John Stevens, Matt. He may be of the other persuasion, attracted to young men but from what I've seen and found out about his activities since he's been in Plymouth, I would hardly put him into the murderer category. It's your interview, I'll just be in there as a witness but also to put you right if you make a faux par.'

'Thanks serg, I do appreciate it. This is my first big case as part of the murder squad.'

'Please call me Jack.'

'Thanks Jack, I can't deny that I am a little bit nervous.'

The interview commenced at 10.11.a.m and the Major had elected just to have the duty solicitor representing him. Matt commenced the interview by asking him to confirm his full name. St John Stevens glanced at his solicitor who nodded, following which he confirmed that he was Major Barnaby St John Stevens but had been living under the alias of Captain

Roger Wilkins since 1960.

'Can you tell me why you decided to assume a new name and how you came to adopt Captain Wilkin's name?'

'It wasn't difficult. I'm sure that you know from your records that I was ex-communicated by the Exeter diocese in 1960 following a case of importuning young men when I was acting as a supply vicar. I was full of remorse and wanted a new start in life.'

Matt was surprised but pleased that the major was not denying who he was and why he changed his name and moved to Plymouth.

'Captain Wilkins was in the same regiment as me, and I remembered his tragic early death from cancer in early 1960. Having lived for many years in a cash only society, I just opened a post office account in his name. My own personal needs are limited, and I have led a good, honest Christian life since then, doing charitable work, helping the homeless by serving in a soup kitchen and giving comfort and solace to those in need in the men's shelter.'

'That sounds all well and good, but here we are again with you being accused of an act of indecency with one of those young men.'

'But it was consensual,' the major retorted.

'That may well be, but it is still against the law. I would now like to turn to your life since you left Barnstable. Have you been back since?'

The Major started to get anxious and started to fidget with one thigh shaking up and down.

'No, why would I?'

'What about your old friends, let me say of similar persuasion.'

'Why don't you just say it detective, you mean gay friends, homosexuals.'

'Well, if you must put it like that, yes.'

'No. I told you. I moved to start a new life. I have been chaste ever since, until now that is when I lapsed because a young man came onto me in the hostel.'

'Ok, let's move on. I believe that you purchased a black hooded cloak from Eve and Ravenscroft.'

'Yes, I don't see how that is relevant, but I still have it. It was well made and is of good quality. It keeps out the winter chill as I make the rounds of the soup kitchens giving respite to the homeless,'

'Have you any objections if I take a look at that cloak Major?'

'No of course not.'

'Then you have no objection if I take it away for forensic examination?'

The Major then looked again at his solicitor who suggested a break might be in order. Matt looked at Jack who indicated that was quite in order and asked the Major and his solicitors if they would like a cup of tea or coffee. The interview was temporarily suspended at 10.20 and Matt and Jack left the interview room.

In their absence, over cups of tea, the solicitor advised the Major that if he refused the request to take away his cloak, they, the police, would only go to a Magistrate and get a court order, so he might as well cooperate. Matt discussed the interview so far with Jack.

'You're doing well Matt; I can see where you are coming from. Keep it up, he may have more to say.'

The interview reconvened at 10.30. The duty solicitor

opened up by saying that his client had no objection to handing over his cloak for forensic tests. He had nothing to hide and wanted it to be noted that he was being fully cooperative with your enquiries.

'Duly noted,' intervened Sergeant Hingham.

Matt continued. 'Are you still a practising Christian, Major?'

'If you mean, do I still believe in upholding Christian values, then I suppose I am.'

'That's not what I asked, do you worship God?'

'There are many Gods, detective constable.'

This is very interesting, thought Matt.

'Have you ever been a member of a voodoo cauldron practicing dark arts and the worship of Voudun at various sites in North Deven?'

'This is preposterous! I don't know what you're talking about. Besides why is it of your concern what religion I believe in?'

'I am talking about a murder Major, a murder most heinous carried out during the debasing of a young woman. It has all the signs of it being carried out by a voodoo cauldron.'

'As I told you detective, I only have an interest in young men, not young women.'

Matt decided that he was not going to get anything further out of the Major, so he terminated the interview.

'Does that mean I am to be released?' asked the Major.

Sergeant Hingham replied, 'It most certainly does not Major. You will be charged with the crime of gross indecency under the Sexual Offences Act of 1956.'

Despite the Major's agreement to hand over the black cloak, Matt decided not to take any chance of him retracting that statement, or saying it was made under duress, and applied for an emergency search warrant of the Major's home.

The search warrant arrived within the hour. The Major's home turned out to be a dingy rented flat near the Devonport Dockyard. Several others in the same block were occupied by known drug pushers and prostitutes. He naively asked Jack why they weren't being arrested and prosecuted, to which he replied that drugs and prostitution were rife in the area, and they would only be replaced by others in a jiffy. It was better to keep them under observation. Besides, some were police informers.

On searching the flat they found more than they were looking for. In a bedroom wardrobe they found the black cloak. Matt was disappointed, it was not torn, and the original label was intact. Jack then pulled out an old leather suitcase from under the bed. Upon opening it, low and behold there was a white hooded cloak emblazoned with the golden image of Bondye on the back.

Matt was taken aback, and he tried to assimilate in his mind what that meant. *So, he is a member of a voodoo cauldron, but probably not the warlock. It doesn't prove that it is the same cauldron that we're investigating, and even if it is, it doesn't prove at this stage that he was present on the night Samantha was murdered.*

They also found a clipped return train ticket form Plymouth to Barnstable dated for 26th and 28th September in the pocket of a coat hanging behind the bedroom door.

'By the look on your face I take it these are both highly relevant to your enquiries, Matt?' commented the sergeant.

'You bet,' replied Matt. 'Let's get the cloaks and the train ticket bagged up as evidence and hot foot it back to H.Q. When we get back, I'll arrest the Major for aiding and abetting the murder of Samantha Billings! I'll require an escort to take both he and I back to Barnstaple Police H.Q, together with the bagged evidence.'

'No problem, I'll see if my boss can spare me to take you. Meanwhile let me buy you a splendid lunch. You must be starving by now.'

On arrival back at Plymouth Police H.Q, Matt couldn't wait to phone Rick.

'Detective Inspector McCarthy.'

'It's Matt, Guv.'

'Good afternoon Matt, you must have started out early. Any news?'

Matt could hardly disguise his delight in reporting back, 'You will not believe it.'

'Go on, get it out, nothing surprises me in this case anymore.'

'I've interviewed the Major and will bring back a copy of the tape and a typed transcript.'

'Good, well done.'

'That's not all, on searching his flat we found a black hooded cloak.'

Rick's ears pricked up and he sat bolt upright.

'I doesn't have a tear and the original label is intact. It also doesn't have anything emblazoned on its back. I have brought it back for forensics to take a look.'

Rick was momentarily disappointed. He thought that they might have made the breakthrough they desperately wanted.

'However, we also found a white hooded cloak with Bondye emblazoned in gold on its back, and a clipped return train ticket from Plymouth to Barnstable dated 26th and 28th September.'

Matt was right, Rick could hardly believe what he was

hearing. 'Jesus, Matt, what a result, get in here, son.'

'I'm being brought back to Barnstable in a squad car by Sergeant Jack Hingham who has assisted me all the way on this. We are bringing the Major with us, who I have charged with aiding and abetting murder at this stage, and we'll bring the bagged evidence.'

'Marvellous, when do you think you'll get back?'

'Well, Sergeant Hingham is treating me to lunch whilst the paperwork is sorted out by his custody sergeant, then we'll be on our way. I suppose it'll be quite late, maybe around 5.30.'

'Don't worry. Dave and I'll be here. You go and have a good lunch, you deserve it.'

'Thanks Guv, see you later then.'

Rick put the phone down and called out from his desk,

'Dave, Dave, get yourself in here, Matt has just called in.' Rick proceeded to update Dave on the main points of the call.

Matt and Sergeant Hingham duly arrived at 5.40 p.m. The Major was booked in, and his fingerprints taken by the custody sergeant. The two bagged cloaks and the railway ticket were sent to forensics together with the Major's prints for analysis, with the Code A1, signifying that their results were needed a.s.a.p.

Matt and Jack joined Rick and Dave in Rick's office. As they walked into the outer operations room they were clapped in, much to the embarrassment of Matt.

'Sit yourselves down, this calls for a celebration,' said Rick as he pulled out a bottle of Jack Daniels from his desk drawer and four shot glasses. As he poured the drinks, he thanked Sergeant Hingham for all his help and support of Matt in Plymouth.

'No bother sir, but if it's OK with you, please call me Jack. You have a good one in Matt. Are all of your team as tenacious?'

'Thanks' Jack. I am very fortunate to have, in my eyes, the best of the best at all levels in the team.'

'No wonder you get the results that you do. You are getting quite a reputation amongst the south-west forces.'

'Enough of self-congratulations, let's get down to talking about what you have found out. I'll read the full transcript of the interview later, and we'll have to wait for the forensic report before we can interview him again.'

Matt and Jack informed them of the assailant points of their interview with the Major.

Matt drew Rick's attention to the question on religion that he put to the Major. I asked him, 'Are you still a practising Christian, Major?' to which he replied, 'If you mean, do I still believe in upholding Christian values, then I suppose I am.'

I then said to him, 'That's not what I asked. I meant do you worship God? which drew the response of, 'There are many Gods detective constable.'

'From that point on he was extremely nervous although he did readily agree to hand over the black cloak for forensic analysis. I became suspicious of this and went for an emergency search warrant of his home. It looks like it may have paid off.'

At that point Adam knocked and was beckoned in. 'Jack, let me introduce you to another one of Dave's proteges, Adam.'

'Pleased to meet you, Adam.'

'And you too Sergeant.'

Adam then gave Rick the message from forensics:

'They appreciate it is an A1 request Guv, but they need a bit more time to compare the results with other evidence found up on the Head. They will be ready first thing in the morning.'

'OK Adam, thanks.'

'The Head? enquired Jack, smiling.'

'Hillsborough Head, the scene of the crime,' piped up Dave.

Gentlemen, may I suggest that we retire to the social club for a pint or two and then go on to The Taj Mahal for a curry afterwards. We can reconvene at, say, 8.00a.m.' They all started to get up to leave.

'Jack, Matt will book you into a hotel or you can stay with him overnight if he doesn't mind.'

'That's fine by me,' said Matt.

It was Dave's turn to smile. Any excuse for a Ruby. Rick gave Kay a quick phone call to put her in the picture and to say that he would be late home. After they'd enjoyed a relaxed evening, drinking, eating, and talking about anything else but the murder case, the manager at the Taj Mahal arranged for two taxis to take them home. The first dropped Rick off, then Dave, who would go back to the Taj in the morning and collect the Dart before picking Rick up at 7.45. The second took Matt and Jack back to Matt's flat from where they could easily walk to H.Q.

When Rick got home Kay was already in bed, reading. She liked a good book and was currently reading Graham Green's novel, The Comedians. As Rick walked into the bedroom Kay looked up from their bed, pulled a face in jest and said,

'Hello gorgeous, have you had a good time? You smell of a mixture of Camel cigarette smoke and madras curry.'

'Sorry babe, I'll have quick shower and brush my teeth, then join you,'

'I don't suppose that will do you much good. The smell of curry will be coming out of your pores all night long. Do you really think curry houses will catch on?'

'They may be a new phenomenon down here in Barnstable, but they have been springing up in Birmingham and London for some time now. In fact, the very first one in London was Veeraswamy in 1949 would you believe.'

'How on earth do you know that.'

Rick laughed, 'There's a potted history of curry in the UK up on the wall in the Taj Mahal.'

'Huh, there's me thinking is there nothing you don't know? Come on, hurry up and get into bed. I have an early start in the morning.'

28

Sunday 6th

There was no chance of a lie-in. Sunday was just another day for a D.I. and his team on a murder case. As per usual, Dave picked Rick up on time at 7.45 and they were in the office by 8.00. Matt and Jack were not far behind them. Mugs of strong coffee from the newly introduced cafetiere in the kitchenet and Colombian arabica ground coffee was the first order of the day, quickly followed by the fresh jam doughnuts that Matt had bought on the way in. The combination not only settled their stomachs but also served to get their adrenaline flowing for the task ahead.

The first task was to review the forensic evidence on the two cloaks belonging to Major St John Stevens. The black cloak yielded nothing. The white cloak was an entirely different matter. As well as the obvious link to Voodooism with the golden image of Bondye embroidered on the back, there were traces of various herbs and drugs that were also found up on Hillsborough Head. There were semen stains on the front of the cloak and traces of pubic hair matched to that of Samantha Billings. So much for the Major's claim that his only interest was in young men, not young women.

The return train ticket had the Major's fingerprints on it and was verified as being used by the on-board ticket collectors having clipped it.

'Well gentlemen, it looks as though we have the Major

banged to rights as to having at least been at the scene of crime in the case of the murder of Samantha Billings. What we have to do now is to interview the Major under caution and present him with the forensics. We need to try and get a confession out of him. In doing so I'll try to elicit who else was involved, and in particular the name of the warlock.'

'Thank you Matt, and you too Jack. Dave and I will take it from here.' With that Matt and Jack got up to leave. Jack shook hands with both Rick and Dave and they left the office.

The interview started at 10.00.am. This time the Major was accompanied by his own appointed solicitor, and Rick was accompanied by Dave. After going through the preliminaries of identification, Rick commenced proceedings.

'Major St John Stevens you are under arrest for aiding and abetting the murder of Miss Samantha Billings on the night of 27th September 1967 on or around 12.00 midnight. You do not have to say anything, but it may harm your defence if you do not mention, when questioned, something which you later rely on in court. Anything you do say may be given in evidence. Do you understand?'

'I do.'

'Major, we have forensic evidence obtained from the white cloak found at your home address in Plymouth that links you to the murder of a young woman up on Hillsborough Head, Ilfracombe. Do you deny that you were there on the night of the 27th September.

'I do.'

'We also found a used railway ticket at your home for a return journey from Plymouth to Barnstaple. The outgoing journey was on the 26th and the return on the 28th September.

Your fingerprints have been identified on that ticket. Do you confirm that it was you who used that ticket.'

'I do.'

'Would you care to tell us the purpose of your visit to Barnstable?'

'It was to visit an old friend.'

'And who was that old friend. Can he corroborate you visiting him?'

'It was Jim Derbyshire, and no, I believe that he is unfortunately no longer with us on this earth.'

How convenient, thought Rick.

'Let us return to the white cloak. It is emblazoned with an embroidered golden image of the Voudun God, Bondye. Do you deny worshipping voodoo and being a member of a voodoo cauldron?'

'No.'

'Are you aware that Mr. Derbyshire was not only a member, but an acolyte of the North Devon Voodoo cauldron?'

'Yes.'

'Oh, come now Major, are you really expecting us to believe that you were not present when the North Devon cauldron met up on Hillsborough Head on the night of the 27th?'

The Major's solicitor intervened on behalf of his client and suggested an interval. The interview reconvened after 10 minutes. Upon recommencement the Major's solicitor said, 'Following advice, my client wishes to retract his answer as to whether he was up on Hillsborough Head on the night of the 27th September. He wishes to fully co-operate with your enquiry and seek clemency from the court.'

'I can offer your client no assurances that the judge will

confer a reduced sentence, but if he co-operates leading to further arrests, I will make such a recommendation to the crown prosecution.'

'Thank you, inspector. Would you care to put that question to him again?'

'Major, we have forensic evidence obtained from the white cloak found at your home address in Plymouth linking you to the murder site upon Hillsborough Head. Do you deny that you were there on the night of the 27th September?'

'I do not.'

'For the purpose of clarity and for the record. Were you up on Hillsborough Head on the night of 27th September?'

'I was.'

'Whilst there, did you participate in a ceremony conducted by The North Devon Voodoo cauldron?'

'I did.'

'Did you participate in the raping of Samantha Billings?'

'I did.'

'Did you administer any drugs or potions to her?'

'I did not.'

'Were you aware that such drugs and potions were administered to her?'

'Yes.'

'By whom?'

'The warlock.'

'Can you tell us who the warlock is?'

'I am afraid I cannot. His name is only known to his two acolytes. At ceremonies he wears a mask to protect his identity.'

'And who might his two acolytes be?'

'Jim Derbyshire and Freddie Fairbrother.'

At last, thought Rick, *confirmation that Freddie Fairbrother is indeed the second acolyte.*

'Were you present when Miss Billings' hand was severed?'

'I was, but I had no knowledge that it was about to happen.'

'Go on.'

'I along with the rest of the celebrants, perhaps with the exception of the warlock, were shocked and momentarily stunned by what happened.'

'Who carried it out?'

'I don't know, it was one of the celebrants.'

'What weapon was used?'

'That I do know, it was a large, long handled axe.'

There we have it, thought Rick, *the murder weapon was an axe.*

'Returning to the warlock, surely you must have had some conversation with Jim Derbyshire as to who the warlock is?'

'Naturally, I had asked him on many occasions, but he was sworn to secrecy and feared for his life should he ever divulge who it was. The most I got out of him was that he was a man of high office in the community.'

That same refence keeps coming up time and again, thought Rick.

Rick terminated the interview at 11.00. a.m. Major St John Stevens was led away to the custody cell pending transfer to Exeter jail to await trial. Rick was as certain as he could be that any bail application would be denied.

After the interview Rick and Dave discussed their observations.

'What do we conclude, Dave?'

'One, Major St John Stevens was present at the murder scene.

Two, he took part in the raping of Samantha Billings.

Three, Jim Derbyshire and Freddie Fairbrother are the two acolytes and they were both also present at the time of the murder.

Four, the murder weapon was a large, long handled axe.'

Five. Other than the warlock, the two acolytes and the person that swung the axe, the remaining celebrants had no knowledge of the intended severing of Samantha's hand.

Six, confirmation that The warlock is someone holding high office in the community.'

'That's about it, Dave. We still don't know who the warlock is, nor do we know who swung the axe that severed Samantha's hand, but we do now know that Freddie Fairbrother was there. Was he the one that met Samantha on Hele Bay beach that night and persuaded her to go up the footpath from the beach to the top of Hillsborough Head? Did he give her LSD on that climb? It's time we brough him in for questioning.'

It was not long after that, just as Rick was about to catch up with the rest of the team, when the phone call that he never wanted to receive came in. The cleaners at the Tumbling Dice Casino, owned by Freddie Fairbrother's father, had discovered a body in the main office.

It was Freddie Fairbrother.

29

The Tumbling Dice casino was located on the seafront at Saunton Sands. Its prominent position was to attract the holiday makers from all along the coast, from Saunton Sands, Croyde and Woolacombe up to Ilfracombe, together with wealthy business clients from Barnstable. The gaming room covered the whole of the first floor of a former Victorian hotel with tinted windows offering a panoramic view of the beach and coastline. The ground floor was a bar and grill room and the second and third floors were bedrooms for late night punters and seasoned gamblers who came from afar to play the machines and tables over a longer stay.

The whole building refurbishment had been architecturally designed to attract clients to walk in, to wine and dine them if preferred, but most importantly, to attract them into the gaming room and keep them there for as long as possible, gambling. The various games consisted of a variety of slot machines, some of which paid out very large jackpots, roulette, blackjack, and dice. The classy entrance was finished in marble, adorned atop with a pair of tumbling dice lit up in neon lights. Its objective was to subliminally send a message to guests that the inside was classy but comfy and inviting. Nothing points out a casino better than a dazzling sign and a colourful display of lights.

The casino space itself covered a wide area, with many

gaming platforms laid out in such a way that it took a considerable amount of time to learn your way around the room. The more you wandered inside the more you got distracted and tempted to try different games. It was all based on tried and tested gambling psychology.

The cleaners at the club had finished cleaning the gaming room, bar, cloakroom, and toilets at the casino. They had opened the door of Mr Fairbrother senior's office, which they only cleaned once a week, on a Sunday. There lying on the floor in a pool of blood was a body. As they approached, they recognised the person immediately as Mr Fairbrother's son, Freddie.

The paramedics who answered the 999 emergency call had pronounced him dead on the scene. In the light of what they found the uniformed police officers who also answered the called reported a suspicious death.

In the early hours, the night before last, Freddie had reached the end of his tether. He swigged down the last of a bottle of gin with a handful of purple hearts and temazepam tablets. In the half light, sprawled on the office floor, the last thing he saw was someone dressed in a white cloak, looking down on him. Speaking incoherently, he mumbled, 'Is that you Sam? I'm so sorry, I never knew, I swear I never knew.'

'You snivelling bastard, you're no better than the rest of them. They are all sadists and rapists, the lot of them. Derbyshire got what he had coming to him. He raped Linda and took advantage of Samantha. You're no better, coming onto Sam until she couldn't say 'No.' You think you can cheat the wrath of God? Well, you are very much mistaken.'

Unaware of whether Freddie had just passed out or had in fact died in front them, it mattered not. The assailant proceeded to turn him over onto his back and remove his trousers and underpants, exposing him like a new-born baby.

Taking the small leather pouch from their pocket, a phial of Ketamine fell to the floor. It wasn't needed, Freddie was comatose. They unzipped the pouch and selected a scalpel from the mobile surgical set and set about castrating him. There was no hesitation, one swift and determined continuous cut was enough to remove his penis and testicles in one go. It was an 'operation' that they had performed before.

Before they left, they stuffed a silver cross pendant in his mouth with a label attached, inscribed Romans 1.18. Dawn was breaking. They left as silently as they came, disappearing into the early morning light.

'No, no!' shouted Rick as he slammed down the phone. Dave rushed into his office.

'What's up Guv, more bad news?'

'Freddie Fairbrother's dead.' Dave remained speechless, but his body language said it all.

Rick thought it was beginning to look like an Agatha Christie crime novel. Four murders, Samantha, Derbyshire, Theo and now Freddie, three without any doubt, one possibly a suicide, in the past two weeks.

'Get hold of Kay and Ethan, you know the drill. We'll meet them down at the Tumbling Dice Club.'

The scene that greeted them was a familiar one. Kay was bent over Freddie's body and Ethan and the SOC team were scouring the room for any evidence. As they entered Kay looked up and acknowledged their presence.

'It looks like the same MO doesn't it Kay?' said Dave.

'Don't be too quick to judge, Dave. Freddie may well have

committed suicide before being castrated.'

Rick almost felt sorry for Freddie. Another life wasted, an aspiring golden career as a boxer ruined by his father's greed for gambling. Unrequited love from Samantha and almost certainly being recruited to the cauldron when he was at a low ebb by Jim Derbyshire. It all contributed to his downward spiral. The final straw was being entangled in the murder of Theo by Tiny Foreman.

'Is that what you think Kay?' asked Rick.

'Well firstly he's been dead for over 24 hours, which suggests that he died the night before last. The cleaners only come in every Sunday, so that would tally. He certainly intended to commit suicide. He appears to have downed a bottle of gin over a short period of time, and by the look of the empty packets, took a substantial amount to purple hearts and temazepam tablets. The big question is whether he was dead or just comatose when the attacker castrated him.' Kay rose up from her squatted position, giving out a sigh. *This is getting ridiculous*, she thought.

'Ethan found a phial of unused Ketamine on the floor which presumably was intended to be used to subdue and render him unconscious. I won't know the timing of events for sure until I get him on the slab and carry out the postmortem.'

As Rick looked closer at Freddie's body, he observed the all too familiar mark of the small circular Bondye branding with an A in the middle under his armpit. Further confirmation that he was indeed, an acolyte of the voodoo cauldron.

'Anything else, Ethan?'

'The label attached to the pendant says Romans 1.18. 'The wrath of God is being revealed from *heaven against all the godlessness and wickedness of men who suppress the truth by their wickedness.'*

'Whoever is doing this, knows their Bible. As well as the Ketamine I have found a footprint in the deceased blood, it looks the same size as the small one found at the smithy.'

Rick commented, 'There is no longer any doubt this is all about revenge. Revenge for Samantha or revenge for some other reason. Either way, the victims' deaths are connected. How about you Kay, anything more you can tell us at this stage?'

'The attacker cut themselves whilst carrying out the castration.'

'How can you tell?'

'There are some drips of blood leading away from the body. They are slightly different in colour. Fairbrother's is darker having ingested so much alcohol and drugs, the liver has struggled to cope with the poisons.

I've taken samples of both blood types for analysis by the lab. I've also found some strands of blonde hair on the body which I have bagged and given to Ethan as evidence. Even through my surgeons gloves they feel soft and wavy. I would hazard a guess to say they are definitely from a blonde female with short wavy hair.'

'OK Kay, let us know your findings from the postmortem. Anything else to add, Ethan?'

'The assailant, and I bow to Kay and say assailant, not murderer at this stage, dropped a small travelling leather pouch containing a scalpel and other medical instruments. Kay is pretty sure it is a travelling vets surgery kit. It presumably fell out of the assailant pocket when leaving in a hurry.'

Rick gave a wry smile. 'OK, thanks both of you. I think we

all know who we think the perpetrator is, and we now have enough evidence to arrest and charge them. I'm sure that the blood, hair, and forensic tests on the medical kit will corroborate that, and provide us with hard, physical evidence. That, together with motive and a plethora of circumstantial evidence, should ensure the prosecution service agree with us and we get a conviction.'

Rick breathed a sigh of relief. This could be the break they were looking for.

'Dave, when we get back to the office can you make an application to the chief magistrate for a search warrant for Strawbridge Farm, including the main house, outbuildings, and grounds. Once we have that you and I will personally serve the warrant and make the arrest of Sarah Cooper-Clarke.'

As they journeyed back to Barnstaple Police H.Q. Rick felt that they were getting close to ending this senseless campaign of horrific murders in the name of God. Murders that looked for revenge against men who had used and abused a younger sister.

Having been groomed by her father from an early age to think having sex with men was how she showed love for them, and that was how they showed respect and love for her, Samantha had lost all her self-worth and pride.

Rick did not know exactly what drove Sarah-Cooper Clarke to embark on such a vitriolic campaign. It was clear that she had a guilt complex for deserting her younger sister, knowing full well that Samantha was still being sexually abused by their father. At some later stage in her life, after she had left home, perhaps she had repented her sins when she became a fervent 'Born again Christian.'

30

Sarah Cooper-Clarke held a small animal veterinary practice at Strawbridge Farm two days a week. It was at the practice one day that Sharon Roberts came in with her pet cat, Tiddles. They got chatting and found that they had one thing in common, Samantha Billings.

Sharon was mesmerised when she first met Sarah. When she went into the surgery, she thought she had seen a ghost. Standing there before her was 'Linda,' *but it can't be, she has changed so much,* she said to herself.

'I don't believe it Ms Cooper-Clarke. You look familiar, just like the sister of my closest friend Samantha, who died recently,' said Sharon. 'You have the same eyes and high cheek bones.'

'A few people have said that since we moved down from London,' replied Sarah sheepishly.

That was the start of a burgeoning friendship. They met frequently over a number of weeks to the point where Sarah eventually confided to Sharon that she was indeed 'Linda.' One evening over a meal and a bottle of wine at the Farm, they were reminiscing about happier days when inevitably the subject got round to Samantha. Sarah knew by then that her sister had left home at 16 to share digs with Sharon, who was her best friend from way back at primary school.

'I knew that you suddenly left home in a hurry when Samantha was only fourteen. It was to go up to London to train as a vet, wasn't it? Samantha was so upset; it was several weeks before she got over it.'

'How much did Samantha tell you about our home life?'

'You're talking about your father sexually abusing her, aren't you?'

So, there it was, the secret in the closet was finally out in the open.

'That's why I left. He came on to me first, but I threatened to tell mum and he backed off. Unknown to me at the time, he turned his attention to Samantha who was not only younger but much more gullible and was easily led.'

'Yeah, she told me everything, but there is more. Something that I am pretty certain you never knew.'

Sarah looked quizzically at Sharon's sad looking face and was now on tender hooks; she knew that something terrible was about to be revealed and feared the worse.

'When Samantha left home at 16, she was pregnant. She came to me, and I arranged for her to have an abortion.'

'Oh my gosh,' replied Sarah.

'It's worse Sarah, far worse. The father of the unborn child was your dad.'

'What? No, no!' she cried out, absolutely horrified. 'I'll kill him, I swear I am going to kill him!'

They talked long into the night about Samantha, how she was finally turning her life around by the time she was murdered and was resisting the unwelcome advances of Jim Derbyshire and Freddie Fairbrother.

'If there is any justice in this world, they got what was coming to them,' remarked Sarah.

Sharon thought that was a strange thing to say, seeing they

were murdered. What surprised Sarah was that Sharon went on to tell her that Samantha had found true love with Jonathon Dukes, and that she adored him. Sarah had been convinced that he too had taken advantage of her sister, but apparently not. Jonathon would never know how fortunate he was at this timely disclosure.

Sharon hardly slept a wink that night remembering what Sarah had said about killing her father. People often say such horrid things when upset or in spite, but somehow she felt that Sarah really meant it. She had been so, so, totally disgusted and appalled she almost threw up when Sharon had told her about the pregnancy. Sarah had said she felt nothing but revulsion for those who had taken advantage of her sister, including her father.

The following morning it was still playing on Sharon's mind. She found the card that Dave had left with her when he came to see her with Detective Inspector McCarthy. *It's no good I have to speak to him about Sarah's threat to kill her own father,* she thought. *I could never forgive myself if she actually carried it out.*

Sharon picked up the telephone in the hotel reception and shakily dialled Dave's private line.

Dave took the call, told Sharon to calm down and tell him exactly what Sarah Cooper-Clarke knew, and what she said she was going to do. After he put the phone down, he rushed into Rick's office.

'That was Sharon Roberts Guv. Sarah Cooper-Clarke knows that it was Sam Billings who was the father of Samantha's unborn child, and she is threatening to kill him.'

'When was this?'

'Late last night.'

'Jesus, let's hope we are not too late.'

'Matt,' he shouted across the room, 'Phone Sam Billings and tell him that Sarah Cooper-Clarke is his daughter Linda, and that she has threatened to kill him. Tell him we are on our way.'

Rick and Dave dashed out of the building and jumped into the Dart. 'Right Dave, now is the time to really see what this beast of a car can do.'

With blue lights flashing and the front mounted bell ringing they sped through the outskirts of Barnstaple up on to the Braunton and Ilfracombe Road and onwards to Hele. It was time to throw caution to the wind, Sam Billings life may well depend on it. They broke all speed restrictions and went through several red lights to get there in record time.

Unknown to them, when Matt put the phone down on Sam Billings, Sarah was already there. She had turned up unexpectantly on the pretence of just dropping by for a coffee on the way to see a client with a distressed goat in Hele. She had a syringe containing the powerful anaesthetic of ketamine in one pocket and barbiturates in the other.

She was welcomed at the front door by her mother. Eileen couldn't believe it as she opened the door. It had been years since she had seen her daughter, and my how she had changed. There was no doubting who this slim, blonde, and elegant lady was though, and she welcomed her with open arms, a big hug, and kisses to both cheeks. Sam stayed in the kitchen.

'Look whose here Sam, it's Linda,' Eileen called out.

Sam got up and poked his head round the kitchen door. He merely acknowledged Linda's presence, there was clearly still an in-built hostility between them from wounds that had remained silent but never healed.

Eileen could never understand why her daughter hadn't been in touch all these years. After the usual pleasantries, over a second cup of coffee and biscuits, Eileen broached the subject.

'Linda darling, why for God's sake have you never been in touch since you left for London?'

'It's Sarah Mum, Sarah Cooper-Clarke.'

Eileen was confused, 'But Sarah Cooper was my mother's name.'

'I changed my name by deed poll.'

'Why on earth did you do that, sweetheart?'

'You never knew mother, did you? You were too wrapped up in your own little world to notice what was going on beneath your nose.' Eileen was taken aback. What was Linda talking about? She didn't understand at all.

'That perfect husband of yours was abusing your daughters for years.'

The atmosphere in the room changed as quickly as a flash of lightening. A deadly silence ensued; you could have cut the tension with a knife, and Eileen just sat there with her mouth open. *She couldn't have heard it right; Linda had got it all wrong* she thought.

The silence has been broken by the ringing of the telephone in the hall. Sam went and answered it. It was Matt.

After he put the phone down, he couldn't think straight. *She doesn't mean it, not our Linda, why now, it all happened so long ago.* He walked into the kitchen confused, but with some fear and apprehension. *Surely, she can't mean it, I'm her father.*

'What is she saying Sam? demanded Eileen. 'Tell me to my face that it isn't true.'

Sarah stood up and launched into a tirade of verbal

accusations. 'Go on, tell her! Tell her why we both left home as soon as we could. Tell her how I rejected your disgusting advances when I was twelve, and how I threatened to tell her. Tell her how you then turned you're fucking paedo attention towards young Samantha. How you brainwashed her into believing that the sexual relationship she was having with you was healthy, loving, and normal!'

By now Sarah was shaking with rage, screaming her accusations at her father. Eileen sat there horrified, she couldn't breathe, her heart was beating so fast she felt it was going to burst. *This can't be true, it can't be true,* she was saying to herself.

'Tell her Dad!' screamed Sarah. 'Tell her how you climbed into Samantha's bed at night and fucked your own daughter! Tell her how she was pregnant by you when she left home and had to have an abortion.'

Sam was shaken ridged. Shaken by the vitriolic outburst of Sarah but moreover shaken by the news about Samantha's pregnancy. He never knew, not that it would have changed the outcome if he had.

'I never knew, I swear to God I never knew,' Sam cried out shedding fake crocodile tears.

Eileen had been reduced to a quivering wreck. With tears flowing and shaking uncontrollably she leapt at Sam beating his chest with her fists. 'You bastard, you filthy bastard. My poor fallen angel.'

'God? You talk of God?' shouted Sarah. 'You blaspheming, snivelling rapist, you are no father to me. You ruined Samantha's life; it was your lust and seed that sent her on a path of self-destruction of all moral compass. She never had a chance to find and witness true love. In the Bible Romans

13.4 says *that if you do wrong, be afraid, for he does not bear the sword in vain. For he is the servant of God, an avenger who conducts God's wrath on the wrongdoer.'*

Sam now feared for his life. 'Don't do this Linda, I beg you, it was so long ago. I loved her, I loved you both. Forgive me.'

'Oh Daddy,' Sarah said as she held her arms out as if to so do.

She put her arms around him and thrust the needle of the syringe into his neck, pushing the plunger fully down.

'Nooo,' he cried out, as the drugs sped around his bloodstream, and he started to feel woozy.

At that moment, the door opened, and Rick and Dave burst in. Quickly realising the situation Rick said, 'Sarah don't do it. Enough blood has been spilt in Samantha's name,' trying to defuse the situation.

Sarah, with a scalpel in hand turned to him and smiled. She stepped towards her father and said, 'God is my witness; I fear no evil.'

'No Linda! Vengeance is mine,' cried out Eileen as she pushed past her daughter and plunged a 6-inch kitchen knife directly into Sam's heart, hitting the main aorta artery. Sam dropped to the floor and began convulsing like a beached shark. His heart erupted like a volcano with geysers of blood spurting everywhere. He died in an instant.

Sarah and her mother clasped each other tightly, sobbing, but with no feelings of remorse.

'It's over Linda, I'm so, so sorry I wasn't there for you. May God have mercy and forgive us for our sins.'

Dave went into the hall, picked up the phone and called in for a squad car. Fortunately, a traffic patrol car in the Ilfracombe area responded and was with them in under 5 minutes. Sarah and Eileen were cautioned, hand cuffed and put into the car.

'Is it really necessary for my mother to be handcuffed?' demanded Sarah.

'I am afraid so; it is as much for her safety as ours,' replied Dave.

Sarah and Eileen were taken back to H.Q and booked in by the custody sergeant. Their fingerprints and photographs taken, they were put into separate holding cells awaiting the return of Rick and Dave.

Later that day they were both respectively charged with murder. Sarah Cooper-Clarke for the murder of Jim Derbyshire and the attempted murder of Freddie Fairbrother. Eileen Billings with the murder of her husband, Sam Billings.

Once again, as Rick and Dave entered the ops room, they were clapped in by the team. On this occasion Rick took no comfort and had wished for a better ending to the case.

'What do you think will happen in the case of Eileen?' asked Olivia.

'She will either be tried for murder or possibly manslaughter as it was not premeditated. That is a decision for the crown prosecution to take. If found guilty I think the judge will take into account her guilty plea, weigh up all the evidence and circumstances surrounding her action and pass the minimum sentence he or she possibly can.'

'In the case of Sarah Cooper-Clarke, I have no doubt she will stand trial for murder. Her defence lawyers might argue that she is mentally disturbed, brought about by the abuse of her father. Albeit in her case she was not actually sexually abused unlike her poor sister Samantha. No doubt if she is found guilty, she will serve a life sentence of no less than twenty years. She is fortunate, if that is the right word, that the death penalty by hanging was abolished two years ago.'

'Right team, we have another case to solve. We still need to bring the murder of Samantha Billings to a close.'

Rick suddenly thought of the weapon used to severe Samantha's hand. 'The axe, Dave. Major St John Stevens said that the weapon used to severe Samantha's hand was a long wooden handled axe. Olivia also said that when she interviewed the Mayor, he showed her a replica axe used in medieval re-enactments. It's time we visited the Mayor. Get hold of a search warrant for his home address and the Mayor's parlour at the Guildhall.'

31

Rick, Dave, Adam, and Matt arrived unannounced at the mayor's home late that afternoon. Rick and Dave had travelled in the Dart and Adam and Matt in a police squad car. The drive up to Ilfracombe and on to Berrynabor seemed an all too familiar one. The house was an old Victorian rectory set back from the lane, which befitted the mayor's standing in the local community.

The mayor was at home with his wife taking afternoon tea in the front sitting room. They had just finished listening to the afternoon play on Radio 4 when both heard a car on the gravelled driveway. Mrs Martin put down her cup, got up, crossed the room to the bay window and peered out through the lace curtains, wondering who it might be.

Upon seeing that one of the cars was a marked police car she turned to her husband and said, 'Andrew, it's the police. What can they possibly want calling late on a Sunday afternoon? I do hope nothing has happened to our Sandra and the children.'

'I very much doubt that darling. They are up in Scotland on holiday with mother, remember? She would have phoned.'

The mayor's heartbeat raced, he got up and went to the window. The significance of two cars, one a marked squad car, was not lost on him. He was aware of the arrest of Major St John Stevens and feared for the worst. His mind started to swirl; *will they find my secret hiding place? Did I leave it locked and pull the old workbench and tool rack in front of it?*

When confronted by Rick at the front door, who duly announced himself showing him both his warrant card and the search warrant, his face turned ashen. It was to all intents and purposes as if he knew that the 'game was up.'

Matt stayed with the mayor and his wife in the sitting room whilst the others conducted the search. The main rooms of the house were immaculate, there was not an ornament out of place, nor speck of dust, with all the furniture polished and surfaces gleaming. There was no doubt that Mrs Martin either loved housework or more likely, had a regular cleaner or even a housekeeper.

The search of the house didn't reveal anything that could remotely be linked to voodoo, the cauldron nor Samantha Billings' murder.

Having searched the upper two floors and the downstairs and kitchen areas, all that remained was what looked like a cupboard in the hallway. Rick remembered there were fanlights below the front room as they approached the front door. *There must be a cellar.*

Indeed there was. Halfway down the hall, underneath the stairs, an old oak door opened onto steep steps down to a cellar. Switching on a dull low wattage light revealed a full height, musty cobwebbed filled space that was probably the size of half of the ground floor. The first thing they noticed was an extensive wine rack holding copious bottles of wine, many covered in dust. A cursory look revealed several old vintages that Rick recognised. They were worth considerable sums of money. There was even a bottle of 1945 Château Mouton Rothchild and a 1951 Petros.

The remainder of the cellar was full of discarded old pieces of furniture, carpets, rugs and other junk. In one corner were piles of old hymn books and other religious ephemera no doubt dating back to when it was the home of the local vicar. On the back wall was a workbench with tool rack above.

'It doesn't look as if there is anything down here of interest,' said Dave.

Rick who had a keen sense of smell and could generally identify most of the single malt whiskeys, thought he could smell something odd. He smelt some sort of cross between ammonia and vinegar permeating its old walls. It was stronger as he approached the workbench. His first thought was that some chemical had been used at the workbench for cleaning a tool maybe. *No, an axe you fool,* he said to himself. He couldn't find anything remotely like a cleaning agent on the bench or the shelves above. He looked around the cellar walls to get his bearings, something was odd, and he couldn't put his finger on it. If the cellar ran the depth of the house, and why wouldn't it, the part they were in was just too small.

'Here, Adam, pass me your torch.'

Rick proceeded to scan the workbench and tool rack. Nothing was obvious, but SOC might find blood splatters on the workbench.

'Help me move the rack and workbench, Dave.' After a few grunts and groans with the odd expletive by Dave, they lifted down the tool rack.

'Eureka,' exclaimed Rick.

There was a door to another room. They pushed aside the bench and found the key easily; it was hanging up on the tool rack. Dave turned the key and opened the door with some trepidation, not knowing what they were about to discover. Hanging behind the door was a white hooded cloak emblazoned with the golden image of Bondye on its back. The cloak on the surface looked pristine, it had recently been thoroughly washed. A search of the room revealed an assortment of Voodoo related paraphernalia ranging from books, cinema and home-made films, and artefacts including a large, long wooden handled axe. There was also an array of ceremonial items including a chalice.

The axe and the chalice both showed signs of having recently been cleaned by bleach, but it was still possible blood had penetrated the wooden handle of the axe. Perhaps it could be matched to the same blood type as that of Samantha.

Amongst the artifacts was a Super 8 cine camera and viewing screen. A small darkroom, with an outside air vent had also been built, containing a sink, film developing equipment and chemicals. It was the chemicals that they could smell in the main part of the cellar.

Amongst the hoard of cinema movie films there were two featuring Voodoo that were of particular interest, in as much that they contained plots with reference to similar practices engaged in by the cauldron up on Hillsborough Head.

The first one entitled *Voodoo Man*, turned out to be a 1944 American horror film featuring Bela Lugosi and John Carradine. The plot involved Dr. Richard Marlowe, (Bela Lugosi), capturing attractive young girls so that he can transfer their life essences to his long-dead wife. He is assisted by Toby, (John Carradine), who under the influence of opium, lovingly leads the drugged girls to a makeshift altar, and then pounds on bongo drums during the Voodoo ceremonies.

The second one, *Macumba Love*, was another American horror of 1960, starring Walter Reed. The film centres on a writer who arrives on a South American island in order to finish his book on Voodoo, Juju, Macumba, Mojo and other cults. He believes they are responsible for unsolved murders on this island, only to find that the local Voodoo queen has other plans for him. Queen Mama Rata-Loi has desires on him and his friends to satisfy her own sexual appetite and blood lust.

The home-made Super 8 films were simply entitled Samantha 1967, Julie 1966, and Susan 1965. Rick was dreading having to watch the films, especially as here was proof that the cauldron had committed similar offences in the past. Julie Taylor had gone missing in August 1966 and Susan Harris in October1965.

Rick decided that Adam was too young and too inexperienced to watch the Super 8 films. He did not want to risk him becoming traumatised by what they might find on them. Explaining this to Adam, he asked him to leave the room and they would let him know when to come back in.

After he'd left, Dave loaded the film titled 'Samantha' and they both sat down to watch. It was in colour, jerky in some places and consisted of small bursts of moving action. The opening scene was that of the makeshift altar, a log fire and white cloaked celebrants dancing around it. The film panned to the edge of the clearing and the coastal path up from Hele Bay Beach. Into focus came Freddie Fairbrother leading Samantha Billings by the hand. Freddie handed her over to someone wearing a white cloak, even though he wore warpaint on his face, there was no mistaking the face of that person. It was Jim Derbyshire.

Later clips included Freddie, now dressed in a white cloak, and the warlock, wearing a black cloak with his back to the camera, holding a silver chalice and administering some form of drink to Samantha.

Suddenly, there was a horrific scene that Rick and Dave found hard to watch. It was the celebrants dancing in abandon, some with erections protruding from the front of their cloaks. The camera panned to Samantha spread-eagled on the alter being raped every which way by each celebrants in turn. One, engaged in anal sex, turned his head towards the camera, leering with his tongue hanging out. It was Jim Derbyshire. The camera panned to an onlooker; it was Freddie Fairbrother being sick. Rick looked closely at the screen and swore that Freddie was crying.

The following scene was jerkier as if it were being filmed by a different person to the rest of the film. It showed Samantha now alone on the altar, comatose, either dead or having passed out. One of the celebrants stood over her holding a long handle axe. He turned to face the warlock as if he were waiting for the command. The warlock raised his right hand, shook his feathered rattle, turned his hand over, looked to the celebrant holding the axe and nodded.

He celebrant slowly raised the axe above his head. In one felt swift motion it fell severing Samantha's right hand. The camera panned to the celebrant holding the bloody axe. It was the mayor, grinning manically and obviously under the influence of drugs. The next scene showed the warlock, disguised by wearing a mask, holding the hand aloft and chanting before casting it into the fire. The final scene appeared to show some form of closing ceremony and that of the full moon disappearing behind the clouds.

The film ended with the film spool continuing to go round and round with the clicking sound as the reel end kept hitting the winding spool. As Dave got up to switch the projector off, he thought just for that moment that it sounded just like when they were kids putting cigarette cards on their bikes so that they clicked in the front wheel spokes as they rode along.

Rick and Dave sat there in silence, taking in what they had just witnessed. Rick lit up a cigarette. They both needed a stiff drink, but that would have to wait. They had witnessed a murder first-hand before. Eileen Billings had stabbed her husband Sam, but the depraved scenes recorded on the film they had just watched had made them both sick to their stomachs.

They could not bring themselves to watch the other films of Julie Taylor and Susan Harris and decided to leave that to the team in the forensic laboratory back at H.Q.

Dave called Adam back into the room to bag up all of the evidence that they had found, and to take it back to H.Q. He had already called up Ethan to get SOC to conduct a search of every nook and cranny of the house looking for any further evidence.

Rick and Dave then returned to the sitting room where Rick charged the mayor with aiding and abetting the murder of Samantha Billings on the night of September 27th 1967. After receiving the mandatory caution, the mayor said that his wife knew nothing of the contents of the cellar, nor had any idea of his pastime as a member of The North Devon Cauldron.

Some bloody pastime, thought Dave.

Rick, inclined to believe him, had no cause to arrest Mrs

Martin. The mayor was handcuffed by Matt and taken out to the squad car to be taken back to H.Q. Rick and Dave both stayed on until Ethan arrived with the SOC team to take over.

On their arrival back at H.Q. the mayor had already been booked in by the custody sergeant and placed in a holding cell. It was getting late in the day and despite an overwhelming urge to get on and interview him, Rick decided that he needed time to reflect on the evidence against him and to let Martin sweat overnight.

Before wrapping up for the day, he went over their findings with Dave, and discussed the approach that he would take in the interview the following morning.

They had still not identified who the warlock was. It was their last chance to crack one of the main participants in Samantha's murder into either naming him, or at the very least, reveal further clues as to his identity.

32

Monday 7th

The interview with Mayor Martin commenced at 10.00 a.m. In the interview room were Rick, Dave, the mayor, and his family solicitor.

Rick switched on the recording device and opened the interview by stating the time of commencement and who was present.

'Mayor Martin, you have been charged with aiding and abetting the murder Miss Samantha Billings on the night of 27th September 1967. For the purpose of the tape recording, I shall now put to the mayor his rights under interview.

'Mayor Martin, do you understand your rights?'

'Yes.'

'Mayor Martin, the evidence recovered from your home address will prove beyond doubt that you were present and participated in some form of Voodoo ceremony up on Hillsborough Head, Ilfracombe on the night of Miss Billings' murder.'

'Do you deny participating in the murder of Miss Billings?'

'Yes'

'Do you deny severing her hand with the long wooden handled axe, found at your home address?'

'No.'

'Yet you still deny the aiding and abetting of the murder charge?'

'Yes.'

'Would you care to explain?'

'The harlot, Samantha Billings, was paying the price for her life of promiscuity and for spreading malicious lies about the existence and ways of the cauldron. As with others who had gone before her, she was to pay the price by being raped and debased by all present.'

Martin was now in full flow and launched into a vitriolic attack on Samantha and any young girls who had sex in abandon.

'Some might even be regarded as fallen angels in their own right, coming from either impoverished or abusive backgrounds,' he said, 'but they are raped for their own good to teach them a lesson, D I McCarthy. Gang raped if you prefer and humiliated. Afterall, simple raping is not a punishment for these girls, these cockteasers. They love it rough and encourage decent men to lower themselves to having sex in public places. In the tunnels to Tunnel Beach, on the beaches, even in the sea, up on Capstone Hill, in the undergrowth on the Head, up against a wall in the town, behind a car in a car park. They were, and are, disgusting creatures, whores by any other name. Temptresses in their shorter-than-short skirts, and not always of the night. Sex anywhere, anyhow, with anyone, providing it wasn't in the decency of the marriage bed. They lead men astray to break vows and they deserved their punishment. In other countries they would be publicly stoned to death, and quite rightly. We show clemency. They feel no pain and are drugged up whilst having sex every which way.'

The mayor shuffled in his seat, pulling himself upright. He was confident and indignant. 'Normally,' he continued 'After we are all satisfied, the whore would be driven up to Exmoor and left there, unconscious, to find her way home in the morning. No real harm done. A little sore, perhaps, but hopefully a lesson learned.'

He lowered his head and thought for a second or two.

'Samantha was different. She had been telling people about the cauldron and spreading lies. The punishment for any disclosure was the severing of a right hand. She was high on drugs on arrival and danced provocatively before the celebrants, following which the warlock administered a concoction of drugs and herbs to her that he had prepared earlier. She felt nothing.'

He fidgeted in his chair again but showed no sign of either remorse or shame. He was enjoying talking about it, boasting, and it seemed to be a turn-on for him. Rick just sat back, letting him rant on.

'All of the celebrants, including myself, got worked up into a frenzy on the drugs and sex. After Derbyshire had finished with her, she was laying prone on the alter. The warlock looked across at me and nodded. I swear that she was alive both before and after I severed her hand. Severing a hand would not kill her.'

Rick tried to remain professional and non-committal. Inside his heart was pounding with disgust for this evil creature that was sat before him. He swallowed hard and continued:

'Let us now come to the warlock. Who is he?'

'I do know, but it would be more than my life's worth to reveal his name to you. To do so would result in a voodoo curse of death being put upon me by the Voodoo God of Creation, our almighty Bondye. However,' he said, sniggering, 'I will say this. He is right under your nose. If you are the great detective that we are led to believe that you are following the capture of the coastal path strangler, then solve the puzzle, D I McCarthy. The clue is on the film.'

His air was superior, arrogant and taunting, his head held high. He was throwing out a challenge.

'Have you anything further to say?'

'Glory be to the supreme God, Bondye, the creator of everything and the source of universal order.'

With that Rick terminated the interview at 10.30. a.m. and Mayor Martin was handcuffed and led away back to his cell. He would be transferred to Exeter jail later that day to be held on remand pending trial.

Rick went back to his office with Dave. A customary cigarette was lit, in this case two, Dave was now hooked on them too. They sat in silence, trying to understand, in some small way, the horror they had just heard.

'Are they all mad, Guv?'

'We might think so, but in the eyes of the law almost certainly not. Many a life has been taken, indeed wars fought, over religion. Their beliefs are just another form of worship of the creator of the universe, albeit an evil creator as opposed to God as we know it.'

'What did Martin say? The clue is in the film. He was really taunting you wasn't he, the evil bastard. He must be referring the 'Samantha' film.'

'Ok Dave,' said Rick, sitting back in his chair. 'I've always enjoyed a challenge. Set up a viewing screen and projector and go and retrieve the 'Samantha' film from forensics, even if they haven't finished with it. We need to see it again. Can you also ask Matt and Ethan to join us for another viewing The more experienced eyes the better for this one.'

The four of them arrived to watch the Super 8 Film of the events on Hillsborough Head on the night of 27th September, culminating in the murder of Samantha Billings.

After everyone was sat down and comfortable, Rick briefed the others about the interview.

'We are particularly looking for clues that might identify who the warlock is. We know from other testimonies that he is a member of some standing in the local community and is, quote, 'under our very noses.' Just say 'stop,' if you notice anything, anything at all. Ok Dave, roll it.'

The warlock is first seen administering a concoction of drugs and herbs to Samantha as the celebrants dance round the fire. Ethan was the first to say 'stop.'

'Look at his left hand, he's wearing a signet ring on his left pinkie finger. It looks like an alumni or regimental ring.'

'Well spotted Ethan. We'll get the forensic boys to blow up the image.'

'Anything else?'

'Yes. His index fingers are longer than his ring fingers. Leading psychologists and police profilers believe that this indicates it is a person who's leader and quick to take charge of any situation. They are the confident and resourceful ones who shine at leading the way.'

'That bears out the belief that he is someone of high office and standing in the local community,' said Dave.

'Good start, lads,' said Rick giving everyone encouragement.

The film continued to the scene where the warlock turns and nods to the mayor prior to the axe falling.

Dave then spoke. 'The cloak, look at the cloak. We know

about the torn label, which has probably been repaired by now, but look at the hood.'

'What, Dave? Am I missing something?' asked Rick. 'What about you two?' Dave asked Matt and Ethan. They both shook their heads.

'The hood is misshapen,' said Dave. 'It looks like the stitching went wrong when sewing it up. Maybe it was sold as a 'second.'

'Christ, Dave, we never thought of that one. Get Olivia on the phone to Ede and Ravenscroft to see if they sold off "seconds."'

Dave then rolled the film on to the closing ceremony.

'Anything here before we wrap up?' asked Rick.

'He has got a slight limp,' said Ethan.

'Roll that scene again, Dave.'

'So, he has,' said Rick. 'Maybe it was caused by an accident.'

'It looks more like some form of congenital deformity to me,' said Ethan.

'Well Gentlemen, we now know a hell of a lot more about our mysterious warlock. Off you go, you know what to do. We'll reconvene when somebody has something positive to report.'

Olivia, as instructed by Dave, had been on the phone. She was the first to report back that Ede and Ravenscroft do have an annual clear-out when they sell off 'seconds.'

'Some cloaks, both black and white, are usually bought by the film and TV production companies, but here's the thing. Three years ago, two were sold to Mayor Martin's re-enactment business.'

'Well, well,' said Dave.

'But we only recovered one,' exclaimed Rick, 'and that one was found hanging in the mayor's parlour. It was examined by forensics and found to be uncontaminated of any incriminating evidence. Where is the other one?'

The signet ring was the next to be identified. It was the Royal Army Medical Core, whose motto was 'in arduis fidelis,' faithful in adversity. The core was jokingly called 'Rob All My Comrades' but when a soldier was wounded in battle and the cry went up 'medic,' they were mighty glad to be seen..

'Hold on Guv.' Matt who spoke up. 'If he was in the RAMC, he probably still works high up in the medical profession. Or in some capacity, surely. That narrows it down a bit, doesn't it?'

'You could be right Matt. Now I know why I like having bright young things in my team. Applying logic is good. It doesn't surprise me that the warlock is an ex-member of the RAMC. If we didn't know better, we would have thought it must be Major St John Stevens, but unless he has attempted to throw us off the scent by the admission in his interview, it's not him. However, the ring does suggest that he is in the medical profession.'

He looked around at his team, all of which gave 110%.

'So, leading lights in the medical profession right under our noses, gentlemen. Once more into the breach my friends, think on and call them out.' They took it in turns to come up with a title.

'GP, consultant, medical director, on the board of governors at the infirmary, maybe even the chairman or the coroner.'

'Good. Anyone we have missed?'

'What about the police surgeon, in fact I believe we have two part time GPs on our books,' said Ethan.

'Now there's a thought. We keep getting told by informants, suspects, and detainees that he is right under our nose. It doesn't come much closer than within H.Q. itself.'

'Your call Ethan get Adam to talk to personnel and get the names, addresses and CV's of both if they have them. Also contact the BMC and see what they have on them.'

'Will do.'

'What about the others?' asked Dave.

'GP's and consultant's would be a long list and I somehow think, without denigrating the fine work that they are doing, that our man holds a higher office in the community. That leaves, the infirmary medical director, the chairman of the infirmary board of governors, and the coroner.'

'Matt, can you look into the background of the medical director, and Dave look into the chairman of the board of governors, bearing in mind whether they were both in the RAMC and their physical deformities.'

'Yes, Guv,' they said in unison.

'I'll talk to Kay about the coroner, although that seems a bit of a long shot, but at this stage we can't rule anyone out.'

Adam was the first to come back to Rick. He had been to see the head of personnel who was initially reluctant to reveal information regarding the two police surgeons, siting issues with breach of confidentiality etc. Although the head of personal was way above Adam's pay grade he stood his ground and told her how embarrassing it would be for H.Q. and the chief if they themselves were issued with a search warrant. When he told Rick this, Rick burst out laughing.

'Well done my boy, you will go far; I shall make sure of it.'

'Thank you, sir,' he said with a smile and feeling very proud of himself. 'Here are their CV's.'

Rick had met both of them in the course of their duties in providing a clinical assessment if it were deemed necessary or requested by a detainee's solicitor. He started to look through them. The first one was Dr Robert Makepeace MB ChB. He trained at the University of Bristol Medical School and went straight into practice as a junior GP. He is now the senior partner of The Victoria Road Medical Centre and works part time as a police surgeon.

The second one was Christopher Wiggins MPhil/PhD/MS, trained at the University of Exeter Medical School, research fellow, now a semi-retired heart surgeon, which allowed him to work part time as a police surgeon. Neither of them served in the armed services.

A similar picture came back on the background of the Infirmary Medical Director, Sir Giles Herringbone. Although he had had an eminent medical career, he did not serve in RAMC. He did, however serve in the navy and rose to the position of commodore-surgeon, head of the Royal Navy Medical Service.

Rick called Dave into his office. 'Shut the door Dave, this is just between you and me.'

'What's up? You're looking very thoughtful.'

'I'm getting seriously concerned that we are running out of leads. You are the only one I completely trust. I just get the feeling that we are now reaching the point of incredulity. What if the warlock is someone so close to us to be almost unbelievable? Where else are we? Unless we find the cloak, it looks like we are going to have to rely on physical identification either by luck or by chance,' said Rick rather dejectedly. 'Any thoughts?'

'Well, we've still got the coroner to investigate. I have checked the army records and I am afraid he was in the RAMC.'

'Ok, well that may give a different perspective to it. I'll talk to Kay this evening, but I am as sure as I can be that she would've noticed something about his behaviour, let alone noticing if he were limping. Something is bugging me. When Adam mentioned the police surgeons, I immediately thought who else could it be that is amongst our ranks.'

'Surely not.'

'Well, it wouldn't be the first time. There are plenty of cases of police corruption, even the odd one involving gangland murder.'

'But not this murder. It's the most heinous we have had to investigate.'

'Here me out Dave.' Rick paused, elbows on his desk, clasping his hands together in front of his mouth. He couldn't believe what he was about to suggest but suggest it he must.

'Who's been right alongside us all the way since Samantha was first discovered on Hele Bay Beach, and apart from Kay, has all the medical and forensic skills? Who is a religious person, and the son of a methodist preacher that has a most detailed knowledge of the voodoo religion and practices?'

'No! No, Guv! I think you are a brilliant detective who sees things that others don't, but I think you are well and truly wrong on this one.'

'That's why this must stay between us until we prove otherwise.'

'But what about the clues we found watching the film of Samantha's murder?'

'Think again Dave. The so-called clues revealed by Ethan

could all be lies to divert our attention to the characteristics of the person he wanted us to look for. If I'm right, he has laid false trails all the way through our investigation. He was the one that pointed out the ring. If it *were* him, he could have worn the ring deliberately to suggest the warlock was in the RAMC. The size of his index finger, again a false trail maybe? The limp, suggesting the warlock has some form of congenital deformity? He could have faked a limp deliberately when performing during the ceremony.'

'Bloody hell.' Dave walked around in circles, his hands on his head. 'I'm sorry but I can't believe it. It's a bit like saying I'm the warlock, or *you* are! We all know Ethan. We all work with him. Surely one of us would have twigged something was odd about him?' Dave was visually shocked at the very idea.

'If you are right, how on earth do we prove it?'

'I don't know yet; I must first talk to Kay about the coroner to hopefully rule him out. I'll share these thoughts with her as she's had to collaborate with Ethan throughout. Maybe he's either made some odd remarks to her or even done something when examining the crime scene that seemed strange to her at the time. In the meantime, keep it to yourself, think about it tonight and we'll pick it up again in the morning.'

As Rick walked into the apartment that evening, Kay already had their evening meal on the go.

'Hmm. smells good, is that a hint of garlic I can smell?

'Pollo alla Cacciatore! OK with you?'

'You know it's my favourite Italian dish. What's to go with it?'

'I'm keeping it simple tonight and serving it with an Italian flatbread filled with spinach and parmesan cheese and a nice cold bottle of Pinot Grigio. In fact, I've already opened the wine and am one ahead of you, so what can I get you?'

'I'm weary babe, it's been another challenging and thought-provoking day, so I think I'll start with a Jameson's on the rocks.'

It's like that eh? I'm sure I can smooth your brow and relax you later on,' she said with a sideways smile.

'Just seeing you does that to me darling, but who am I to resist - later?'

Kay poured Rick his Jameson's and whilst she was at it, topped her own glass up. After a second glass Rick started to relax. Over dinner he decided to broach the subject of the coroner.

'We are running out of leads as to who the warlock is,' said Rick somewhat dejectedly. 'Dave, Matt and I sat down as a team to look at the film the mayor took of the voodoo ceremony that led to the murder of Samantha. We looked for anything that we may have missed. As you know, all the way through the case we have kept getting told by informants, suspects and detainees, that he is someone high up in the community and right under our noses.'

He took another mouthful of the delicious chicken before continuing. 'This is gorgeous babe. Are there any seconds?'

'No, we've eaten it all. So where d'you go from here?'

'We've run out of suspects, unless.' He stopped there, hesitating. 'Our only other thought is that it might be someone within our own ranks. Several observations were made whilst watching the film, one of which was that he was wearing a signet ring on his little finger bearing the insignia of the RAMC.'

'OK, I can see where you are going with this.'

'It was also noticed that he walked with a slight limp, and Ethan suggested that it was probably from some form congenital deformity. He also said his index fingers are longer than his ring fingers. What do you think Kay?'

'Well, I can confirm that the coroner was in the RAMC, and he does wear their insignia ring. In fact, he wears it with great pride, and we have often talked about his illustrious army career. However, he most definitely does not limp, in fact I know that he regularly plays squash so he could hardly do that with such a condition. I can't say I have noticed the length of his fingers, but I am sure I can establish that if you deem it that important.'

'I don't think that will be necessary at this stage. I have another hunch that you are going to find difficult to accept.'

Kay, sat back in her chair, her glass of Pinot in her hand and looked Rick in the eye, not knowing what bombshell he was about to reveal. 'OK. Who?'

'Ethan.'

'Ethan?! You have got to be kidding!' she spluttered, half laughing and choking at the ridiculous thought.

'You do realise that he is the founding member and chairman of the nationally recognised charity 'Freedom'.'

'I have vaguely heard of them, tell me more.'

'They are one of the fastest growing charities in the South West. They promote freedom of choice. Choice of race or creed. Choice of religion. Choice of sexuality and the relaxation of drug laws for personal use. They resonate with the youth of today and have supporters in high social and political circles.'

'Do they indeed,' said Rick.

'In fact among their patrons are none other than music

icons Bob Marley and John Lennon and the MP for Taw and Torridge, James Wellby.'

'I hear what you say Kay, I won't give you all my reasons yet, but I would like to hear if you have ever noticed anything odd when working alongside him. Any strange remarks about the case, any misconstrued observations regarding the evidence discovered, or otherwise.'

'Well, I am afraid that you are going to have to tell me your reasons. I have come to regard Ethan as a friend over the past couple of years, not just a colleague, and him being a warlock and a murderer is the most ridiculous idea you have ever come up with.' Kay was annoyed, and taking a long drink, emptied her wine glass. She was almost angry that Rick could even entertain the idea.

'Look darling, I know that this is hard for you, but can you just trust me on this one. I may well be wrong, and I suppose deep down, I hope I am. What if his observations of the film were made deliberately to mislead us? What if he is the warlock and he was deliberately wearing a RAMC ring and pretending to limp?'

'But that could apply to anyone. Absolutely anyone, couldn't it?' She wasn't sure whether she was still angry or just upset at the thought of her friend even being a suspect.

'If we are to accept the idea that the warlock could be someone within our own ranks, who, apart from you, has all the medical and forensic skills to uphold such a position. It has to be someone who has an intimate knowledge of poisons and has a religious background.'

Rick got up and refilled his glass. He knew everything he was saying sounded crazy and he didn't like upsetting Kay. He liked the guy too; thought he was good at his job and had contributed a great deal on all murder investigations. Kay worked closely with him, respected him, trusted him, but something was niggling Rick, and he didn't know what. He continued:

'Ethan's father is a methodist preacher with an incredibly detailed knowledge of occult practices and in particular Voodoo. Maybe that's where Ethan gets it from, maybe he has disowned the methodist faith for whatever reason.'

Kay had calmed down and walked over to where Rick was sitting. She perched on the arm of his chair, saying;

'Of course I trust you, love conquers all, and I do love you, but this sounds crazy to me. I just hope you disprove your theory that's all.' She got up and kicked a pouffe towards Rick's feet, sitting down to face him.

'Now I come to think of it there was one occasion, not long after we started working together. It set me back a bit to the point of asking myself whether the partnership was going to work or not. You know it's paramount that we, Ethan, and I, have a 'hand in glove' professional relationship with total trust in each other. A bit like you with Dave I suppose. Anyway, it was on your first big case, the coastal path strangler. Ethan particularly wanted to see the victims, the women's bodies. I mean part or completely naked Rick. Sometimes he even touched them. I considered that it was my job to establish whether they were raped or not, but he made some excuse about looking for forensic evidence. I sensed he gained some form of sexual pleasure out of it, and I didn't like it.' It was Kay's turn to refill her glass, and with her back to him she continued:

'Also, over the past two years he often talked about his sabbatical year, backpacking around central South America and the Northern Islands of the Caribbean. He told me he was a lapsed methodist, and all about his father being a lay preacher. He wouldn't say what the circumstances were, but I sensed he had broken their strict code of conduct. He took great joy in telling me all about the religions of the countries he visited, particularly the remote Afro Caribbean Indian tribes.'

'Thanks Kay. I have only shared this thought with Dave up until now, and tomorrow we are going to delve into it further.'

Nothing more was said that night on the subject. After they cleared away the dishes, cracked open a second bottle of wine and chilled out listening to some cool jazz, Rick took Kay up on her promise.

33

Tuesday 8th

The next morning on the way into the office Rick briefed Dave on his conversation with Kay.

'It wasn't an easy one Dave; Kay was quite tetchy at first as you can imagine. the coroner was in the RAMC, but he doesn't have a limp and Kay can vouch for him. She was even more staggered when I ushered the thought of Ethan being the warlock.'

'I can imagine! She has got very close to Ethan in the relatively short space of time they have worked alongside each other. He joined us not long after I did if I remember. What was he doing before?'

'He came highly recommended; he was deputy head of forensics up at Taunton. Personnel checked him out. Before that he was on some kind of sabbatical. One thing Kay told me was that he'd had a falling out with the methodist church where his father was the lay preacher. I am assuming that is the one up at Marwood where Pastor Jeremiah is now the preacher.

Before we do anything else and set any hares running, I think that we should pay the pastor another visit to try and find out what happened between the church and Ethan. Before we do that can you get hold of an emergency search warrant for Ethan's home address. We might as well either prove my hunch or put to bed the idea that one of our own is the warlock.'

After the morning's team meeting to check if anything else

relating to the case had emerged overnight, they waited for the search warrant to arrive. An hour later, search warrant in hand, the pair set off for Marwood. On arriving at the methodist chapel, they were received by Pastor Jeremiah.

'Gentlemen, this is a surprise. Do come in, has something come up in your enquiries that you need further assistance with?'

'Yes Pastor,' said Rick, almost apologetically, 'and please forgive me if I start raking up old embers.'

Pastor Jeremiah led them into his private parlour. It was clear from his changed demeanour that he knew what they might be alluding to.

'It's about Ethan, is it?'

'I am afraid so. I am led to believe that he had a falling out with the church and renounced his methodist faith some three years ago.'

'Not so much that he renounced it inspector, he was banished by the elders after being found guilty of several offences in breach of Wesleyan rules. You see, he had an affair with the wife of another member of the church and was charged under The Book of Discipline of The United Methodist Church.'

'And what charges might they have been, pastor?' enquired Rick.

Pastor Jeremiah got up and crossed the room to his library shelves. Scanning the numerous books, pamphlets, and articles, he found what he was looking for.

'Ah yes, here it is,' as he reached up and pulled out a copy of The Book of Discipline.

Returning to his desk he placed the book down and thumbed through to the relevant passages relating to lay members of the church.

'There are eleven chargeable offences, A to K. Ethan was charged with clauses A, D, and F.'

The Pastor read them out.

A) Immorality, including but not limited to, not being celibate in singleness or not faithful in a heterosexual marriage.

D) Disobedience to the order and discipline of The United Methodist Church.

F) Sexual misconduct, including the use or possession of pornography.

'I am so sorry pastor. Are you now reconciled to your son?'

'I am, he is family, and he has repented to me. However, he will never be welcomed back into the church again. He told me that he has found his own religion whilst on his travels, and I thank the Almighty for that.'

'What about his travels, did he keep in touch?'

'No, not as such. I hadn't heard from him for over six months after he left, and then suddenly I received an odd postcard.'

'Oh yes?' asked Rick. 'What was odd about it?'

'It was one of those touristy ones, you know the type, 'Wish You Were Here' and all that, but it was posted in Haiti. It was a picture of the Voodoo God, Bondye. It just said 'I've been listening to *Sinnerman* by Bob Marley and The Wailers; it reminded me how your God drove me away. I'm now at peace with the true God of Creation.' It was just signed, Ethan.

'What did you make of that?'

'I just shrugged it off and prayed for him. As you know from what I had previously told you, we learned and talked together about alternative religions including Voudun. I expect whilst on his travels he was experimenting with all sorts of hallucinatory drugs and the cultures of remote tribes.'

'How was he on his return?'

'A changed young man. Still loving of course, but he seemed more at peace with himself and with whatever salvation he had found. He did a refresher course on forensics and got a job with Taunton police force. He did very well for himself there, and then moved on to join your team in Barnstable as Head of SOC.'

'Has he ever mentioned any of his close friends in the North Devon area?'

'We don't see him that often. The only friend that I know that he has mentioned is the mayor of Ilfracombe. I believe that he even participated in some of the re-enactment events that the mayor's production company put on.'

Rick and Dave exchanged knowing glances.

Pastor Jeremiah continued, 'Surely you don't think that Ethan had anything to do with murder of the poor young girl on Hillsborough Head, do you inspector?'

'I'm sorry to have to say pastor that I can't rule anything out at this stage. No doubt it will soon be public knowledge, but the mayor has been implicated and charged with aiding and abetting the murder of Samantha Billings. We are following up all known acquaintances of his, and Ethan's name popped up.'

The pastor was clearly shocked. The blood drained from his face, and he started shaking. For a moment Rick thought that he was going to have a heart attack or a stroke. The pastor got up from behind his desk and without saying another word walked across the room and dropped to his knees in front of the Holy Cross. He bent his head and crossed himself and in a low muffled tone, he uttered a prayer.

'Dear Lord, You are a forgiving and merciful Lord, abounding in love to all who call upon You. Thank You for granting forgiveness so freely to us who are so undeserving. I pray that You overwhelm my son Ethan with awareness of how much he is forgiven, and that he be able to grant the same mercy to others who he believes have wronged him or done wrong. Open his eyes to the trap set by the devil himself and enable him to find freedom by following Your example. In the name of Jesus Christ, I pray. Amen.'

He then rose and turned to Rick and Dave.

'I shall pray for Ethan; you must do your duty inspector.'

With that Rick and Dave got up, bid the pastor goodbye, and left the house in a sombre mood. The mood continued as they drove back towards H.Q. On their way they called at Ethan's flat down on Taw Warf in Barnstaple. They knew nobody would be home, so Dave had to force an entry, allowed by law under the terms of the search warrant.

They had come to terms on the drive back from Marwood that Ethan was now their prime suspect for Samantha's murder. They did not imagine, given Ethan's skill in detecting evidence at a crime scene, that on entering the flat they would find any evidence openly displayed and linking him to the murder.

Wearing surgical gloves so as not to contaminate the scene, the first thing they found hanging up behind the entrance door was a black cloak, emblazoned with the golden motive of Bondye on the back, complete with its misshapen hood. Hanging with it was a white mask and a feathered rattle.

It was at that moment that Rick knew for certain that it

was all over, they had their man. He turned to Dave, shook his hand, and just said, 'We've got him!'

The kitchen revealed a number of jars and bottles of various labelled herbs and poisons together with a large stone mortar and pestle. They continued to search the rest of the flat. In the bedroom came their biggest surprise, the icing on the cake, the coup de grace. There, carefully laid out on the top of a dresser were three items. Jewellery belonging to Samantha and his previous victims, Susan and Julie was shining in the sunlight that streamed through the window. There was what appeared to be the missing silver ankle bracelet, engraved with the name Samantha, a silver clip-on earring belonging to Susan with the letter S, and a 'Best Friend' choker necklace; Julie's half of a butterfly that matched the other half worn by her best friend.

Rick looked at Dave in wanton disbelief. Dave, with lips closed just swallowed hard and shook his head.

'Trophies Dave, the bastard kept trophies. The trait of a serial killer, not the Ethan that we have come to know.'

When they arrived back at H.Q. there was an eerie silence. The word had got round that Rick and Dave were up at the Marwood Methodist Chapel talking to Pastor Jeremiah and that Ethan's flat had been searched. Ethan was waiting for them in Rick's office with the blinds down.

That sixth sense, that foreboding feeling had come over the rest of the team.

Rick and Dave raced up the stairs two by two just wanting to get it over with. It was the end of two weeks of high intensity police work. Highs, and lows, eureka moments and red herrings. Great detective work from the CID team backed up by faultless forensic pathology from Kay, and not forgetting the work of the SOC team led by Ethan. Ethan, who played his part so well in solving of the murders of Jim Derbyshire and Theo plus the attempted murder of Freddie Fairbrother.

As they entered the outer office the whole of the rest of the team were standing to attention. There was no clapping on this occasion, just wonder and amazement at what was about to happen, and relief that it may be over.

Rick opened his office door and entered to find Ethan already there with tears in his eyes. Ethan knew that with the searching of his flat, the game was up, it was all over.

The Devil had entered Ethan's body and consumed his soul long ago in Haiti, during a Voodoo ceremony. He turned to face Rick and just said, 'You know, don't you, sir.'

He had led them all a merry dance, but knew for certain that:

When the Devil wants to dance with you,
you had better say never,
because if you dance with the Devil,
he will take your soul and consume you forever.

(Dance With The Devil : Immortal Technique)

Ethan's demeanour suddenly changed as he moved across the room towards Rick. He sneered and spat out his words in an evil smelling, distorted voice:

'Damn you and your God! Do you think you have beaten ME? Lucifer, Prince of Darkness? Think again! This is only the beginning; we shall meet again.'

Rick took a deep breath and just said, 'Ethan James, I am arresting you for the murder of Miss Samantha Billings,' following it with the mandatory caution.

Ethan fell to the floor in a fit, his body writhing, jerking and frothing at the mouth. Suddenly a foul- stinking vapour drifted out of his mouth, accompanied by maniacal laughter, which became quieter and quieter as it evaporated into nothing.

Ethan came too, staggered up from the floor, and with a hint of a smile, said,

'What took you so long, sir?'

Epilogue

Ethan James was found to be of sane mind and fit to plead at his trial for the murder of Samantha Billings. He was found guilty and given a life sentence.

Major St John Stevens and ex-Mayor Martin were found guilty of rape, grievously bodily harm and aiding and abetting the murder of Samantha Billings and were each sentenced to fifteen years imprisonment.

John, 'Tiny', Foreman was found guilty of the manslaughter of Theo Clarke and sentenced to 20 years.

Sarah Cooper-Clarke was found guilty of the murder of Jim Derbyshire and the attempted murder of Freddie Fairbrother. The judge accepted mitigating circumstances and sentenced her to 15 years' imprisonment.

Eileen Billings was found guilty of the manslaughter of her husband Sam Billings. The judge accepted exceptional mitigating circumstances and gave her a three years suspended sentence.

Sarah was allowed out of prison on day release, accompanied by prison officers, to attend the funeral of Samantha.

His Honour Judge Simon Beverley QC put on record his thanks to the team that brought Ethan James, Major St John Stevens, Andrew Martin, John Foreman, Sarah Cooper-Clarke and Eileen Billings to justice. Detective Inspector Rick McCarthy, Detective Sergeant Dave Elliot, and Forensic

Pathologist Kay Stone were given individual praise for their diligent work on the case. He said the entire team had reflected an outstanding level of investigation. He added: 'Detective Inspector Richard McCarthy gave clear support and direction to his team throughout, and the whole of the team reflects his own high personal standards.'

Jonathon Dukes created a beer in memory of Samantha, named *Fallen Angel*.

"To conceive the horror of my sensations is,
I presume,
utterly impossible;
yet a curiosity to penetrate the mysteries
of these awful regions
predominates even over my despair
and will reconcile me
to the most hideous aspect of death."

Edgar Allan Poe